THERE ARE TOO MANY
TERRIFYING QUESTIONS . . .

Bradley—The CIA agent who always put his job first. In the past it had cost him his wife and child. What would the price be this time?

Sylvie—The stunning French art student no man could resist. Each of her lovers had died violently. Would Bradley be next?

Hardy—The ruthless security chief whose dangerous game could destroy years of careful planning. How far was he willing to go to win?

Suvorov—Was he the craftiest Russian spy ever to match wits with the West . . . or part of a dirty double-crossing deal?

THE ANSWERS ARE ALL HIDDEN IN . . .

THE DEADLY DOCUMENT

THE
DEADLY
DOCUMENT

Michael Bar-Zohar

A DELL BOOK

Published by
Dell Publishing Co., Inc.
1 Dag Hammarskjold Plaza
New York, New York 10017

Dell ® TM 681510, Dell Publishing Co., Inc.

ISBN: 0-440-12165-5

Reprinted by arrangement with Delacorte Press

Printed in the United States of America

First Dell printing—January 1981

CONTENTS

THE
DEADLY
DOCUMENT

Prologue

PANDORA

Her fingers twitched nervously as she buttoned the heavy white coat over her black woolen suit. The clock of the Kremlin chimed seven; the Moscow sky was a thick black mass pressing against the windows of her tiny living room. It was time to go. She checked the contents of her purse for the last time and mentally repeated her instructions. She drew a deep breath and slowly raised her eyes.

The face that looked back at her from the mirror was definitely not that of a Mata Hari, she conceded, valiantly trying to fight her rising anxiety with a wry jab of self-mockery. There was nothing of the *femme fatale* in those sharp, aquiline features, in the hollow cheeks, the too-small mouth, the sallow forehead topped by a taut bun of straight blond hair. It was just an ordinary face, prematurely aged, with a web of tiny cracks and wrinkles almost visibly expanding around her eyes and the corners of her mouth. Even the large brown eyes, her only beautiful feature, had long ago lost their golden specks of laughter; now they reflected only worry and resignation.

No, she was definitely not one of those glamorous adventuresses who so abundantly and conveniently populate spy novels and films. But then, she had never believed all that nonsense when she joined the CIA ten years ago. Her experience had taught her that the less attention she attracted, the more ordinary and unimportant she looked, the better her chances of carrying out her assignment. She had been the only one to escape from Prague after the breakdown of the Karlovy ring, just because none of the security officers at the Austrian border had thought it necessary to search the sad-eyed, plain girl sitting by herself at the back of the tourist bus, with the blueprints of the new Skoda T-76 amphibious tank taped to the skin of her thigh. Nobody in East Berlin had suspected that she was the Mülder courier; she had made the exchange practically under the Vopos' noses and had calmly walked past their ambush and through Checkpoint Charlie, this time with the Leica Laser gunsight safely tucked in her battered handbag.

Of course, things were quite different now, she reflected as she double-locked the door of her apartment and stood waiting for the old-fashioned elevator to take her down to the lobby: She no longer enjoyed the shelter of anonymity, and her position on the embassy staff exposed her to the unremitting attention of the KGB. They were nobody's fools, and they certainly might suspect that she was something else besides the assistant attaché in charge of cultural exchanges with the USSR. They almost certainly hadn't figured out, however, that she was an important field agent, possibly *the* most important operating inside the Soviet Union. And her assignment—the odds against their guessing that one were almost high enough to be reassuring. Still, it was simple enough—four deliveries and four pickups at a carefully arranged drop, once every six months. She would never meet the contact, would certainly never know his name, if he had one. Perhaps this mole, this alleged key Soviet intelligence official, didn't really exist. She certainly had no proof, either way; and it was just as possible that she was simply playing decoy, while somebody else, somewhere else, was making the real contact. Things like that did happen.

She got into the elevator and tried to concentrate on her evening's mission. There was nothing to worry about, she repeated to herself, irritated by the sudden dampness of the palms of her hands. It was bound to come off, just as it had the last time, in May. God knows, they'd certainly put in the practice.

The elevator started thumping and grating its way downward, and she didn't hear the telephone ringing in her apartment.

She parked her small car in Revolution Square, threw a quick glance at the brightly lit magnificence of the Spasskaya Tower beyond the Kremlin wall, and strode purposefully toward the Lenin Museum. It had started to snow again and a myriad of snowflakes were gracefully descending on the domes and monuments of the city. She entered the huge lobby of the museum and joined the merrily chatting queue of Russians and foreign guests in front of the small cloakroom. She divested herself of the shaggy white coat and climbed the winding staircase to the mezzanine and a receiving line of Soviet dignitaries, headed by the Minister of Culture himself. Moscow was celebrating the anniversary of the October Revolution, and for a couple of weeks foreign diplomats and Russian leaders were mixing almost daily at lavish receptions thrown by the various branches of the Soviet government.

She handed her invitation to the balding, thickset usher, who proclaimed in a stentorian voice: "Miss Emily Hobarth, assistant attaché for cultural affairs of the United States of America." She passed down the line with an artificial smile, murmuring the usual pleasantries. Out of the corner of her eye she observed the guests already leaving through the door on the left, presumably on their way to other receptions and dinners in town.

Still, every one of the twenty-two galleries of the Vladimir Ilyich Lenin Memorial Museum was packed, as she had expected. She absently took a glass of champagne from the tray of a passing waiter and pushed her way through the crowd. Louise, a colleague from the embassy, was expecting her under Petlukhov's bronze bust of the young Lenin. They smiled and deftly exchanged their cloakroom tickets. Emily Hobarth zigzagged through the noisy throng, occasionally smiling at an acquaintance, slowly retreating toward the exit. Eleven minutes after Emily entered the museum, she was back in the cloakroom. The stooped old woman behind the counter didn't even look at her face, just handed her Louise's shabby black overcoat and shapeless wool hat. She pulled it down over her ears, the Russian way, completely concealing her blond hair.

She hurriedly crossed the cobblestone square, and went down the escalator into the Revolution Square underground station. When she boarded the train for Komsomolskaya, Emily Hobarth was sure she was not being followed.

Emily emerged a few minutes later in the chaos of Komsomolskaya Square—the classical cornices of Leningrad Station, the ugly Czarist gingerbread of Yaroslavl Station, the massive modernist bulk of Kazan Station, and the enormous Stalinist Gothic spire of the Leningradskaya Hotel across the square. More important, all three great stations were disgorging hundreds of travelers into the square, and no one was likely to notice a lone woman in a black coat threading her way through the slow-moving crowd, beckoning, and stepping into a battered Moskvitch taxi.

"*Gostilnitsa Ukraina,*" she said, imitating the Russian accent to perfection. The slant-eyed driver, a Kirghiz or Kazakh from Central Asia, nodded and carelessly gunned his car, almost grazing a group of elderly women who were busy shoveling the new-fallen snow.

The taxi crossed the deserted Lermontovskaya Square, down Kirova Street, and finally turned into Dzerzhinsky Square. The driver was simply trying to bypass the congestion in the main streets adjoining the Kremlin, but Emily shivered involuntarily when she saw the dark mass of the notorious Lubyanka prison looming on the far side of the square. And the bright lights burning in the three top floors of the new wing of Lubyanka seemed even more foreboding. This was the headquarters of the KGB, and she couldn't suppress the thought that at this very moment the most ruthless counterintelligence organization in the world was on the alert, perhaps watching her, scheming to destroy her before she could accomplish her mission. She shook her head angrily, as if to shake off the grip of an irrational fear. She glanced out the back window. The street stretched back behind her, empty and peaceful.

The cab passed by the American Embassy on Tchaikovsky Street, crossed the Moskva River, and came to a stop on the Taras Shevchenko Quay, by the entrance of Hotel Ukraina. She paid the driver and walked into the hotel. The enormous lobby was crowded, as usual, mostly with visiting Eastern European officials. Emily elbowed her way across the lobby, into the restaurant and out by the Kutuzovsky Prospect entrance. A group of provincial party members, on what was apparently their first visit to the capital, were waiting docilely at a bus stop. She boarded the bus with them, found a seat in the back, and rode all the way across the tiny Luzhniki peninsula, into the oldest part of Moscow, the Zamoskvorechye. The bus was virtually empty by the time it reached the entrance to the Gorky amusement park. The crowd dispersed quickly into the cafés, restaurants, and exhibition halls of the park; only Emily turned away and doubled back toward the river. Ahead of her, in the dim light, was the object of her long trip: the Krimsky Bridge.

Her heartbeat quickened. In a few minutes it would be all over. She had some difficulty mastering an instinctive urge to hasten her stride, but she kept walking calmly and steadily. She glanced attentively around, but the bridge was deserted, except for a few pedestrians who quickly scuttled past her. She was on the bridge now. She put her right hand in her purse and quickly removed the paper wrapping from the object she had received from Washington in the diplomatic pouch. It felt like an irregularly shaped stone with a rugged, uneven surface.

Another ten paces to go. She spotted the drop: a roughly rectangular fissure in the stone parapet of the bridge, about a foot beyond the sidewalk. She reached the spot and stopped. Her heart was pounding like a sledgehammer in her chest. She bent down, as if she were having trouble tying her shoe, and stretched out her hand to thrust the stone into the gaping hole in the wall.

And then it all happened, with stunning speed. She heard shouts, running steps, and somebody jumped on her from behind while a hand tightened on her wrist, immobilizing her before she could throw the stone into the river. She collapsed heavily on the wet sidewalk. The shock paralyzed her and her scream died in her throat. She looked up in panic. She was surrounded by five or six men, mostly young, dressed in civilian clothes. The one who had caught her wrist pulled her close to him. His red face was glistening with sweat, and his breath carried the odor of foul tobacco. She didn't try to struggle; it was too late. They ordered her to her feet. She obeyed meekly; her knees were trembling. She had been caught *in flagrante delicto* by agents of Soviet counterintelligence, by SMERSH, exactly as she had always dreaded, as she had seen it over and over again in her most chilling nightmares. There was only one thing left for her to do—she had to alert her contact in case he was still lurking nearby. "Let me go!" she screamed, in a high-pitched voice she hardly recognized as hers. "I am a foreigner! I am a diplomat! I have immunity!"

On the other side of the bridge, a tall, slightly stooped man walked into a phone booth and dialed the direct number of the second secretary in the political section of the U.S. Embassy. "Is that the Pekin restaurant?" he asked.

"Wrong number," the secretary answered, and replaced the phone on its cradle. Then he looked up at the two others sitting in his office.

"That was our stakeout," he said. "She's been caught."

Shortly before 2:00 A.M. a solitary ZIL limousine entered the inner court of the Kremlin by the Nikolskaia Gate, drove up the alley by the Hall of the Supreme Soviet, and came to a smooth stop in front of the main entrance of the administrative building. A medium-built man, holding a brown leather attaché case, emerged from the car. He wore neither an overcoat nor a hat, despite the fierce cold. "Wait for me here," he said to the two men sitting in the front seat. He spoke with the casual authority of one accustomed to command.

"Yes, Comrade Andropov," one of the men said.

Yuri Andropov, director of the KGB, walked quickly into the building. Two officers of the guard, eyes puffed with fatigue, jumped to attention. Another officer, a fresh-faced major, smartly saluted. "The Secretary General is waiting for you, comrade. I'll escort you to his office."

Andropov grunted and followed the officer through the maze of corridors. An elevator took them to the fifth floor. Andropov was wearing a black double-breasted suit, but his shirt was wrinkled, his tie crooked, his thin, graying blond hair disheveled, and his waxen face badly in need of a shave. Twice during the ride up he pulled a large blue handkerchief from his trouser pocket and mopped the beads of cold sweat from his forehead.

The two men walked quickly past the armed guards posted along the corridors. Andropov was staring ahead with glazed, unseeing eyes; he didn't return the guards' salutes. A sour-faced matron dressed in black approached them and led them through a succession of expensively furnished anterooms and offices. Finally a young male secretary appeared through a heavy oak door. "This way, please, Tovarishch Andropov."

Brezhnev's working office was small and surprisingly modest: an Uzbek carpet of rough wool, a small portrait of Lenin between two bookcases, a medium-sized desk surrounded by a few leather armchairs, a wornout sofa in the far corner. The only touch of luxury seemed to be the magnificent view over the onion-domes of St. Basil's Cathedral, rising on the far side of Red Square.

Brezhnev himself was slumped behind his desk in an old-fashioned armchair. He did not wear a tie, and the collar of his shirt was unbuttoned, revealing a triangle of hairy, sunburned skin. He didn't rise to greet his visitor. At this late night hour the cruel marks of fatigue and illness were clearly written on his powerful face. The skin under his eyes sagged in heavy, wrinkled pockets, and massive doses of cortisone had left him with unnaturally puffed cheeks and swollen jaws. Still, the deep furrows on both sides of his belligerently protruding upper lip gave an unmistakable impression of brutal, unrestrained power. His eyes, bloodshot and contracted to narrow horizontal cracks in the broad, tired face, were as steely and watchful as ever, and his cavernous voice still carried a crushing authority.

"Well, Yuri Vladimirovitch, show it to me," he grumbled, without preliminaries, straightening his bulk with some effort and leaning forward over the desk. Andropov wordlessly opened his case and removed the stone that his agents had seized a few hours ago from Emily Hobarth. He opened his mouth to speak, but was interrupted by the entrance of an elderly woman in a gray dress. She nodded respectfully, sat down at the far end of the desk, and placed a memo pad and a pencil in front of her. Andropov's expression didn't change and his pale blue eyes remained cold and indifferent, yet he knew that the presence of a stenographer at a confidential meeting with the Secretary General of the Communist Party could only mean trouble. Brezhnev had summoned the stenographer out of caution. And Andropov understood that tonight he would have to fight for his life.

But nothing of this showed in his even voice, nor in the precise movements of his long fingers as he turned the stone in all directions for Brezhnev to see. "Plastic, American made, perfect imitation of the stones in the parapet of the Krimsky Bridge," he explained. With a swift movement he snapped the fake stone into two unequal hollow halves, from which he carefully extracted a few objects which he laid on the desk. "Special R-7 ultraminiature camera. We use almost the same thing for documents. Two rolls for a B-19 miniature camera. It seems that our man has already one in his possession. Wad of hundred thousand rubles, worn bills, compressed to fit into a very small space. Instructions in code, on two separate sheets of paper."

Brezhnev wiped his glasses on the lapels of his jacket and replaced them on the tip of his nose. He picked up the thin sheets of paper and glanced at the unintelligible succession of letters and numbers.

"You broke the code, you said."

Andropov nodded. "The counterintelligence lab cracked it, but it was not an easy job. We have it here." He took a typewritten sheet of paper crossed with a red diagonal line from his briefcase and handed it to Brezhnev. The Secretary General took a long time reading the document. His heavy jaws tightened; he spoke without taking his eyes from the papers. "You know what this means, Yuri Vladimirovitch."

A mortal pallor settled on Andropov's face. "Yes," he said in a low voice.

"Say it, then," snapped Brezhnev suddenly, and crashed his heavy fist on the desk. "What does it mean?"

Andropov said slowly: "From the questions and instructions we can infer that the . . . the individual to whom they are addressed is a high official of the KGB."

"How high?"

Andropov swallowed. "Very high, Comrade Secretary."

"Could that mean one of the top twelve in the KGB supreme council?" Brezhnev was taking a morbid pleasure in the cat-and-mouse game he was playing with Andropov.

"I'd say it could, yes, Comrade Secretary."

"Any hint of his identity?"

"None, Comrade Secretary."

"And the American woman, what does she know?"

Andropov cleared his throat. "She knows nothing, not even a code name. She was just a courier."

"How did you spot her?"

The KGB director moved uneasily in his chair. "She had been under surveillance for the last month. The Second Directorate had some vague indications that the Americans were preparing something, and last night they tailed six people who were on the most suspect list."

"So it was just a stroke of luck," muttered Brezhnev.

Andropov didn't answer.

Brezhnev leaned back in his chair and tilted his head slightly to one side, watching Andropov through half-closed lids. "How long have you been director of the KGB?" he asked suddenly.

Andropov wiped his forehead. "Twelve years."

"Twelve years," Brezhnev said slowly, and turned to the right and left, as if to catch the reaction of an invisible audience. "Twelve years. And during all that time you have been unaware of the presence of a spy, a traitor in your own organization!"

Andropov tried to protest. "Comrade Secretary, I strongly doubt that he has been operating for so long."

Brezhnev cut him short, jerking his hand impatiently.

"All right, all right. So you either inherited him from your predecessor or the CIA recruited him right under your nose. Both ways it could cost you your position, comrade, and more than that." He glanced at the sheets of paper he was still holding in his hand. "Yes, much more than that."

But Andropov didn't give up that easily. He had already outlasted two regimes, and there was little that Brezhnev, or any other politician, could tell him about the realities of Soviet power. When under attack, his cunning mind was desperately seeking a way out. And he knew suddenly that he had found it: the threat to Brezhnev named Gusnov. Obviously, Gusnov and the other Cold Warriors would start howling for Brezhnev's scalp as soon as they got wind of this business. This was the politicians' problem, too; it was time for them to start sweating.

"It could also mean the end of détente, of the SALT talks, of the grain deals . . ." Andropov said, in a barely audible voice.

Brezhnev looked at him sharply. "What do you mean?"

"Well, if this matter is brought before the Politburo, this is exactly what Gusnov and the rest are waiting for to prove they've been right all along, that the Americans are a bunch of gangsters, spying on us, taking advantage of détente to lull us into complacency, just to hit us harder in the end. You know Gusnov. He would gladly exploit this incident to discredit our current foreign policy; and as one of the architects of that policy, you yourself, Leonid Ilytch, would find yourself in . . . in quite a precarious position."

Brezhnev leaned back and closed his eyes. His stubby peasant fingers clutched the arms of his chair. He sat motionless for a long while. Then he rose to his feet and with a slight nod dismissed the stenographer. "What do you intend to do?" he asked.

"I intend to convene the KGB Supreme Council first thing this morning," Andropov replied, regaining some of his calm. "I shall tell them everything. I shall tell them I am convinced that the mole is one of them, and if I don't get his head on a platter I'll make them all pay for it. They'll jump down each other's throats, you can be sure of that."

Brezhnev looked at him dubiously. "And you think they'll find your man?"

"Quite soon, you can be sure of that, Leonid Ilytch," Andropov said firmly. "They'll be fighting for their lives, you know."

"Like you did for yours, just now," Brezhnev murmured ironically. "All right, let's try it that way. Go and do it."

Andropov quickly collected the spy equipment from the desk and replaced it in his case. He turned when he reached the doorway. "What should we do with the American woman?"

Brezhnev sighed heavily. His eyes wandered absently from wall to wall. "We can't do much, can we? She has immunity, and this isn't the right moment for a spy trial. Have her photographed with all her equipment."

"I already have," Andropov said promptly.

"Fine. Then try to get a confession. Maybe she'll break down. And have her out of the country by tomorrow night."

As Andropov turned to go Brezhnev laid a heavy paw on his shoulder and pulled him back, until their faces were barely inches apart. "And get me that traitor, Andropov," he hissed, "because if you don't, Gusnov or no Gusnov, I'll skin you alive."

Andropov's pale cold eyes blinked nervously, then he was gone.

Two weeks later, in the late evening, the telephone rang in the private apartment of the Second Secretary of the U.S. Embassy political section. A muffled voice said in

English with a clipped Russian accent: "Red . . . Achilles . . . close . . . Pandora."

The KGB team monitoring the secretary's telephone had no trouble pinpointing the origin of the call: a phone booth in the Karl Marx Street, behind the Kolizey cinema. But when two cars of the counterintelligence department arrived, the booth was empty.

The Marine band struck up "Hail to the Chief." The two-hundred-odd guests rose to their feet and loudly applauded as the President of the United States and his foreign guest solemnly descended the main staircase to the great ballroom of the White House. The two dignitaries and their wives, in formal evening dress, were preceded by two stony-faced Marine sergeants in impeccable parade uniforms. While he flashed his famous smile and waved absently at the cheering crowd, the President reflected that at least this ridiculous pomp and circumstance seemed to be having the desired effect on his guest. An oblique glance at the bulky figure pacing solemnly beside him confirmed this impression. General Luis Francisco Santander y Diaz appeared to be very happy indeed—massive torso swelling with self-importance, squarish head, which rose abruptly from his bulging shoulders, held stiffly erect, chubby hands swinging in time with the martial strains of the band. The general's face hardly suggested the conventional military man, however—coarse, raven-black hair, wide cheekbones, small, bright piglike eyes. He was said to have started his career as an illiterate conscript from a remote Indian village. His brutal efficiency had quickly brought him to the notice of his superiors. Not too many years later he was planning the coup which toppled his predecessor's regime. Today he managed his tumultuous officers' corps well enough to guarantee his country's stability for years to come, and he had shown considerable shrewdness while negotiating a very favorable economic and military aid package.

Santander had every reason to be happy, the President thought, as they finally took their seats at the central table and began sampling the hors d'oeuvres. He had gotten the complete Latin-American statesman's package tour: reception in the White House garden, speeches, national anthems, full military honors, then a private talk in the Oval Office, and a public announcement of the new development loans and assistance programs. The republic's strategic position was crucial; Santander depended on the loyalty of his generals, and the United States had no choice except to pump millions into his treasury, which passed easily and efficiently into the generals' numbered accounts.

Well, there was only tonight's dinner left and Santander's visit would be just another unpleasant memory. Then the President noticed Santander's wife on his right, and suddenly felt a twinge of embarrassment. Auburn-haired, green-eyed Señora Graciella Sarita Santander was surprisingly young, astonishingly beautiful, and obviously very keen on displaying her advantages. Furtively glancing at the provocative cleavage between her half-exposed breasts, the President sighed inwardly and wryly concluded that his biggest problem tonight was going to be Señora Santander's décolletage, although for a reason she couldn't possibly have imagined.

As if she had guessed precisely what he was thinking at that moment, Señora Santander pouted her full, glistening mouth and expertly flickered her long, silky eyelashes in his direction. Yet it was not her physical attractions that worried him as such; it was something rather trivial, but nevertheless disquieting. After dinner there would be dancing, and he was bound to invite the general's lady for the first dance. And no matter how old-fashioned the dance might be—some sugary waltz or the traditional "Tea for Two"—

and how sedately he behaved, he would have to hold the Señora by her bare shoulders and back. The last time he had danced with a similarly-attired foreign visitor, some smart photographer had blown up the picture of his hand resting on the silky skin of his partner. And hundreds of newspapers all over the country had printed it over captions like "DIPLOMACY WITH A PERSONAL TOUCH" and "PRESIDENT ESTABLISHES CLOSER TIES WITH FRIENDLY POWERS." That picture had done a lot of damage to his popularity in the Midwest and South. As that old lady in Atlanta had put it: "A President who spends his time dancing with half-naked women can't be really serious." It had taken him quite a while to burnish up his image, and tonight it was going to happen all over again.

But it did not. He was already halfway through dessert when he suddenly noticed an all-too-familiar figure at the far end of the ballroom, standing well away from the guests' tables, but in full view of almost everyone present. Barely concealing his irritation, the President got up, mumbled excuses to his guests, and quickly walked out of the ballroom and up the staircase. The other man quietly followed suit, and a few minutes later entered the Oval Office and softly closed the door behind him.

The President's fury exploded. "What the hell are you doing here? You must be out of your mind! Do you want your picture in tomorrow's papers? You're their best proof that the CIA is running every corrupt regime in South America!"

William Hardy, director of the CIA, didn't seem affected by the President's outburst. "I'm afraid you attach too much importance to what the media might say, Mr. President," he observed, his deferential tone softening the impertinence of his remark. He went on appeasingly: "I am truly sorry, sir, but something very disturbing has happened, and we need a decision from you."

The President's fury died down as quickly as it had flared. He sat on his swivelchair and crossed his feet on the desk. "O.K., Bill. You must have a pretty good reason for bursting in here like that. Do you want me to call anyone else?"

"No, sir, nobody else. Just you and me," Hardy said, then added quickly: "For the moment at least."

The President unfastened his tie and let it hang loose on the starched bib of his dress shirt. "Let's have it, Bill."

Hardy was a lanky New Englander with short-cropped salt-and-pepper hair and a stern face. His voice was low and rasping; he spoke directly and to the point. "As you know, we have an agent very high up in the Supreme Council of the KGB. We refer to him as Pandora. A few weeks ago, because of a mishap involving one of our subaltern agents, the KGB became aware of his existence. His existence, not his identity. There must be a very thorough investigation going on in Moscow right now. Last night, my man in Moscow got an emergency call from Pandora. He is convinced that one of the KGB chiefs—we call him Achilles—suspects that he is our agent. He asked us for immediate help. I have to ask you to authorize a crash operation to save Pandora."

The President raised one hand. "Before you go any further, let me get it straight, Bill. This Pandora of yours, is he reliable?"

"Absolutely, sir. He's been working for us for a few years. He is virtually invaluable. Especially now, with the next round of SALT just about to start."

"So when you speak of saving him, you mean maintaining him in his present position."

"That's right, sir."

"In other words, you want to remove Achilles."

"To remove him, that's the right term, sir."

The President fiddled for a moment with a few sharpened pencils in a tray on his desk. "How urgent is all this?" he asked.

"Quite urgent, sir. Pandora used the emergency procedure. He called my man at his house and spoke practically in clear. So if you just gave me your approval . . ."

The President preferred to pursue his own train of thought. "You believe that Achilles has got some substantive evidence against your man?"

Hardy didn't answer immediately. "No," he said finally. "If Achilles had the evidence, Pandora would be dead by now. I'd rather say that Achilles might be on the verge of getting the evidence."

"And evidence does exist somewhere, right?" The President's penetrating gaze didn't shift from Hardy's face for a second.

"Yes," Hardy said carefully, "such evidence does exist."

"So if you could get at it and destroy it before the Russians find it, you would save Pandora, wouldn't you?"

Hardy shrugged skeptically. "I wouldn't count on that, sir."

The President threw back his head and seemed to contemplate the ceiling. "Is there no other possibility of saving Pandora? Whisk him out of Russia?"

"That would be a last resort," Hardy protested. "It would be infinitely preferable to retain his services in place."

The President nodded. "Yes, of course." He got up, went to the window, and stood for a long moment, deeply immersed in thought. "And your plan is to kill Achilles, in Moscow, as soon as possible," he said without turning around.

"I think we can do it by the end of next week," Hardy said quickly. "We have people on the spot, we have unmarked weapons, we have escape routes—and I believe we'll have the opportunity."

"So the operation will be safe."

"As safe as can be, sir."

The President's voice lashed back at him with heavy irony: "As safe as can be. The exact words one of your predecessors used to drag Jack Kennedy into the Bay of Pigs. Dammit, Bill, I thought you were smarter than that."

He turned back and came to face the CIA director. His face was hard and taut. "What the hell are you thinking of?" he said furiously. "The world is not what it used to be, Mr. Director. You just don't run around Moscow shooting people. This is an intelligence agency you're running, not Murder, Incorporated. So let's have more intelligence— and less murder, for Christ's sake!"

Hardy pressed his lips, but didn't utter a word. The President started rearranging his tie with quick, nervous gestures. "I will not authorize this operation," he said firmly, "and that's final. Sometimes it is inevitable, and I know that. But in this particular case, if anything goes wrong, the results might be disastrous. You'd better go back home and come up with a more workable plan. Maybe beat the Russians at the race for the evidence against Pandora. I don't know. But murdering people in Moscow can't be the only solution."

Hardy remained motionless for a short while. Then he started to speak. His voice was hesitant, but a curious, sly glint flashed in his eyes. "We could devise an alternative plan, sir. Concerning the evidence in a way. But it would be pretty rough. It might turn out to be even messier than the one I just suggested."

"Tell me about it," the President said.

Hardy spoke for a few minutes. When he had finished both men remained silent for several seconds.

The President gave Hardy a long dubious glance, then started pacing up and down the office, his forehead furrowed in deep concentration, his arms crossed on his chest.

Hardy stirred uneasily. "Should I start an operation along these lines, sir?"

The President looked at him gravely. "All right," he said finally, and at that moment he spoke with the voice of a tired, overburdened old man. "I hate this conversation, Bill. I resent giving those orders. Yet I understand that sometimes there's no other way. I just cannot authorize the killing of a Soviet official by our agents. I have to consider the political implications. If there is no other choice, go ahead with that alternative project of yours."

"May I have your instructions in writing?" Hardy asked softly.

A flash of anger exploded in the President's eyes, but in a second it was gone, and he acquiesced with a shrug. "Yes, of course." He scribbled a few words on a sheet of paper embossed with his seal and handed it across the desk. "I guess that settles it." Hardy read the note carefully, then folded it neatly and put it in his pocket.

The President took a deep breath and drew back his shoulders. "Well," he said in a different tone, "I guess I have to return to my guests now." He suddenly chuckled. "Let's hope that the dancing is over at least."

Hardy threw him a perplexed look. "I don't understand."

"Oh, never mind." The President grinned. Hardy followed him through the outer office and along the deserted corridors. At the top of the stairs the President abruptly turned back to face him: "Why didn't you want anyone else to be present at our conversation?"

Hardy's reply was almost a whisper. "Well, sir, I believe that if we've got our Pandora in Moscow, they've got their Pandora in Washington."

The President glanced at him sharply, then nodded and turned away.

On his way back to the ballroom the President kept

thinking about the paper he had just signed. He had no doubt that his signature had just sentenced several people to violent death. He wondered fatalistically how, where, and who was going to be killed in order to save a spy, a renegade, and a traitor to his own country.

Part One

THE
BOOK
OF SYLVIE

1

STILETTO

A sudden icy gust swept the empty sidewalks of Fleet Street and raced up the Strand. Richard Hall shivered in his worn trenchcoat and quickened his pace. He had rarely seen London so bleak and dreary, its streets so deserted and hostile under a low, leaden sky. Yet one could hardly expect anything else on the morning of January the second. Most people had been partying, gorging, and guzzling for the last two days, and it would take them a few more hours to sober up and realize that New Year's Day was finally over. He hurried past the tiny Twining's teashop and the Temple Bar Memorial, where a hideous bronze griffin brooded over the gloomy statues of Queen Victoria and Edward VII. For himself, he would have preferred the original Temple Bar gateway, even taking into account that former sovereigns had enjoyed the ghoulish hobby of sticking the bloody heads of criminals and traitors on the spikes that topped its picturesque facade. He crossed the street by the main entrance to the Law courts, a whole dirty-gray block of needle-sharp domes and towers, which an architect friend of his had once contemptuously referred to as "the Persian market of Gothic art." A solitary bobby was making his rounds on the sidewalk, obviously freezing beneath his inadequate blue uniform. Richard turned left into Chancery Lane, past the small Victorian shops of law books, stationery, and attorneys' wigs and gowns, and entered the arched porch of the Public Record Office. He showed his reader's card to the warden and hurried into the pleasant warmth of the dark entrance hall.

He exhaled a sigh of contentment. He had been fascinated by this place ever since that day in his early teens when he had visited the small museum inside the thirteenth-century chapel by the main archway. His eyes had devoured the collection of historical documents displayed in the glass cases faintly glowing in the semidarkness of the old house. He had spent the whole day in the museum, darting from one showcase to another, thrilled over and over again by the discovery of the Magna Carta in its final form, Shakespeare's testament, the original reports of the mutiny on the *Bounty*, Marlborough's dispatches from the battle of Blenheim, Wellington's message from Waterloo, Dr. Livingstone's letter describing his meeting with Stanley. . . . It was on that day that his passion for history had been kindled. Even today, a graduate student halfway through his thesis, he was still under the spell of those yellow-edged, timeworn bits of paper that made the past come back to life before his eyes.

He felt at home in the labyrinth of corridors, passages, staircases, and reading rooms of the PRO. He had spent most of his last two years here examining dusty old files, scanning thousands of documents, preliminary research for his thesis which dealt with diplomatic relations between Britain and Czarist Russia in the years before the First World War. Today, as at the beginning of every year, the classifications would run out on an enormous quantity of documentary material which would finally be open to examination by scholars and students. And he could hardly wait to plunge into the bundles of Foreign Office correspondence and ambassadorial reports hitherto kept in utmost secrecy in the vaults of Her Majesty's archives.

The history reading room was almost empty. Only one other reader had preceded him—a heavy, stocky kind of fellow, dressed in black, who was sitting uneasily at a corner desk, his small, dark eyes riveted on the archivist's booth. There was something vaguely disconcerting about him; he just didn't seem to belong to this place. Richard quickly filled his yellow slip—he knew the reference numbers by heart—and put it in the wooden box on the archivist's desk. There was only one other slip in it—probably the other fellow's. The archivist, a thin little man with sparse white hair and a gaunt, emaciated face, smiled with pleasure when he recognized him. "How are you today?" Richard asked warmly.

The old man mumbled something completely unintelligible in his dreadful accent, which had won him the nickname of "Old Cockney" among the habitués of the reading room.

Richard patted him affectionately on the shoulder. "Well, happy New Year." Old Cockney was a fine old man, he thought, taking his usual place by the window; he was also the most absent-minded living thing he had ever met. Old Cockney was notorious for his perpetual fits of mental abstraction; his powers of confusion were unrivaled. Richard smiled at the thought that even though there were only two readers in the room, he would certainly mix up their slips and give both of them the wrong file.

Richard had just started to relax in the pleasant warmth of the wall radiator, after pulling his pullover sleeves up to his elbows, and stretching his legs blissfully under the desk, when Old Cockney materialized on his left and dumped a file in front of him. He smiled, revealing two missing teeth, and croaked something which by a very liberal interpretation could mean, "Here you are, Mr. Hall." Then he was gone, leaving Richard to savor his first pleasure of the new year.

Richard impatiently unfastened the straps that bound the documents together, encased in the customary cardboard jacket. The papers varied in size, and except for a few printed circulars, were all handwritten. The document on top was a memorandum from the First Lord of the Admiralty to Prime Minister Asquith concerning a delay in the construction of two cruisers for the Royal Navy. Richard, puzzled, leafed quickly through the succeeding documents. They all dealt with naval matters, and they had nothing to do with the subject of his research. He checked the number on the cover, and the perplexed expression on his face slowly metamorphosed into an ironic smile. Blast Old Cockney, he had done it again! He had brought him the other chap's file.

Richard looked up and waved his hand, trying to attract the old man's attention; but Old Cockney was standing beside his booth, busy explaining something to the man in black, who, to judge by the look on his face and the nervous motions of his hands, didn't seem to understand a thing. Sighing stoically, Richard rearranged the documents in the file. As he retied the frayed canvas straps, his fingers brushed against a thick sheet of paper, attached with the blank side outward to the back cover of the file. He turned the file upside down. There was a document, a single folded sheet, fastened to the cardboard jacket with two paper clips. That was quite unusual; someone in the vaults downstairs must have placed it there by mistake. Richard detached the document and unfolded it. What he saw made him blink with disbelief.

It was a handwritten report, signed by General Sir Archibald Montague, Head of His Majesty's Secret Service and addressed to the King. It was dated November 15, 1910. A red stamp on its upper right corner certified that the document had been classified for forty years. A second notation in red ink read: "Classification extended for 25 years, by personal instruction of the Director of the Intelligence Service, November 15, 1950." And under it, in a darker ink and a different handwriting: Classification extended for 10 years, November 15, 1975." The signature was illegible.

It was a mistake all right, and a serious one. Somebody had inadvertently attached this top secret document to a nonrestricted file, long before its classification had run out. Deeply intrigued, Richard started to read the document. Its contents were amazing. He had never seen anything like it.

On the spur of the moment he decided to copy the report before returning the file. He took several sheets of paper and a sharpened pencil out of his briefcase; pens were not allowed on the premises of the PRO. The sound of footsteps on the linoleum floor made him look up. Old Cockney and the man in black were walking in his direction. The archivist held a voluminous file under his arm; the stranger looked quite agitated. His face was flushed and his small eyes gleamed with anger. They had certainly found out about the switch in the files and were coming to straighten things out. On a sudden impulse, Richard surreptitiously slipped the classified report between a few sheets of virgin paper, and quickly stuffed them into his briefcase. He had never stolen a document before; but he had never been tempted before. And then, he said to himself, nobody would ever connect the disappearance of this document with him—if and when they found out about it. It had been put there by accident—and it was just his good luck.

When Old Cockney and the man in black reached his desk, he was already on his feet. "There must have been some mistake," he said to the archivist, smiling boyishly, "This is not the file I asked for." Old Cockney nodded with relief and mumbled something. The other man glared furiously at Richard, but did not speak. They exchanged files and Old Cockney insisted on carrying the navy file to the other reader's desk, obviously trying to make amends for his blunder.

The reference number on Richard's file was correct; the documents inside were exactly what he had hoped for. But his enthusiasm had suddenly evaporated. Tremendously excited by the secret paper safely tucked in his briefcase, he had completely lost interest in his work. He spent barely fifteen minutes on the file, absently taking note of its contents, jotting down dates and subject headings. Glancing occasionally at the other reader, he saw him nervously leafing through his file. He also turned in Richard's direction, their eyes met, and Richard read a growing hostility—or maybe it was suspicion—in the man's face. Just for a moment a rather strange thought crossed his mind: could he be looking for the document that was in his briefcase? He quickly dismissed the idea. There was no possible way anyone could know about this report. He felt, however, that he had had enough of this morning's adventure. He got up from his chair, stretched lazily, and returned the file to the archivist's desk. In the staircase he met a few students he knew on their way to the reading room.

The street scene was a little more animated and a pale winter sun was desperately trying to pierce the gray canopy that spread over London. Richard Hall strolled happily home, occasionally stopping to glance at a nicely decorated shop window. In a candy shop, he bought a big box of Swiss chocolates and asked the salesgirl to wrap it in gift paper.

Even though he glanced back occasionally, he didn't notice the man who expertly tailed him all the way to his small flat in Tavistock Street.

Actually, there was a second reason for his sudden urge to get home, which was moving lazily beneath the eiderdown spread over the double bed, stretching her slender arms, and inquiring in a sleepy voice with a delicious French accent: "Did you go out? What day is it?"

Sylvie. She was the most stunning girl he had ever known. They had met at a Christmas party a week ago, and since then he had felt himself drawn deeper and deeper into an overwhelming involvement with her. He had had quite a few affairs before; he was good-looking, funny, and had an easy way with girls. Two of them had lived with him for quite a while, one for more than a year. But thanks to what he thought of as his inbred British cynicism, he had always played it cool, and had never got emotionally entangled with a woman. He liked to repeat that to himself, and even to boast about it in front of his girl friends—just in case they were tempted to get ideas. He was a brilliant young historian, his career came first, and all the rest was just pleasant, casual play. Yet since he had met Sylvie at a friend of a friend's house, his inbred British cynicism had vanished without a trace. And what was even more surprising, he didn't care. He felt he was falling in love, and he liked it. This French girl was something special. He didn't know very much about her.

Sylvie was an art student, the only daughter of an aristocratic family who lived outside Paris. She had come to London to spend the holidays with a girl named Jennifer, whom he knew vaguely. Sylvie was tall and slim, with a perfect body: long legs, thin waist, full breasts, softly rounded shoulders. Her long silky black hair formed a perfect background for the oval contours of her lively face, lit by two enormous blue eyes. It might have been the artificially pretty porcelain face of a doll, were it not for her slightly protruding jaw and full, soft lips, which introduced a note of pure carnality. When he had first seen her, it was her beauty that had attracted him. But what had transformed his purely sexual urge into a deeper, serious feeling, was her quick intelligence, her sharp wit, and her tremendous love of life. And for the first time in his life

Richard Hall felt that he wanted to hold on to a girl for good.

Her thoughts, as she watched him sleepily from her cozy nest under the quilt, were rather different. She had come to like Richard. He was a nice boy, smart and witty; in his company she felt relaxed and at ease. She found him quite handsome; in a way he reminded her of a younger Michael Caine. He was surprisingly good in bed and sufficiently inventive to make the aftermath of their wild sexual adventures an experience in itself. They had spent some marvelous nights together. He was indeed a good sport, as Jennifer would say. But it all stopped there. If she hadn't broken off with René in Paris a month ago, she would never have let him pick her up so easily. Actually, he was exactly what she needed after the end of her year-old affair: a solid therapy, healthy sex, good laughs, warm attention. He had made her feel loved, admired again, and thanks to him she had partially recovered her emotional equilibrium. Well, it was almost over. It had been a pleasant interlude that would end tomorrow, when she boarded the early-morning flight to Paris.

She clapped her hands gaily, like a little girl, when he handed her the box of chocolate. She quickly arranged the heavy, soft pillows into a pile behind her back and wormed herself up to a sitting position. The eiderdown slipped down from her shoulders, exposing her breasts, but she didn't care. She impatiently unwrapped the box and bit into a creamy-brown chocolate bar. She closed her eyes delightedly. "Hummm . . . *délicieux*," she trilled, and put one in his mouth. "That was a good idea." She worked her way hungrily through half the box. "Richard, darling, may we have some coffee now?" she pleaded.

He smiled at her: "I have something better." He went into the kitchenette, and she grinned knowingly when she heard the familiar popping sound. A moment later he was back with a small tray, on which stood a bottle of Dom Pérignon champagne and two glasses. "Nothing better to start the day with," he remarked.

She nodded eagerly. "Once in St. Moritz I practically lived for a couple of weeks on caviar and champagne for breakfast. It was heaven, although it does make you dizzy all day long." He didn't ask her who had joined her in this unconventional diet, but she noticed the quick spark of jealousy in his eyes. They drank the ice-cold champagne and he refilled their glasses. "Where did you go?" she asked.

The old excitement swept over him again. "I must show you something." He opened his briefcase and took out the document he had just stolen from the PRO. "Listen to this!" He started reading, becoming more and more animated with each phrase. But when he looked up to observe her reaction, he noticed that she was not really listening. Her face was flushed, her lips were parted, and her eyes shone behind their half-closed lids. He bent over her and kissed the full red lips. She purred contentedly and lay back, arms outstretched. He started kissing her and felt the passion building in him. The report slipped from his fingers on the far side of the bed. He undressed slowly while she lay motionless, her face buried in her long dark hair. He removed the quilt and caressed her palpitating, responsive body with the tips of his fingers. They made love slowly, tenderly, until their inner tension exploded and they reached a wild climax that left them blissfully exhausted.

They lay side by side in quiet satisfaction. Richard felt utterly spent and closed his eyes. He didn't respond to Sylvie's obvious initiative to start all over again. When she began caressing his shoulders with her warm mouth, he mumbled drowsily: "Orson Welles used to say there were three things in life he couldn't tolerate: lukewarm champagne, cold coffee, and overexcited women." He turned his back to her and sank into a light sleep. Sylvie made a face at him, then jumped out of bed and noiselessly walked into the adjoining bathroom. She closed the door and turned the tap on.

The secret report was nowhere to be seen; it was buried under a heap of sheets and pillows on Richard's bed.

He awoke with a start, and heard a curious grating sound that seemed to come from the outer door. "Who's there?" he asked languidly. "Sylvie, is that you?" There was no answer. Instead, he heard light, muffled footsteps. Someone was tiptoeing through the tiny vestibule. "Hey, what's going on?" He jumped out of bed and reached for his clothes. The door opened quietly and two men came into the room.

Richard looked at them in utter amazement. He recognized one of them—the man in black he had seen that morning in the PRO. The second was a tall, blond man wearing a gray suit over a black turtle-neck pullover. His thin wispy hair was combed to one side over an obvious bald patch. His light gray eyes were narrow and expressionless, but his thin lips were stretched tightly in a death's head grin.

"What the hell . . ." Richard blurted. His eyes blinked with bewilderment as his hands tried to conceal his nudity. The man in black grasped him by the shoulders. "The letter you stole this morning. Where is it?" He had a thick foreign accent.

"What letter?" Richard stuttered, still in a state of shock. "I don't know what you're talking about."

The man in black pushed him brutally aside and his eyes quickly surveyed the room. He picked up Richard's briefcase that lay on his desk, emptied it, and examined every paper inside it. The PRO document wasn't there. "Where is it?" the man in black repeated.

With swift, feline movements, his blond companion closed in on Richard. A long thin blade suddenly materialized in his right hand. "Where is the letter?" he hissed. "Tell us or ..."

Richard stared at the weapon with horrified eyes, suddenly realizing the danger. He looked around him in panic, but couldn't recall where he had put the letter. "I don't know," he shrugged helplessly. "I . . . I must have put it somewhere. . . ."

"Where?" the blond man asked again.

Richard tried to think, but fear confused his thoughts. "I don't remember . . ." he mumbled. "Honest, it must be here, somewhere. . . ."

Those were his last words. The blond man exchanged a quick glance with the man in black, then drove his hand forward. Richard opened his mouth, but his scream turned into a horrid groan as the stiletto slashed his throat and his blood spurted out in rhythmic pulsations. He started falling backward, but the killer wouldn't let go. Moving adroitly aside to avoid the thick stream of blood, he steadied the shoulder of the collapsing boy with his left hand and with his right viciously thrust his knife into Richard's chest. Again and again, he stabbed the naked boy, even after he crumpled to the floor, arms and legs twisted grotesquely. The killer's right hand rose and fell mechanically; tiny beads of sweat appeared on his pale forehead and his breathing came in quick, gasping groans. Only when the man in black barked out a curt command did he release his victim, leaving the dead boy lying like a broken doll in the center of a widening pool of blood.

Slowly emerging from his trance, the killer wiped his knife on the bedsheets, slipped it into the oblong leather sheath that was strapped to his forearm, and joined the man in black, who had already started the search. Expertly, systematically, they tore the room apart. They checked every book in the big cabinet, dumped the huge pile of research files on Richard's desk onto the floor, and examined every document one by one. The man in black went through Richard's clothes and removed his wallet, then picked up a leather pouch from the nightstand. He pocketed both articles, although he hadn't found what he was looking for. The blond man furiously pulled the drawers from the desk and the chests and emptied their contents on the floor. The document wasn't there.

In growing irritation, they started to tear off strips of wallpaper. Suddenly the watchful eyes of the killer caught a slight movement to his right. He motioned to the man in black and pointed with his finger. The knob of the bathroom door was turning slowly. They exchanged a stupefied glance—somebody else was in the apartment.

The man in black hesitated for a split second. He had assumed that the boy was alone and could be easily dealt with. But other people in the apartment meant trouble, and maybe even capture. He looked at the killer and jerked his head toward the door. They darted quickly through the vestibule and out of the apartment, slamming the outer door shut.

Wrapped in a huge towel, Sylvie came out of the bathroom. Her eyes opened wide at the sight of the terrible havoc in the room. "Richard?" she gasped. She stared around her, dumbfounded, and took a step forward. Her bare foot stepped in something warm and sticky. She looked down at the savagely butchered corpse of Richard Hall and screamed.

Gasping, sobbing, shivering with panic, she ran aimlessly through the ransacked apartment. Her eyes were wild with terror; incoherent thoughts rushed through her mind. The towel slipped to the floor as she trampled through the litter of papers and clothes, as if she were searching for some clue which would make her understand the senseless horror of the scene. But there was no clue. She could only see the blood, and she could only understand one thing: She had to get away from here.

She ran back into the bathroom and washed Richard's blood from her foot. The image of Richard's butchered body still clung to her like a shadow. The folding mirror over the washbasin threw back a reflection of the sickening chaos in the bedroom. She felt an uncontrollable surge of nausea.

She vomited into the washbasin; her throat was on fire, and tears were streaming down her cheeks. She went back into the bedroom, being careful to avoid looking at Richard's body, and began to collect her clothes. She found them in a pile by the bed: jeans, panties, and sweater. The embroidered sheepskin coat that René had brought from Turkey was hanging in the closet. She threw it over her shoulders and pulled on her knee-high boots with trembling hands. She couldn't find her pouch. Her frightened eyes swept the room. She had left it on the nightstand by the bed, but it wasn't there. Maybe whoever had killed Richard had taken it? Or maybe it had fallen onto the bed? She yanked off the sheets and covers and threw them aside. Something white fluttered for a second in the air and came to rest by Richard's body. Its edge touched the puddle of blood and a red stain quickly spread on the paper's porous surface. Overcoming her aversion she picked it up: It was the document that Richard had started reading to her. It must be important—she had rarely seen Richard as excited as when he showed it to her. If it was really important, could it be the reason for Richard's murder? Were the killers looking for it when they ransacked the apartment? Confused thoughts rushed through her mind. She tried to concentrate on the document. The words danced before her eyes and she had to read it over several times before she could grasp its meaning. It was very odd. . . .

The telephone rang. The shrill, insistent sound sent a tremor of panic through her body. She crumpled the letter and stuffed it into her jeans pocket. The pouch, where was the damn pouch? She had everything in it—her passport, the rest of her money, and her ticket. She looked helplessly around her. The telephone rang over and over. She stumbled to the door, dashed down the stairs, and out into the street.

As she ran down the wet sidewalk and turned right into Wellington Street, a man got out of a dark blue Austin sedan parked on the corner and set out after her.

It had started to rain, a typical ice-cold London drizzle. Sylvie half walked, half ran through the narrow streets around Covent Garden. The few passersby stared in dismay at the beautiful young woman hurrying past them, her clothes in disorder, her face streaked with tears. She barely seemed to notice, and kept walking stiffly ahead, like an automaton. Several times, when the persistent images of blood, of destruction, of pursuit, became too strong to shake off, she glanced back anxiously over her shoulder, almost without breaking her stride. She stopped walking when she caught sight of the comforting uniform of a London policeman in front of the Bow Street Police Court. Her first impulse was to run to him, ask him to protect her. She even took a few steps in his direction. And then she remembered those other British policemen, that dreary police station, two years ago, and she quickly crossed the street. No, she couldn't go to the police.

There was only one place she could go, and that was Jennifer's house. She was the only person in London who could help her. Her flat was at Berkeley Square, in Mayfair. But how could she get there? It was quite a distance. She had to take a cab. And her pouch, with all her money, was gone. She searched her pockets. In the outer pocket of her sheepskin coat she found a pound note and some silver. She sighed in relief and turned back to look for a taxi. And suddenly she felt the same maddening, paralyzing fear returning. She realized that she was being followed.

It was nothing tangible, just a sequence of impressions she had recorded unconsciously, which reappeared now to form a disturbing pattern in her memory. A stocky figure in a black overcoat and hat walking behind her as she turned from Tavistock Street onto Wellington; the same figure, much closer now, reflected in a shop window as she stepped over the curb across from the police court; and again a glimpse of the black overcoat disappearing into a doorway when she turned to hail a taxi. She began to tremble and her knees felt as if they were made of cotton. My God, she thought, he's after me now! Fighting her panic, she started walking again, past the Garrick Club, trying to pull herself together and to think straight. He wouldn't try anything on the street, that didn't make sense. He would certainly follow her to a place where he could kill her and easily escape. But then, she couldn't go to Jennifer's; there she would be a sitting duck, completely at his mercy. She must find a way to shake him off. But how? She didn't know anything about this sort of business. And yet, straining to recall, she began to retrieve odd bits and pieces of conversations among Sean and his comrades that she had overheard long ago. There was a taciturn fellow with a gray beard, the one they called "the Librarian," who had said one night: "If you want to duck a tail, the first rule is to find a shop or a restaurant with a few exits."

She glanced over her shoulder. Garrick Street was almost empty; she and the man in black were the only people on the rain-beaten sidewalks. Her pursuer wasn't bothering to conceal himself anymore, and was quickly closing in on her. She looked around for help. A car was slowly crawling up the street. It was a dark blue sedan. She thought of dashing out into the middle of the street to flag it down, when it suddenly occurred to her that the car was moving very slowly, as if the driver was trying not to overtake the man in black. Could this car be tailing her too? She could take no chances. She broke into a run and quickly covered the last two hundred yards to the crowded intersection of Long Acre Street. A cabbie noticed her outstretched hand and stopped. "Spink's," she blurted out quickly, "St. James's Street."

"That's right, miss," smiled the young driver, looking at her appraisingly under his leather cap, and he put his meter on.

She turned around sharply and stared out the tinted rear window just in time to see the man in the black overcoat jump into the blue car, which quickly pulled out into the heavy stream of traffic behind them.

In the safety of the taxi she tried to think—to make some sense of the chaos that was swirling in her brain. Who had killed Richard? A burglar? Something to do with drugs? Or somebody who was after the strange document he had brought this morning? The first two possibilities could be ruled out—she hadn't seen the killers, she couldn't have identified them, not till they started chasing her, anyway. As for the drugs, she didn't know everything about Richard, but his tastes seemed to run more toward sherry and the odd bottle of Dom Pérignon, and he never seemed to have much money. But why was he butchered like an animal? Why were the killers hunting her now? And why had they taken her pouch? There was almost nothing in it, just a few pounds and her papers. The document, everything, seemed to point toward that document. But why kill a man for a letter written so many years ago? She unfolded the crumpled sheet of paper and perused it attentively. It was certainly fascinating, but could it be worth killing for?

The taxi turned left at Piccadilly, continued all the way down St. James's Street, and stopped. Spink's, dealers in coins and exquisite art objects, occupied an immaculate eighteenth-century house in the corner. Sylvie got out and managed to smile at the driver. "Will you wait for me just a moment?" The cabbie nodded pleasantly. She glanced furtively to the left. Barely a hundred yards away, the blue sedan was closing in slowly.

She ran up the steps and went into the shop. Rare pieces of jewelry, antique Chinese daggers, and heavy damask draperies embroidered with golden thread were artfully displayed in big glass showcases. A handwoven silk Qum rug cascaded like liquid gold from a concealed stand. A poster announced an exhibition of early Persian art. She flashed a dazzling smile at the white-haired gentleman wearing tails and a silvery ascot who came forward to greet her, then brushed past him through the two big exhibition galleries—and out by the second exit into King Street.

Ten minutes later she ran breathlessly down the steps of the Green Park underground station. A crowded train took her to Knightsbridge. She stepped out of the train into a throng of busy Londoners. At the first landing she waited until the last man who had gotten off with her disappeared up the stairs, and finally she exhaled with relief. She'd lost them, and she was on her own at last.

She went into a little Italian sandwich shop and gulped down two double espressos. On the wall, under a decorative string of dried red peppers, there was a public phone. She knew Jennifer's number by heart. Her friend answered immediately. "Sylvie!" she exclaimed when she recognized her voice. "Thank God! Where are you? I've been so worried about you."

"Worried? Why?" She had no reason to worry, Sylvie thought quickly. As far as Jennifer was concerned, she was still with Richard.

"Well . . . some people were just here, they said they were looking for you, that it was quite urgent."

"People? What kind of people? Was one of them wearing black?"

"Yes . . ." There was a puzzled note in Jennifer's voice. "A man in black and a younger man with blond hair—looked rather nervous. Sylvie, what does all that mean? You sound funny."

"I'll call you later," Sylvie said, and quickly hung up.

A cold shiver ran up her spine. So they had been to Jennifer's place already. They were quick and thorough, real professionals. They must have checked her address book, in her pouch, and found Jennifer's address; or maybe they found the letter in which Jennifer invited her to come and spend the holidays. After they lost track of her at Spink's, they must have driven straight to Jennifer's flat. And they certainly hadn't gone away. They must be lurking in the neighborhood, expecting her to turn up, sooner or later.

She went back to her table. She couldn't go to Jennifer's. Not now. Perhaps they would tap Jennifer's telephone if they were that serious—would they be able to do that? She couldn't go back to France, she had no passport and no plane ticket. She would have to find a place to hide for a few days and then think of a way to get out of here.

But first she needed money. She couldn't survive in London with just the few coins she had in her pocket. As she left the restaurant she recalled that Harrod's was just down the street, which suddenly gave her an idea. It would mean violating one of her most sacred principles, but as her mother used to say, *"à la guerre comme à la guerre."*

Harrod's winter sales had just started that morning and an unusually large crowd, mostly women, was besieging every counter. For half an hour Sylvie wandered through various departments until she found the best setting for the execution of her plan. The ladies' shoe department looked like it was the busiest, as the salesclerks were virtually submerged in the crush.

Sylvie joined the crowd of women milling past the plastic display stands which held every imaginable kind of ladies' shoe. She pretended to examine these attentively, but she was actually more interested in the other customers who were sitting patiently in a long row of padded chairs. The most interesting of these was a stout, matronly woman wearing a light-gray turban and an expensive chinchilla coat who had annexed two chairs—one for herself, one for her large black handbag and a clutch of miscellaneous parcels. She was busy torturing a thin, aging saleswoman, ordering her back and forth with countless pairs of shoes. She was never satisfied and walked frequently over to a nearby mirror to extend a plump leg and critically examine her latest selection. Sylvie watched for an opportunity and when the neighboring seat was vacated, she quickly slid into it, removed her sheepskin coat, and threw it casually over the chair that held the woman's parcels. Her coat almost completely covered the black handbag. Sylvie sat still and waited. A few minutes later her neighbor majestically sailed toward the mirror with a new pair of shoes. Sylvie got up, shrugged as though she were disappointed with the inadequate service, grabbed her coat with her left hand, and unhurriedly walked away. Nobody noticed that she had also snatched the black handbag, which was safely concealed beneath the folds of her sheepskin.

Her heart was beating wildly, but she forced herself to walk slowly out of the ladies' shoe department and into the ladies' room. In one of the cubicles she examined the contents of the bag. She ignored the cards, checkbook, cosmetics, and the other articles one would expect to find in any woman's bag. But the bulging wallet contained more than two hundred pounds in cash, and that was exactly what she needed

She left the handbag in the ladies' room, stuffed the money into her pocket, and hurried into the elevator. Now that she had some money, her confidence was returning rapidly. And she knew exactly where she was going to hide for the next few days.

The white-haired lady that opened the door of the modest Victorian house in Kensington Gardens didn't recognize her immediately.

"How are you, Mrs. O'Shaughnessy?" Sylvie inquired sweetly.

The old lady in the long black dress blinked a few times, then her china-blue eyes lit up with recognition. "Oh, dear," she muttered and clasped her hands. "Well, it's our beautiful French lass. What a surprise! Come in, come in, love. Let me see—why, you haven't been here since . . . since . . ." Her voice trailed off helplessly.

"Since Sean was killed," Sylvie said softly.

The old woman avoided her eyes. "Yes," she whispered. "What a tragedy. What a loss." She suddenly turned back to face Sylvie, thrust her chin up, and looked straight into her eyes. Her eyes were filling up with tears, but the glint of steel that blazed in them reflected a stubborn, unbreakable will. "But the struggle goes on!" she announced defiantly.

"Yes," Sylvie murmured as she bit her lip, "the struggle goes on." *It does for her*, she thought, looking at the small, thin, hollow-chested woman, so frail and defenseless—and yet so strong and dedicated with all the inner fire mirrored in her angular face—stubborn chin, thin lips that seemed to have been carved in stone, blue eyes shining like hard unyielding crystals. Sylvie felt she could see in this woman's face her people's whole history of bloody, fanatical, and yet noble warfare.

"Have you seen any of the group lately?" Mrs. O'Shaughnessy asked eagerly.

Sylvie looked off to one side. "No, not lately."

"Come in, come in," the old Irishwoman urged, and Sylvie followed her down the stairs to the basement. She pushed open a door marked *Office*, which led into a modest room furnished with a desk, a few chairs, and a telephone switchboard. "I'll fix you a cup of tea," Mrs. O'Shaughnessy said, scanning her face critically. "You look ghastly." She moved into the next room, and Sylvie heard her rattling cups and saucers.

"Do you still rent furnished flats?" Sylvie asked loudly.

The old lady reappeared bearing two steaming cups of tea, a pot of cream, a small silver bowl full of sugar cubes, and biscuits on a large tray. "Of course I do," she replied, placing the tray on the desk. "We rent now by the week and even by the day. Business is quite good and I always keep a flat ready for our people. The police almost never bother me."

Almost never, Sylvie thought, *except for that last time when I was here. With Sean.*

"Now then,"—Mrs. O'Shaughnessy took a sip of tea, then raised her eyes to look straight into Sylvie's—"what brings you here, love? You need a flat, don't you?"

Sylvie nodded.

"Trouble?"

She nodded again.

"It's all right," the old woman said softly. "You're one of ours, you'll always be." She put her half-empty cup down on the desk. "You must be exhausted. You could do with a hot bath. Let me take you up to your flat. It's a nice one, the one you had with Sean."

"No, not that one," Sylvie pleaded.

Mrs. O'Shaughnessy sighed and turned away, embarrassed by the raw pain she read in Sylvie's face. "I'm sorry," she said in a dull voice, "it's the only one left."

In the small residents' lounge on the ground floor a lanky middle-aged man was watching the BBC news, his eyes fixed on the big color television set. Sylvie gave him an indifferent glance and had already started up the stairs when something she heard made her stop dead in her tracks.

". . . resulted from multiple stab wounds," the newscaster was saying. "The police are looking for a girl of about the same age, who has apparently spent the last few days in the apartment of the deceased. An anonymous phone call identified the missing girl as Sylvie de Sérigny, a French art student, on a short vacation in London. Another crime was committed last night in Chelsea, where . . ."

"Come on, love, let's go up," Mrs. O'Shaughnessy said impatiently, taking the trembling girl firmly by the elbow. "You've got your own telly in your flat. No use hanging around here." There was nothing in the inflection of her voice or in the sealed expression of her face to show that she had actually heard the news broadcast. Yet Sylvie knew the foxy old woman well. And she could swear Mrs.

O'Shaughnessy had heard and memorized the news piece, every single word of it.

The black ZIL limousine rolled smoothly away from the porch of 2, Dzerzhinski Square, and turned to the right, on its routine itinerary to Andropov's apartment house building on the fashionable Kutuzovski Prospect. But after a few blocks, the driver spun the wheel sharply to the right, drove on for several blocks, past the TSUM state department store and the Moscow Circus, and slowed down at the corner of Samotechnaya Avenue. Two figures wrapped in heavy winter coats detached themselves from the crowd flowing in and out of the huge Moscow central market, front and back doors flew open, and almost instantaneously the two slid into the still moving car. The doors closed noiselessly, the ZIL smoothly accelerated, still heading north. "Just circle around town, Volodya," said Yuri Andropov. "Avoid the center."

The driver nodded. "Certainly, Tovarishch Director."

Andropov turned to his two passengers. "I judged it better to hold this meeting in the car. I still don't know who this man is, and I don't want anybody drawing any conclusions from any unusual meeting in my office."

Both passengers remained silent. The taller of the two, a square-shouldered, brawny colossus, sat woodenly on the front seat, his small eyes staring fixedly ahead. The man sitting beside Andropov in the back seat calmly took off his gloves and his fur-lined Astrakhan cap. He was a middle-aged man of slim build, long legs, and the cruel face of a bird of prey: cold, watchful eyes, wry mouth, and a prominent beaked nose. His scrubbed skin was stretched tightly over his jawline, then sagged and wrinkled around the prominent Adam's apple in loose vulturine folds.

"We still don't have the document," he said. His voice was very deep, but surprisingly well-cultivated.

"Explain, Alexei Sergeievitch," Andropov said curtly.

Alexei Sergeievitch Kalinin, chief of the First Directorate of the KGB, took out of his inner pocket a pack of Gauloises, and lit one with slow, deliberate gestures, cupping his left hand around its glowing tip. The smell of strong black tobacco immediately filled the interior of the car. Andropov wrinkled his nose in disgust, but said nothing.

"As I reported to you three weeks ago, we learned that an unequivocal indication about the identity of the American mole could be found in a certain classified document in the Public Record archives in London. We conceived a plan to get the document with the cooperation of a member of the archival staff. The paper was to be removed from its original file and attached to a declassified file which one of our agents was to request through the customary channels."

"Yes, yes, I know all that," said Andropov impatiently. "The transfer was to take place this morning."

"That's right," Kalinin continued, unperturbably. "A very simple operation. However, our man was given the wrong file. The file containing the document was mistakenly turned over to a young Englishman for a short while—enough time, though, for him to read it and . . . abstract it from the file before our man could correct the error."

"What?" Andropov roared. "What kind of a story are you telling me now, Kalinin? Do you expect me to swallow that nonsense?" He had some difficulty mastering his fury and scornfully spat between his clenched teeth: "A young English student found the document and stole it. Rubbish!"

"That is the truth, however," Kalinin said, and there was a note of apology in his voice. "I deeply regret it, but in the circumstances our man was entirely helpless. You know that Polevoy's people are the best. He can vouch for them."

The huge man in the front seat turned around. "And I trust them completely, Tovarishch Andropov," he said reverently. His hollow, cavernous voice suited his mountainous aspect. "I sent to London the best agents of the operational squad."

"Who?" Andropov asked quickly.

"Korchagin and Muller as front-line operatives, Gorsky, Zaitzev and Chovakine as back-up team, Furtseva from the economic mission, Harris and Spears as local contacts."

Andropov grunted. "Go on."

"When Korchagin and Muller found that the student had stolen the document, they followed him to his flat and liquidated him. They searched the apartment but didn't find the document. They were interrupted in the middle of their search and had to evacuate the place."

"Who interrupted them? The police?"

"No. There was another person in the flat. Our people were unaware of her presence."

"Who was that?"

"A woman, a French girl. Her name is Sylvie de Sérigny." Anastas Polevoy had some trouble pronouncing the French name. "She escaped from the flat, and succeeded in eluding our surveillance. We are convinced that she has the document in her possession."

Andropov turned sharply to Kalinin. "Who is she? Do we know her?"

"No, we have no record of her," Kalinin said carefully. "I checked with the French and British sections."

"We have her papers," volunteered Polevoy. "She is an art student from Paris. We have the address of a friend in London she was staying with and her family's address in France, too."

"Where is she now? Did she go to the police?"

"No," Polevoy said. "She apparently panicked and went into hiding. But she'll come out soon. She has no money and no papers. She will either contact her mother, in France, or try to reach her friend in London. We are watching both places."

"That's not enough," Andropov grunted. "She might hide for weeks, even months. We have had cases like this. Even inexperienced people can live underground when they have to. You'll have to smoke her out."

Polevoy nodded. "The British police are already looking for her—we gave them the name and description, anonymously of course, to save them the trouble. We expect her to surrender to them or try to contact her friend in London. As soon as she comes into the open, we'll get the document."

"And if she goes to the police?"

Kalinin smiled, baring his tobacco-stained teeth. "That will suit us perfectly, Yuri Vladimirovitch. As you know, we have excellent contacts in the British police."

"That's settled, then," Andropov said. He looked out of the car window. The driver had completed a half circle around Moscow, and had reentered the capital by the highway leading to Vnukovo Airport. They passed by the brilliantly illuminated domes of Smolensky Cathedral; Andropov threw an indifferent look at this architectural masterpiece and said to the driver: "Stop here."

The ZIL came to a stop near the Tolstoy Museum. Kalinin and Polevoy silently got out of the car.

"Kalinin!" Andropov called softly. The head of the First Directorate walked back to the car.

"Don't disappoint me again, Kalinin." Andropov's voice was quiet and controlled, but Kalinin didn't miss the tensing of Andropov's jaws, the lines of strain at the edges of his mouth, and the cold fire that burned in his eyes.

"Be careful this time," Andropov said quietly. "Get that document. And kill that girl."

3

BOMB

As she stepped into the flat that she had once shared with Sean, she was caught up in a whirlpool of raw, vivid memories and her entire body was wracked by a spasm of unbearable pain.

Sean came to life before her eyes, the way she had first seen him and had always remembered him since. It had been on a Friday night in midwinter, about three years ago. She had taken the late flight to London to spend a weekend with Jennifer. The plane was full, and she had been among the last to board. The man sitting in the next seat was completely hidden by the unfolded pages of a newspaper, which appeared to be absorbing every particle of his attention. She only noticed the shabby leather bag that he clamped firmly between his legs on the floor. The flight was rather rough—it was a beastly night, with storms and heavy rain, and the flight attendants had trouble getting the refreshment trolleys up the aisle. Just after Sylvie had gotten her orange juice, the plane suddenly dropped into an air pocket, her hand trembled, and the sticky liquid spilled over the sleeve of her neighbor's jacket.

"Oh, I'm terribly sorry," she mumbled, in English. She was deeply embarrassed. The man beside her slowly lowered the paper and turned his head toward her. She found herself looking into the most striking pair of eyes she had ever seen: big, coal black, nestled between long curly lashes and bushy brows, and radiating a fierce, almost palpable magnetism. He had a lean, swarthy face, a patrician nose, and a well-shaped mouth. There was something granite-hard and indomitable in the firm setting of his jaws and the grave look in his eyes. He was about thirty, and he wore a rather shabby tweed jacket over a spotless white turtleneck, which enhanced the darkness of his skin.

"Sorry?" he said politely.

"I am sorry, I spilled my drink over your jacket. Let me clean it off."

He glanced casually at the wet stain on his sleeve. "Oh, never mind, no harm done." He smiled, an extraordinary smile that completely transformed his face and gave it a carefree, boyish air. "But you are very kind indeed."

His smile broadened and after a pause he said, "Anyway I am very pleased that it was you who spilled your juice on my jacket. My name is Sean, Sean Brannigan."

"Oh—"

He anticipated her question instantly. "Yes, you're right, I'm Irish. From Derry."

"Londonderry?" she asked quickly.

He gave her a reproving look. "We just call it Derry."

She couldn't help laughing. "So you, too, are a diehard revolutionary?" But when she noticed the sudden blaze of anger in his face, she added quickly: "I am sorry. Ireland is no joking matter. I know. And furthermore, how could I? We happen to have some common blood."

He looked puzzled.

She explained to him that her mother's family was from Brittany, and her Celtic ancestry made her feel a vague kinship with the Irish. "I also inherited from my grandfather some of his dreams for Breton independence. He was a fervent separatist. When I was still a child, he taught me to scribble in my copybook 'Breiz Atao'—Free Brittany —and to recognize the symbol of the Breton rebels. It seemed a cruel symbol to me then: an owl's carcass crucified on a barn door. I think the dreams of the Bretons and the Irish are quite similar."

He smiled vaguely and asked a few questions about her family and her life in France. They chatted pleasantly until the aircraft landed in a rainswept airstrip at Heathrow. She felt rather intrigued by this handsome Irishman, and she would have liked to see him again, but he didn't give her his address or ask for hers.

They disembarked quickly and started the usual trek down the endless concourses of the airport, Sean Brannigan walking close behind her. The airport was almost deserted, but there seemed to be a record number of policemen posted all along their way, as well as a great many other men who she imagined might be plainclothesmen. By the time they reached the immigration desks it was obvious that something was wrong. A cordon of policemen appeared to be hovering over every incoming passenger. "What do you think about—" She turned to Brannigan and stopped in midsentence. All the blood had drained from his face, and his eyes darted nervous glances up and down the corridor. Once she had ridden with a hunt near her family's château in the Orléannais; she had come quite close to the fox, cornered by the wildly barking dog pack. She had seen the frantic sparks in the fox's eyes, and knew how to recognize the look of a hunted animal.

She suddenly understood. "Give me that," she hissed, without thinking, and almost tore the leather bag from his grasp. "I'll meet you outside the terminal."

"No," he murmured, his eyes still shifting anxiously. "It won't be safe. Take the airport bus to the Cromwell Road terminal, and then a cab. Twenty-seven Kensington Gardens. Wait for me there."

She moved ahead, quickening her pace, while he fell back to put distance and people between them. While giving routine answers to the immigration officer, a bored young man in horn-rimmed spectacles, she glanced over her shoulder and saw Sean, surrounded by policemen, disappearing through a side door. She was quickly checked through and she had no trouble reaching the house in Kensington Gardens. The old woman—who she later learned was called Mrs. O'Shaughnessy—treated her with cold reserve, didn't react when she mentioned Sean's name, and didn't speak to her during her long wait in the residents' lounge. Only when Sean came in, hours later, and warmly took Sylvie's hands in his, did she smile at her. A few minutes later she reappeared with a tray of delicious sandwiches and delicately perfumed tea. Sylvie followed Sean up to his furnished flat on the third floor. He was jubilant. "They had to release me," he said. "My papers were in order, and they didn't find anything in my bags."

"But they were waiting for you," Sylvie said.

"Yes. They must have got a tip."

"Why, Sean? What is in this bag?"

The same hard, grave expression she had seen before returned to his face. "My dear girl," he said in a low voice, "you have just smuggled a ten-pound bomb into London."

She was surprised by her own reaction. She was not revolted, and she didn't feel any guilt or shame for what she had done. She felt even relieved that the bag didn't contain any drugs, which she loathed. She looked intently at Sean's face and realized that he had been watching her closely.

"Then you *are* a revolutionary?"

He smiled. "The BBC calls us terrorists, but back home the correct term is 'murderin' Fenian bastards!' "

"Why did you tell me? About the bomb, I mean?"

His face was pensive. "I don't know, really. I suppose I just trust you." He took off his jacket and started pacing around the room. "As a rule, I'm very suspicious, you know. But tonight I was absolutely certain I could rely on you. Why? I think you would have to call that my Celtic intuition. Underground life tends to make one a keen judge of character."

She looked at his athletic body, his handsome face, and felt an almost physical thrill of real adventure. Nothing like this had ever happened to her before, not in the exquisite dullness of her parents' château and certainly not in the Catholic girls' college of Saint Amboise. Even the last two years on her own in Paris, studying at the Sorbonne and decorating the exquisite flat her mother had rented for her on the Ile Saint-Louis, had scarcely been teeming with excitement. And here she was, on a tempestuous London night, in the hideaway of an Irish underground fighter, a live bomb within her reach.

"You should go now," he said. "I imagine you must be expected somewhere."

Jennifer must be worried to death, she thought, but she didn't care.

"Your . . ." she hesitated. "Your operation, is it for tonight?"

"No," he said. "Why do you ask?"

She kicked off her shoes, squatted comfortably in one of the deep armchairs, and smiled at him. "You know what I'd really like? A big glass of brandy and the life story of Sean Brannigan, freedom fighter." It sounded quite artificial, though, and she added spontaneously, "I want to know more about you, Sean. I like you."

He gave her a long, strange look. "You look like an elf to me," he said softly. "All huddled up there, in the middle of that great chair, with your long hair and your mischievous eyes and the innocent frankness of a child. . . ." His voice faded away.

He went to the other room and returned with a decanter and two bell-shaped glasses. He poured the brandy into her glass and cupped it for a while in his hands. As the amber-colored liquid warmed up, it diffused a fragrant aroma. He handed her the glass and sat on the floor by her feet. "I like you too," he said. His voice was very slow, very peaceful. "I'd like to talk to you."

She could never tell, later, how long they talked. Two hours? All night? He began to tell her about his boyhood in Derry, as the sixth child—and fourth son—of a poor Catholic family. The Brannigans were fiery, relentless fighters, and had been considered by the British government to be a pack of perennial troublemakers. Several of Sean's forefathers had ended on the gallows. His own father had been killed and his eldest brother wounded in the ruthless confrontation of Protestant against Catholic which had spread across Northern Ireland in the last ten years. His sister and nephew were killed when a bomb went off in a restaurant where they were celebrating the boy's eleventh birthday. "On their graves I swore to carry on the fight," Sean said. These words could sound like the flimsiest clichés, and yet in Sean's mouth they carried a solid ring of truth. He had joined the IRA and fought in the streets against British soldiers in Belfast and Derry. Advancing quickly through the ranks of this clandestine army, he had become one of the leaders of the radical wing, who advocated "bringing the war home to England"—by the bombing of military objectives—barracks, headquarters, and transmitting stations. He was sent to London with a select team of his comrades. Their main base was to be this house, owned by Mrs. O'Shaughnessy. The old woman had dedicated her life to the Irish cause, after her husband was shot on the steps of St. Patrick's church in Belfast a few minutes after their wedding.

Sean told her that they would hit their first objective over the weekend. But she didn't hear the end of the story. She was fast asleep, curled up in the cosy armchair, dreaming that he was holding her close, pressing his warm body against hers, and making love to her as no man ever had.

They didn't make love that night or the next. Only after midnight on Sunday, when he came back, triumphant, and found her asleep in the narrow bed by the window, did he touch her. He gently removed the covers and woke her, caressing her all over with his burning lips. She lay still, not even opening her eyes, reliving the erotic fantasies of her dreams. He made love to her exactly as she had imagined, and she climaxed in an explosion of ecstasy she had never known before. And while she still held him tight, her hands clutching his back, his brown curly head nestled in the hollow of her shoulder, she realized that she had fallen in love with this Irish rebel.

It was more than that. Sean Brannigan had become so much a part of her that nothing else mattered. She did not return to Paris; she stopped seeing Jennifer and only communicated with her family when she needed money; she became indifferent to her mother's anguish and incomprehension. She traveled everywhere with Sean and gradually came to share more of his secret life. She succeeded in overcoming the suspicion of Sean's companions; they spoke with genuine affection of "the French lass" who had joined their struggle. Sean declared fervently that she had "got under me skin," and he was clearly devoted to her. On one point only he remained adamant: she was never to engage in any secret activity, never to smuggle any arms or explosives, or take part in any of their operations. When she protested the decision, he put his hands on her shoulders and said softly, very tenderly: "I have given Ireland all I have, even my own life. You are the only thing I want just for myself. Please, try to understand."

She had acquiesced, accepting the edict as the price of her happiness, of being on his side, in his struggle. And she had been happy that year, a wild, almost savage kind of happiness, tasting life every minute of the day, drinking it to the lees. And yet now and again she would awake in the middle of the night bathed in cold sweat, suddenly realizing that this couldn't last forever. Two of Sean's comrades, the big, burly Neil and the soft-spoken Kevin, had been killed in the streets of London; one of the girls, Maureen, had been arrested with a gun in her purse. And when once in a while they would enjoy a relaxed evening in their flat, she would hold him tightly when the youngest of the band, clear-eyed Ryan, picked his guitar and intoned a sad Irish ballad.

Oddly enough it was Sylvie who provoked their first real disagreement. A few months after they had started living together, strange visitors began coming to their flat, mostly at night, to confer with Sean: dark, taciturn Arabs, polite but secretive Japanese. In the newspapers there were rumors of a secret alliance between the IRA, the PLO, and the Japanese Red Army. She questioned Sean about this, and he admitted stiffly that there had been meetings with representatives of other revolutionary groups. She was shocked. "Those people are terrorists of the worst kind, Sean," she said heatedly. "They don't hesitate to murder civilians, to kill for the sake of killing. It's a shame for the Irish fighters to be associated with them."

"They are freedom fighters," he countered angrily. "They have their own ways of fighting."

"You call that fighting? Blowing up planes and slaughtering women and children? Sean, don't you think that even freedom fighting should comply with certain moral principles?"

The row ended when Sean rushed out of the flat, slamming the door behind him. But their argument on this subject became increasingly violent and painful. When the Palestinians hijacked an Air France plane to Entebbe, and an Israeli task force liberated the kidnapped passengers, she was appalled to find that Sean sided with the hijackers.

"For heaven's sake, Sean, how can one help admiring what the Israelis did?" she cried. "And can you possibly justify those sadistic killers?"

"Why don't you just stick it, then!" he snapped back brutally. "Those people are fighting a war. Stop bellowing around like a child who found out that Father Christmas is dead." She started to cry, deeply hurt, and although he managed to soothe her with caresses and tender concern, her frustration didn't fade away. What disturbed her even more was the painful sense of having awakened from a dream, the realization that her Sean was changing before her eyes, and that she couldn't do anything to stop it.

And then, one day, the thing she most dreaded had actually happened. For security reasons, he never told her what the next objective would be. And she had never questioned his decisions, since that night when the bomb she had brought from Paris had damaged the London Post Office tower. But that morning she saw the newspaper photograph of a young woman's shattered body lying in the wreckage of a London restaurant. It was just as if someone had pointed an accusing finger at her and said: "You are to blame for this!"

"You did it, didn't you?" she asked Sean when he came back to Kensington Gardens. It was a late autumn afternoon. A cold wind was blowing outside, sweeping the fallen leaves off the sidewalks and spinning them around like damned souls joined in a *danse macabre*.

"Yes," he said, "we did it."

"But Sean, look at that girl! She is not a soldier, she's not a combatant. She might not even be English. Why did she have to die?"

"We decided to intensify the struggle," he said quietly.

"Intensify the struggle? By throwing bombs into crowded restaurants? My God, Sean, that's plain murder! You told me you were going to hit only military objectives. What is that poor girl—a military objective?"

"Now, take it easy, Sylvie." It was clear that he was struggling to keep his own temper from erupting. "You know what the British are doing to my people. We can't let it go on, don't you see? We alert public opinion, we must use terror as a warning. . . ."

"As a warning against what?" she interjected bitterly. "That you might kill more people? More innocent men and women who just happened to be in a restaurant that you picked out of the telephone book?"

"You don't understand." His face was livid and his voice quavered on the edge of fury.

"Maybe I don't. You know that I support your struggle with all my heart. But you'll never make me condone murder. That makes you as low as the lowest criminal!"

She ran sobbing from the room and for the first time in a year she stayed overnight in Jennifer's flat. Jennifer was tactful enough not to ask questions. She lay awake all night, her soul in torment, listening to the shrill wail of the wind outside. At the first light of dawn she got up, hastily scribbled a note to Jennifer, and hurried out to the street. She called Sean from a phone booth. He sounded like he was just as miserable as she. "I love you, Sean," she whispered into the phone.

"I love you too, my darling. Please come home. I must talk to you. I have something to tell you."

What had he wanted to tell her? She never found out. When she came back to the flat he had already gone. Mrs. O'Shaughnessy told her that he would return in the early afternoon.

But in the early afternoon a police radio car stopped in front of the house. Two officers appeared at the outer door.

"Is this the house where Sean Brannigan lived?" one of them asked formally.

* * *

He had been killed instantly, blown to bits by the explosion of a plastic charge outside the Regency restaurant in Baker Street. The only eyewitness, an elderly cleaning woman who was on her way to the nearby underground station, gave a detailed but still somewhat puzzling statement to the police: "I was walking on the other side of the street, I was, minding my own business, and there I saw this young gentleman, a very presentable young man I should say—he looked Italian to me, or Greek. Now I happened to notice him because I think it very queer for him to be just standing there, with all that nasty weather, raining cats and dogs, as it was. But he was looking at his watch, and I thinks to myself, maybe he's waiting for his girl and he doesn't want to go in before she comes. And just then a taxi stopped right in front of the restaurant and I think to myself again, maybe his young lady's coming now, but it was just a couple with their children, two little boys, I think, and they went into the restaurant. Then he moved over to the window and he sort of held something under his coat, and he raised his hand, and suddenly he seemed to hesitate and then everything exploded and there was a big ball of fire—just like in the blitz, when a German bomb came down in my street and killed little Derek Bartley."

Sylvie was held for forty-eight hours at the police station and questioned at length, first by two police inspectors, and later by a superintendent of the Special Branch. They couldn't establish anything against her except that she had been Sean's girl friend, which she admitted freely. Finally, they let her go.

From the station she had taken a cab straight to Heathrow and had flown back to France. By the time she reached her mother's château, the deep cuts in her lower lip, which she had almost bitten through more than once, were beginning to heal over. And her eyes were dry.

* * *

It was a year before she came back to life, a year she spent in the Sérigny château, almost never leaving her room. Her mother had only learned what had happened from the accounts in the newspapers, but Sylvie obstinately refused to say anything. For the first few months she was just a shadow of herself, sinking deeper and deeper into apathy and despair. She rarely touched food, she stopped reading, and her favorite records gathered dust on the shelf. She would sit for hours by the window, her long thin hands resting limply in her lap, and her hollow eyes staring unseeingly at the low gray sky of the Orléannais. Her mother feared that she might try to kill herself and spent many nights in the corridor outside her room, often coming to the door to listen for her breathing. But Sylvie was made of stronger stuff than she herself suspected. Slowly, painfully, she emerged from the nightmare. She returned to Paris, found a new apartment, and, instead of going back to the Sorbonne, she signed up for a program of art courses. She gradually started seeing her old friends, going to parties, traveling, laughing again. On her first flight to London she trembled with anxiety on the way over. But her visit was a pleasant one, Jennifer was as friendly and peppy as ever, and she found to her surprise that her wounds had healed and she could still love London. Yet it took her a long time before she could go to bed with a man again. And when she met René Dumas, and let herself be seduced by him, she realized that something deep inside her had died with Sean Brannigan, and she would never feel the same passion for a man that she had for her Irish lad.

René was blond, tall, full of laughter, supremely indifferent to politics. It sometimes occurred to her that she had subconsciously chosen him because he was so completely different from her dead lover. René ran a highly successful advertising agency; he was brilliant, original, self-indulgent, and rich. Essentially he was a pleasure seeker—the best food, the best wine, the best clothes. His appetite for the bizarre and the unexpected had taken him all over the world—now Sylvie went with him. They had a glorious time together, whether they were in Paris or the Upper Amazon. He was very much in love with her; she was never in love with him. She enjoyed being with him, traveling with him to the most enthralling places, staying in the finest hotels, the most exclusive resorts. He knew how to make her laugh and taught her to enjoy herself again, and yet she felt that their relationship had only one dimension, that there was nothing beneath the surface that might have created an emotional bond between them. He was an expert lover who knew all sorts of ways of exciting her and of gratifying her sexual needs. But she felt that he had perfected his art to such a degree that he was more of a performer or a technician than a real lover. She found herself some nights yearning for a less thrilling performance, but one with a little more spontaneity, for some genuine explosion of love on his side that would make him lose his head and forget, just for once, his technique. But the nights were always perfect and René very proud of himself when he made her climax, scream, and lacerate his back with her fingernails.

And then one night in Paris, as was bound to happen sooner or later, she realized the futility of it all. She left him casually, without real emotion, and the last evening they spent together strangely resembled the first. She had missed him, though, during the last few weeks, but more as somebody she enjoyed having around than as somebody she needed. A week ago she had come to London, met Richard Hall, and this morning a new nightmare had begun.

She sank into the armchair where she had spent her first night in the flat with Sean and closed her eyes.

* * *

She was awakened by a gentle tapping on the door, and dimly remembered the prearranged code: three knocks, a pause, and three again. The pale morning light was filtering through the drawn curtains, and she suddenly realized she had fallen asleep in the armchair, without even taking off her boots. She got up and hastily tried to smooth out her rumpled clothes. All her bones ached. "I'm coming," she called. She had a sticky, bitter taste in her mouth and her head felt heavy. She opened the door.

"Morning, love." Mrs. O'Shaughnessy marched into the sitting room humming cheerfully, carrying a tray laden with tea, buttered toast, and jam. "Here's some breakfast for you," she said, putting the tray on the dining table and pulling the curtains open. She glanced quickly at the untouched bed in the alcove, but didn't say a word. Only after she had poured out a first cup of tea for Sylvie did she speak to her, in a very soft voice, like a mother talking to a badly frightened child.

"Listen to me now. Your name is all over the morning papers, but I know you and I'm sure you had nothing to do with it. If you did, you certainly had a good reason. I told you yesterday this house is yours, and you can stay here as long as you want to. I understand that you are hiding from someone. If someone is the police, this house won't do. They found you here the last time, and they won't have forgotten where to look. They will certainly come here during the day and search the house. Now I've thought it over, and I know a place where you can stay, where you'll be perfectly safe. It's another safehouse of ours—the police have never called there yet."

Sylvie smiled with gratitude and touched her thin white hand. "Thank you. Really. But I can't, Mrs. O'Shaughnessy. I can't go on hiding. I'd go crazy. I think it would be better if I called my friend Jennifer and talked things over with her."

"Can't you go back home?"

She shook her head. "No passport."

"Then we'll have to find you another," Mrs. O'Shaughnessy observed calmly.

"Yes, I believe you could," Sylvie said thoughtfully. "Maybe I'll ask you for that favor. But not right now. I want to try to sort things out with my friend first, all right?"

"Suit yourself," the old lady said.

In front of Baden-Powell House, in Queensgate, there was a row of red phone booths. Sylvie dialed Jennifer's number.

"Hello?" Jennifer's voice was thick with sleep.

"Don't talk, Jennifer, just listen. I have to meet you. We'll have to pick a time and place, but I think there's someone else listening to your phone. If you follow me, say yes, just yes."

"Yes," gasped Jennifer, now wide awake.

"Fine. Now think of some place that only you and I know about. And then just give me a hint."

There was a silence at the other end of the line.

"Think, Jennifer."

"What the hell do you think I'm doing?" Jennifer was back in her usual form.

Another long pause.

"I've got it," Jennifer announced triumphantly. "The little gray cells are still working."

"Then where?"

"Remember the lady with the red-striped gown? The one who had lost a very important part of her anatomy?"

"Tell me more."

"She kept shouting: 'Bring me light! Bright me light!' "

Sylvie tried to concentrate. "I think I do remember," she said slowly, then: "No, I'm sorry, Jennifer. I remember her quite well, but I can't recall the place."

"Forget it," Jennifer said briskly. "I'll give you another one. Are you sure you're with me, now?"

"Oh, yes, I am," Sylvie answered eagerly.

"Now, let me think. Do you happen to recall the place where the mad old woman went looking for her children. Where the eternal rest of the inhabitants was disturbed by . . . No, that's too far. We couldn't make it out there."

"Try again," Sylvie said.

"Just a moment. Yes, I think this will do. Remember poor old Anne?"

Sylvie hesitated. "Anne . . . Anne Bee, you mean?"

"That's the one. Now, she left for her final trip from a place where she was heard crying. Remember?"

Sylvie burst into relieved laughter. "Of course. I remember. She went down the steps."

"Exactly."

"How clever, Jennifer," Sylvie exclaimed admiringly.

"Clever as ever. Well, same time, same place?"

"I'll be there," Sylvie said. "But, please, be awfully careful when you go out. I'm sure you're being watched."

"Don't worry. See you later. Bye now."

"Bye." Sylvie put the phone back on its hook.

In a Dairy Maid van parked in Berkeley Square KGB agents Harris and Chovakine took off their headsets. They exchanged puzzled glances.

"Play it again," Harris said.

Chovakine pressed the rewind button on the tape recorder. The spools revolved quickly with a low hum. Chovakine pressed stop and play in quick succession. They listened again to the taped phone conversation between Sylvie de Sérigny and Jennifer Soames.

"The place where she was heard crying," Harris repeated slowly. "Now what the hell does that mean?"

4

GHOST

Jennifer Soames replaced the receiver on the cradle and looked down at it for a moment with a contented smile. She stretched her arms, yawned luxuriously, and vigorously rubbed her eyes with her small fists, like a child. She slid regretfully out from beneath her satin sheets—she liked indulging in small luxuries—and tiptoed to the kitchen, naked and shivering, to put the kettle on the stove. She was an alert, vivacious redhead with a freckled face, a small upturned nose, and laughing green eyes. She was not beautiful, and she knew it; she was petite and plump, and there was nothing glamorous about her short arms and legs. Still, she thought, her small, compact body was very attractive in a kittenish sort of way—but not a patch on Sylvie's. She knew she would never live dramatic love adventures like Sylvie—but on the other hand she would never be as lonely as she was. Sylvie's beauty frightened people as much as it attracted them, and only the boldest dared to approach, while Jennifer's easy, pleasant manner put them immediately at ease. Men enjoyed her company, liked going to bed with her, and they had started taking her seriously since she had proved to be an extremely shrewd businesswoman.

She ground a handful of coffee beans and prepared a huge mug of strong black coffee, humming an old Beatles song and beating time with her left foot. If her professional colleagues could just see her now! She had started her business venture barely two years ago, and today was unchallenged in her field. It had been a matter of sheer luck, combined with a touch of imagination. While strolling with a friend through Berkeley Square one evening, she had noticed a For Sale sign on an ordinary-looking Georgian house. She hadn't honored the four-story building with a second glance, but her companion, a journalist, had exclaimed, "Ghost house for sale! Who'd ever want to live in a place like that?"

"Ghost house? That one?"

He had stared at her in disbelief. "Come on, Jenny, don't you know that this is the most famous haunted house in London?"

They sat down on a bench and he had told her how in the middle of the last century the house had been deserted in panic by its owners, when the ghost of a child, dressed in a Scots kilt, had started to appear on the staircase at night, crying and wringing its tiny hands. That was the first ghost. A few years later a young girl was seen several times at the top-floor window, desperately clinging to the windowsill and screaming horribly. That was supposed to be the ghost of a girl who had thrown herself to her death from the window, to escape being raped by a perverted uncle.

One girl who spent a night in the house in 1870 was found quite mad with horror the following day; a man who had made a bet he would survive a night with the ghosts was found dead in the morning. That same year two sailors, noticing the house was empty, had taken shelter from a winter storm in its empty rooms. But in the middle of the night they were awakened by blood-chilling groans and the sound of steps in the deserted corridors. They saw the door of their room slowly open and "something shapeless and horrible" crawl in. Terror-stricken, one of the sailors had fled from the house, but the other one was found dead, impaled on the spiked fence surrounding the garden. Since then, the house at 50 Berkeley Square had become notorious all over England for its ghastly secrets.

Jennifer had taken the story with a grain of salt. "If you'd asked me, I would have given you a far better explanation. Both sailors were drunk, there was a row, one got killed, and the other needed a good story to tell the judge. 'Something shapeless and horrible,' indeed!"

"Maybe and maybe not," her friend said. "But people do believe in these things. You know that crowds of tourists gather here, almost every day? People will do almost anything for a good scare, after all."

The last words had given her an idea. A week later, mobilizing all resources, she bought the house and transformed it into the headquarters of a new travel agency, Occult London, of which she was sole proprietor. She then collected all the books she could find on ghosts, haunted houses, the scenes of atrocious crimes, notorious prisons, hanging trees, and places of execution all over London. Her next step was to insert a very modest ad in several travel magazines, offering "a night of horror" to small, select groups of tourists. Barely two weeks later she knew that she had struck gold.

It was at a time when America was raving about anything horrid, diabolical, or weird. Movies like *The Exorcist* and *The Omen* were attracting huge crowds; TV films about witches and sorcery got top ratings; books on ghosts, possession, and demons had conquered the best-seller lists. Haunted London, with its solid reputation for bloody crimes, eerie apparitions, rattling skeletons in torture chambers, ghoulish secrets buried behind the walls of medieval castles, soon became a must for American visitors to England. And to see all those places of horror, they were ready to pay the most delightful fees.

Jennifer's staging of the haunted London tours was masterly. Shortly before midnight the tourists were picked up at their hotels by sinister-looking guides, all in black, who led them to chauffeur-driven black limousines. They then set out for the principal attractions of ghostland: the Tower of London, haunted by the flower of the English nobility—hanged, beheaded, immured, or drowned in its dark recesses; the Elms at Smithfield, where felons and heretics had once been roasted (or boiled) alive; the suicide tree at Green Park, where the spirits gather at nightfall; St. James's Place in Pall Mall, haunted by the bloody phantom of the Italian Sellis, whose throat was cut by the Duke of Cumberland himself; the Isle of Dogs, with its skeletal horseman and black-draped figures lurking on the foggy wharfs; and on to a multitude of haunted palaces, cemeteries, parks, and houses. Some of the tours included a nocturnal rowboat trip on the Thames and its canals; every rowboat was equipped with muffled oars that allowed them to glide noiselessly through the black waters. The brochure for this trip was headed by a quotation from Heinrich Heine, who observed that the Thames "had already swallowed up such floods of human tears without giving them a thought. . . ."

Even when they didn't see or hear any ghosts—which was frequently the case—the tourists returned to their hotels in the eerie light of dawn, deeply thrilled by the expedition to dark houses, deserted cemeteries, parks full of mysterious shadows, and brooding medieval fortresses.

Soon Jennifer found herself at the helm of an extremely prosperous enterprise. Her staff was constantly expanding, and even some of the stuffier London hotels made discreet inquiries about special ghost tours for the guests. After Occult London's initial success Jennifer was approached by several movie and television production companies that needed a London consultant to arrange backgrounds and locations. Lately she had created a new department entirely devoted to the preparation of newsletters and illustrated guides to haunted London.

Jennifer herself very rarely appeared at the offices of her firm. She preferred to manage the business from her apartment on the fourth floor of the "haunted house" in Berkeley Square, where she lived alone, shamelessly ignoring the horrid creatures who were reputed to share her lodging. She avoided giving interviews about the business, or being photographed. As she remarked, "If they put a picture of my funny little face in just one article about Occult London, all my clients will desert me."

She giggled loudly now and going into a parody of a voluptuous dance, writhed seductively over to the full-length mirror in her bedroom. She raised her mug to her reflection and chuckled again, imagining a centerfold photograph of herself, naked little body, flaming red head, and all. "Jennifer," she announced loudly to the mirror, "Queen of Occult London, Play Ghost of the Month."

Today, though, Occult London had served in a good cause: it had helped her to improvise a code for communicating with Sylvie. She and Sylvie had gone out on a few private tours of haunted London; she could only hope that whoever was listening to Sylvie's phone call did not know as much about haunted London as she did.

She was genuinely relieved that she was going to see Sylvie again, and especially to hear the story of what had happened in Richard's apartment. The papers had made much of the "multiple stab wounds" and the "fugitive art student" business, but she had an absolute faith in Sylvie. She had almost started firing questions as soon as she picked up the phone, but if Sylvie thought there was somebody listening in, then so be it. She admired Sylvie's good sense, and she loved her very dearly. Even though she lived in France, and even after that frightful year which she called "my Sinn Fein experience," Sylvie still was—and always would be—her best, most beloved friend. In fact, Jennifer couldn't recall a time, even in her earliest memories of childhood, when she hadn't loved and even worshipped Sylvie de Sérigny.

It had started as a family friendship, long before she and Sylvie were born. During the Second World War her father, Major Jeoffrey Soames, was a liaison officer with the Free French, attached to General De Gaulle's staff. His opposite number, Comte Hugo de Sérigny, was one of the first French officers to rally to the Free France standard. The two of them had struck up a warm friendship. The Count was a frequent weekend guest at the Soames cottage in Surrey, and after the war, Jeoffrey and Elizabeth Soames had spent several splendid summers in the Sérigny castle in France. After Jennifer and Sylvie were born, only a few months apart, it was only natural for them to become friends as well. The ties between the two girls became stronger after Colonel de Sérigny was killed in Algeria. Sylvie, who had been close to her father, could hardly bear the lonely life with her mother in the château, and it became a habit for the two girls to spend their vacations together, either in France or in England. After Sylvie graduated from Saint Amboise, she stayed with Jennifer in London for an entire year; both girls agreed that this had been the happiest of their lives.

Jennifer often looked back at that bygone year in deep nostalgia. How joyful and carefree they had been then, two young girls with shining eyes, sailing into maturity while the world opened before them like a flower, offering its beauty and its pleasures. She must have been very naive then, but she'd certainly thought Sylvie would have had a better time of it. After all she was beautiful, clever, not to mention filthy rich, and she knew how to enjoy herself. Not that she'd had much chance—first Sean, and now this business with Richard.

She finished her coffee, and her natural optimism banished these gloomy reflections. They'd find a way out of all this. They'd talk about it all, and even if someone had listened in on the phone, how would he figure out what the bloody hell they were talking about?

The little man took off his rain-soaked hat, shook his umbrella, and squinted through thick glasses at the frosted glass door, then noticed the brass plaque on the wall beside it. He read the Russian inscription first, then the English— just to be sure he'd got it right: *SOVTORG, Trade Mission of the Union of Soviet Socialist Republics.* Below that, in smaller characters: *Staff Only.* He unbuttoned his heavy woolen coat, took a large gray handkerchief from an inner pocket, and mopped his bald head. That beastly rain had soaked his hat through and ruined it completely. He couldn't recall ever having had a more unpleasant journey; commuters piled onto that damned train like net fish on a barrow, taxis scarce as hen's teeth, crawling along down Oxford Street, and one final outrage—ten minutes in a stalled elevator. He pressed the doorbell and almost immediately a blurred shape materialized behind the thick glass and two locks opened in rapid succession.

"Yes?" The man in the door, Reed thought, did not exactly fit the stereotype of "faceless Soviet bureaucrat" or "all-in wrestling champion," but seemed to fall somewhere in between. At any rate, he was large, powerfully built, clad in the regulation badly cut blue suit (though much too small, rather than baggy), and virtually expressionless.

He cleared his throat. "I'm here to see Mr. Blake."

"There is no Mr. Blake here." The heavyweight spoke with a remarkably thick accent, stringing the words together as if he had learned the phrase by rote.

"Today there is. He is expecting me. Accounting Department? Room seventeen?"

"Your name?"

"Reed. Professor George Reed."

The Russian bowed formally. "Just one moment, please." He ushered Reed into a small vestibule and disappeared through a door on the right. A minute or two later the Russian returned. "Will you please follow me?"

They went through a large office; six employees—two women and four men—were busy with typewriters and calculating machines. Only one of them, a pretty, black-haired girl, looked up and then quickly looked back at her keyboard. The Russian led him through another door and into a corridor. He knocked on a door that was plainly marked *nine*. *Well then*, Reed said to himself, *I didn't expect to actually have the pleasure of meeting Mr. Blake, but I thought at least there might really be a room seventeen. I suppose that means that if I'm picked up and interrogated, our people can say I blundered in here by mistake or perhaps that I must be suffering from the delusion that I'm a Russian spy.*

Room nine was very small: just a rectangular conference table, with a telephone in the corner, and five upright chairs. Dark-brown curtains covered the only window; an old Aeroflot poster of a gleaming Soviet jetliner was the sole ornament on the light-gray walls.

Three people were seated around the table. A fourth, a stout middle-aged fellow, with reddish skin, who had opened the door, warmly pumped his hand. "Professor Reed, how good of you to come. Let me take your coat. My, you're dripping wet. I called you this morning. My name is Jones."

Probably not his real name, reflected Professor Reed, but then, these were the most elementary precautions. When he had called him this morning he didn't identify himself. He just used the code word—"Doctor Slater sends his greetings"—and summoned him urgently to London.

"I had to cancel two classes," Reed said reproachfully. "It was very annoying indeed."

"I am sorry. I am sorry," Jones apologized in a placating tone. "You must forgive us. As I was just explaining to this lady and this gentleman"—he made a quick motion toward the table—"it is an emergency, and we have an important job for you."

He showed him a vacant chair. "Please be seated, Professor."

Reed found himself sitting between a woman and another man—both English by the look of them. Opposite them was Jones's empty chair and a third man—almost certainly a Russian.

George Reed had been an enthusiastic party member in the thirties, had taken the trouble to learn Russian fairly well, and had even fought in Spain. There he had been approached by the KGB. Reed spent the war years in London as a captain in the British Army Intelligence Branch—the MI-6—seconded to liaison duties with the Soviet Military Mission. His nominal responsibilities consisted primarily of interpreting at low-level briefing sessions and finding hotel accommodations for Russian officers. In fact, he had provided a great deal more aid and comfort to the Soviet Mission while serving in an unofficial capacity.

Since his return to Oxford after the war Reed had been more or less inactive. A lecturer in logic had considerably less to offer than a captain in the MI-6, though he was called on occasionally to perform fairly routine services. The cryptic summons he had received that morning was the first such call in several years.

Jones sat down opposite him. "This lady and these gentlemen, professor, have already examined the record in front of you. It is a transcript of a telephone conversation between two young women. They are arranging a meeting which will almost certainly take place today, perhaps tonight. They've improvised a sort of personal code and I've asked you all here to crack the code. It is imperative"—he looked at the taciturn Russian and corrected himself—"*absolutely* imperative that we find out where and when the meeting is going to take place."

The professor was tactful enough not to ask why.

He bent over the transcript that had been typed triple spaced, so was easy to read. He went through it quickly at first, then read it again, much more attentively.

He adjusted his glasses. "I have a few questions," he said. "May we know the identity of these women, their ages, some personal details about them?"

Jones threw a quick look at the Russian, who nodded.

"I can give you some answers," Jones said, adding quickly, "up to a point, that is. Both women are young, as I said, about twenty-five, twenty-six. The one referred to as Jennifer is Jennifer Soames, an Englishwoman, who runs a kind of tourist agency called Occult London. The other one is French. Her name is of no importance. She has been hiding and obviously wants to meet her friend some place where she will not be seen."

George Reed nodded thoughtfully. "How close is the relationship between these two young ladies?"

"We have checked that," Jones said. "They are the best of friends."

"And how long has their relationship existed?"

"Since early childhood, it appears."

The professor pursed his lips. "That makes things awkward. They can refer to any past common experience."

"Excuse me for butting in," said the man on Reed's right. He was a well-built, well-dressed man who looked like a caricature of the Englishman as depicted in early American movies; three-piece pin-striped suit, old Etonian tie, carefully trimmed reddish mustache with waxed, up-turned edges, and an expression of utter boredom on his long horsy face. He was addressing Mr. Jones. "You seem to have done quite an extensive research job on these women, and you know more about them than you are ready to tell us Wouldn't it be more fruitful if you tried to decipher that phone conversation by yourselves? You don't really need us for that."

If Jones took offense at his words, he didn't show it. Quite the opposite: He smiled suavely. "Come on, sir, you certainly understand," he said indulgently. "You know that many of our people here are not English. Even if they know this country well, this particular sort of work requires people who know the English habits, the forms of speech, the use of certain words. . . ."

"Just a moment!" This was the woman on Reed's left, an obese white-haired woman of about sixty. She was fair-skinned and her fat face bore almost no wrinkles. Her features were quite ordinary but her eyes were sharp, and her strong voice carried a natural authority. "Did you say forms of speech? Well, there are a few expressions here that might be helpful. First of all, when the French girl understands what Jennifer is trying to convey to her, she says: 'How clever, Jennifer.' She wouldn't have said that if Jennifer had reminded her of some . . . some ordinary experience they had had. These words point at something particular, something special. But there is more. If you return to the beginning of the conversation, you'll see that although Jennifer fails to convey to the French girl the first meeting place, she asks: 'Are you with me now' and the French girls answers: 'Yes, I am.' This indicates that they speak of a particular category of common experience they have had."

George Reed nodded in agreement and with precise gestures started lighting his briar pipe. "Yes, I agree with you. Now, let's try and see what kind of particular experience that might have been." He plunged his head into the transcript, and so did the others. After a long silence he raised his eyes. "There is something definitely strange about the words used," he said. "Look here." He waved his transcript and pointed. "Oh, I'm sorry. That's page two, at the top. 'The lady with the red-striped gown . . . who had lost a very important part of her anatomy.' She must mean she has lost a leg or an arm."

"Maybe they had been together in a hospital?" the man in the pin-striped suit suggested.

"No, no," Reed said impatiently. "In a hospital she wouldn't have shouted, 'Bring me light!' So it must have been a dark place."

"I don't know about this first place," intervened the stout woman, "but the second one they talked about was certainly a cemetery."

Reed scanned the transcript. "Yes, you're right," he said. "The place where 'the mad old woman was looking for her children,' and where 'the eternal rest of the inhabitants was disturbed.' "

" 'Eternal rest' can mean only a cemetery, I agree with you," Pin-striped suit said. "But who could disturb the peace of the dead?"

"Maybe you don't know it, but you are leading us in the right direction," the stout woman said. "A little farther along in the transcript there is a question of poor Anne Bee who left for her final trip from a place where she was heard crying. 'Her final trip' hints that she was going to die. And yet I see that when transcribing the conversation somebody has put here in parentheses the word *laughing*. Does it mean that when these girls were talking about Anne Bee going to her death, they were laughing?"

"Yes," Jones said. "That's right. They were laughing and they were very pleased."

"Well, I think that we have here a common and very unusual element. The two girls speak about a woman who has lost a part of her body, about a madwoman looking for her probably deceased children in a cemetery, about somebody going to die and crying—and they are laughing! They couldn't have seen those things happen, they are too macabre to make anybody laugh."

"Maybe they were referring to some stories or legends," Pin-striped suit said.

"Yes . . ." Reed slowly mumbled. "Legends connected to places . . ." He suddenly raised his head. His eyes were sparkling. "What was the name of the agency Jennifer Soames runs?"

"Occult London," Jones answered.

"Why that particular name?"

"They specialize in night tours at places renowned as haunted or where . . ." Jones stopped in midsentence and his face lit up in sudden realization. "Oh yes, of course, now I see! Ghosts! They were speaking about places supposedly haunted by ghosts!"

"May I use your phone?" the stout woman asked.

"Who do you want to call?" said Jones.

"The Ghost Club of London, my dear man."

Only when he heard her well-modulated voice oozing smoothly into the phone did George Reed suddenly remember where he had seen the stout woman, many years ago. On the stage, of course. He didn't recall the name she had been using then, but he had certainly seen her performing.

"Is that the permanent undersecretary?" she was saying, in a serious, respectful voice. "Mr. Higginbotham? My name is Mrs. Drake, from the educational department of BBC Television. I need your help. You see, we have recently approved a project submitted to us by a young man to teach the children of London about their city by means of a sort of ghost-hunt, or, to be more correct . . . a quiz about haunted places. Yes . . . Yes, we also think that it is a charming idea. But there is a small problem. For technical reasons, we shall have to record the program early tomorrow morning. Now, this young man has never done work for us before, and we would like, if possible, to check a few of the questions with you, or with somebody else in the Ghost Club. . . . Yes . . . Yes, of course. We shall be delighted to give the club full credit as consultant. That's right. Could I read you a few of the questions over the phone and call you back this afternoon? Thank you, it's awfully kind of you."

She covered the mouthpiece with her hand and said, excitedly: "He is going for it. He'll do it!" Then, into the phone again: "First question: Where could one see the ghost of a lady in a red-striped gown, who has lost an important part of her body, and who was heard shouting, 'Give me light! Give me light!' Yes . . . What? You think she was headless, you say? Please try to make sure, and find also the place, will you? Thank you.

"Second question: In which cemetery was the ghost of an old woman looking for her children seen? Oh, you know that by heart? Really?" She listened for a few seconds and said: "How very nice of you indeed." She turned to her companions again and her mouth silently formed the name "Highgate."

"And the third question: Where did poor Anne Bee start her final journey, crying and walking down the steps? What? Yes, that's what it says, Anne Bee. Oh, I see what you mean. Just a second." She covered the mouthpiece again. "He asks if Bee is the name of the person, or if it stands for the letter B, the first initial of her name."

"Of course," groaned Professor Reed. "Could you get me an encyclopedia or a history of Britain? I think I have it."

Long before the stout woman was supposed to call the obliging Mr. Higginbotham again, he had the answer. "The lady in question," he told his audience, contentedly puffing on his pipe, "was tried for adultery in a certain palace in London by Archbishop Cranmer. She was sentenced to death and dragged, crying and sobbing, down the stone steps to the Thames. At the stroke of midnight, a barge took her on her final journey to the Tower of London, where she was beheaded, as we all know."

He couldn't help keeping his small dramatic effect for the end. " 'Poor Anne Bee' was of course Anne Boleyn. And the place—is Lambeth Palace on the Albert Embankment."

He nodded with finality and got up. So did the others. The only man who remained seated, a stony smile painted on his blank face, was the Russian.

"I do thank you," Mr. Jones said formally, shaking their hands and dispensing his unctuous smile. "Please, don't leave together, but at intervals of a few minutes. And thank you again. Really, it was a brilliant piece of deduction."

Professor George Reed was the last to leave. While closing the door of room nine behind him, he saw the Russian reach impatiently for the black telephone.

He crossed the secretaries' pool and went out. His hat had dried, and he was in high spirits, exhilarated by his part in cracking the code.

He didn't know that by his "brilliant piece of deduction" he had just sentenced an innocent French girl to death.

5

TRAP

Ivor Carmichael, warden of Lambeth Palace, was making his last rounds before locking up for the night. *That's when those tourists should come and look at 'er*, he thought, *on a fine foggy night like tonight, with no moon showing*.

It was true that Lambeth Palace was sadly eclipsed in daylight by the cluster of slabbing concrete buildings that had sprung up on three sides, even on the site of old St. Thomas's Hospital. But the palace was not merely a relic, as Carmichael well knew, but a vital memory of another age—when the Archbishops of Canterbury sat in judgment at the assizes in the Great Hall. Carmichael took particular relish in showing visitors the secret burial place in the crypt beneath the chapel and the pathetic inscriptions scratched by the prisoners on the walls of Lollards' Tower.

He locked the heavy door of the smaller Laud's Tower, and peeked into the Guard Chamber, which, with its portrait gallery and its impressive beamed ceiling, was always the first stop on the guided tour. The portraits of Archbishop Warham by Holbein and of Laud by Van Dyck had pride of place, and they always seemed to put the tourists in a suitably reverent frame of mind before they trooped on to look at the priceless collection of books and illuminated manuscripts in the Great Hall.

He heard something rustling in the deserted garden and smiled to himself. That would be the Cardinal's fig trees, he thought. Planted by Cardinal Pole himself in the sixteenth century, and patiently nursed through many an illness by Warden Carmichael in the twentieth—and the Warden had often expressed the wish that all those stinking factory chimneys and motorcars on the bridge should be placed under the ban of the Church.

He walked to the fuse box at the right of the arched entrance and shut off the electricity. His steps echoed in the cobbled courtyard. Nothing had changed in four hundred years—a thought that the Warden found very agreeable. Everything damaged or destroyed in the Great Fire or the blitz had been lovingly restored in minute detail. Warden Carmichael walked on, then turned to survey his domain. The ragstone tower of Saint Mary's parish church and the Tudor chimneys were authentic; the castellated gatehouse with its handsome white facings, the gently pitched roof of the Great Hall, and the palace turrets were restored. The only visible change from Cranmer's time was the retreat of the riverbank, now a few hundred yards to the west. In years past, the archbishop's barge used to be moored quite close to the entrance to the palace. Today one had to cross the road in order to get to the River Police pier, down by Lambeth Bridge.

He locked the street gate and set out toward the Lambeth North underground station. On his right the Archbishop's Park was dark and silent. He was walking purposefully up Lambeth Place Road, when the sound of quick footsteps made him glance across the street. A girl, wearing boots and a white sheepskin coat, her long black hair floating in the wind, hurried by him, gazing the other way. He shook his head, wondering what in heaven's name a girl could be doing out here at this hour of the night.

The girl was Sylvie de Sérigny.

The taxi crossed Lambeth Bridge, turned left, and stopped by the stone steps that led down to the river. "Thank you," Jennifer said, getting out. "Will you please wait? I'll just fetch my friend—won't be a minute." The driver nodded and looked at his watch—five minutes to midnight. Jennifer had hardly taken five steps when Sylvie appeared in the diffuse yellow circle of light cast by a street lamp, barely fifty yards away. "Sylvie!" she shouted happily. "Over here!" Sylvie saw her and broke into a run, hands outstretched to embrace her friend.

What happened next was like a nightmare come true. Two men emerged from the shadows and pinned Sylvie's arms; one clapped a hand over her mouth. Jennifer screamed and hurled herself forward. "Sylvie! Help, somebody, help!" A third man caught her from behind and flung her to the ground; her head struck the pavement.

"What the hell's going on here?" the taxi driver muttered and started to get out of the cab, when he was brutally pushed back into his seat and a gun was thrust in his face. "One more word and you'll be dead."

Sylvie writhed and kicked furiously, but she was no match for her two captors. She heard a sudden screech of brakes behind her, and felt herself being dragged over toward the pavement. Frantically, she bit her abductor's palm and a high-pitched shriek burst from her lungs as the man pulled his hand away, cursing in an unintelligible language. She felt the cold touch of metal on her back— in another moment they'd have her inside the car. She wrenched her left hand free, groped for the other man's face, and scratched it hard, raking her nails savagely across his cheek. She heard a cry, then a heavy fist crashed into her face and she gasped in pain. The fist struck out again; she tasted blood, and as if from very far away, she heard Jennifer cry out. She opened her eyes.

As soon as the car appeared, Jennifer's assailant pulled her to her feet. She didn't resist, let her head loll forward— the man spoke some words she couldn't understand, another voice answered. Crying out, Jennifer lunged forward blindly and started to run. The man raised his revolver and fired twice. Jennifer pitched forward and fell heavily to the sidewalk.

Sylvie felt her knees give way, then rough hands bundled her into the car. Suddenly, one of her captors gave a startled exclamation and released his grip on her arm. The other man spun around, and Sylvie slumped to the pavement. She painfully raised her head; she was dimly aware of three shapes misting in the darkness, not far away. She tried to focus her eyes and saw a heavy body, which she assumed was that of her abductor, crash heavily by her side. A tall man stood over her, holding her second assailant by his collar and ferociously battering his head against the roof of the car. At that moment the driver of the car started to get out, his right hand going for the gun in his belt. He never reached it. The tall man blocked his movement by shoving the slumping body of the man he had overpowered against him, then swiftly moved forward and dealt him a vicious blow on the side of his neck. He completed the onslaught on the stunned man with a punch in the face. The driver slowly collapsed and lay still.

The stranger bent over Sylvie and took hold of her hand. "Come on." He paused to catch his breath. "Let's get out of here!" She started to struggle. "You fool"—he was almost shouting—"I'm trying to help you." He pulled her to her feet. "My friend"—it was so hard to talk—"Jennifer . . ." He broke into a trot, pulling her along behind him. "No time! They'll kill you. Run, for God's sake!" She tried to follow, stumbling, rising to her feet again, his powerful hand still clutching her arm. They crossed the street and started to run. Close behind them she heard the sounds of a car engine, shouts, and rapid footsteps. Three shots rang out and she faltered, almost fell. He kept running, dragging her behind him. Now they had gone past the palace; she saw the indistinct outlines of bushes on their right—Archbishop's Park. "Here!" He crashed into the thicket; Sylvie hesitated, then plunged in behind him.

She stumbled many times in the tangle of roots and low branches; thorns snagged her coat and tore at her legs; dead twigs tugged at her hair. The man in front of her was blazing a trail for her, only a few paces ahead. She knew her face was bleeding again. Her heart was racing and her throat was on fire. She felt a stab of pain in her left side with every breath she took. And yet, she ran, docile, pulled by a violent man she didn't even know, who might be her enemy as well as her friend.

Suddenly, she stepped out of the bushes; they were in a lane she did not recognize on the other side of the park. He didn't slow down until they reached a wide street. There was almost no traffic, and for a second the stranger looked around indecisively. Then, he dashed to a blue Vauxhall parked near the corner, and to her astonishment he put his fist through the window on the driver's side. The glass shattered and splinters rained onto the sidewalk. Blood spurted from a diagonal cut on the back of his hand, but he didn't seem to notice. He thrust his hand in, groped for the handle, and opened the door. "Get in!" he barked, and she obeyed, running around behind the car. He reached over to unlock the other door; she pulled it open, and slid into the front seat. His fingers deftly explored the underside of the dashboard. With an abrupt, violent tug, he pulled out the torn ends of two wires, and pared away the insulation with a fingernail. He fumbled impatiently in his pockets and swore under his breath. "Got any chewing gum?" He spoke without turning to look at her. She stared at him uncomprehendingly. "Did you hear me?" he repeated. "Have you got any *chewing gum?* Or *cigarettes?*" She shook her head, then remembered. "Cigarettes . . . yes, I have some." She reached into the pocket of her jeans and fished out a crumpled package of cigarettes. "Good," he said, then tore the package open, and carefully peeled the thin layer of foil away from the fancy wrapping. He bent over the steering wheel and connected the torn wires, wrapping them tightly in the foil. On their right, at the far end of the lane, quick footsteps were approaching and she looked up with a start. He gave no sign that he had heard. The engine suddenly coughed once, twice, and came to life. He pushed the gas pedal to the floor; the engine roared and the car hurtled forward.

When they reached Westminster Bridge he turned the headlights on. He sped through Whitehall and joined the growing stream of traffic at Charing Cross Road, aggressively overtaking the cars ahead of them, glancing watchfully from time to time into the driver's mirror. Neither of them spoke until he pulled up at a stoplight. He turned around to observe the five or six cars behind him; then, he appeared to relax. He turned to her and smiled. "Hello," he said pleasantly. "My name is James. James Bradley. And who are you?"

Now the interior of the car was lit up by the intermittent red reflections of neon billboards overhead. Sylvie turned her head stealthily to study James Bradley for a moment before answering. She knew already that he was tall, strong, and fortunately, very resourceful, but that was all. Now she saw that his thick, dark-blond hair was graying at the temples—prematurely, she suspected, since he didn't look much older than thirty-five. His face was very tan, his eyes deep-set—gray, she thought, although it was difficult to tell in the flickering red light—and she noticed a hairline scar running from the corner of his left eye down the middle of his cheek. *But he doesn't look very fierce—just serious—and a little sad, at least until he smiled just now.* His candid smile lighted up his whole face, suddenly painting a web of laughter wrinkles around his eyes and mouth.

"You have an American accent," she said self-consciously.

He nodded. "That's right." He shifted into gear and the car moved forward, quite slowly now, through the lively streets of Soho. "I come from California originally, but I've lived in Washington and in Europe for the last few years." His voice was deep and clear, yet his tone was reserved.

"What happened to my friend? Did you see?" She was beginning to remember again . . . Jennifer crying out . . . then the gunshots.

"I saw them shooting at her, and I saw her fall."

She covered her face with her hands. "They've either killed her already, or else they're going to kill her now," she whispered.

"If your friend is still alive, they won't do anything more to her," he said firmly. "It's you they're after. They must have cleared out right away, and the police will have certainly got there by now."

They had just crossed Regent Street. "I asked you a question before," he said, and now there was a distinctive edge to his voice. "Who are you? What's all this about?"

"I . . ." she bit her lip. "I'm French, and my name is . . . Françoise Delorme." She didn't look at him, but she was sure he had noticed the slight hesitation.

"May I see your papers?"

She suddenly burst into tears, sobbing with despair. "Who are you to ask me for my papers? A policeman? Let me out of here!" Impulsively she threw herself against the door, got it open, and tried to jump out of the car. But he was quicker and stronger. With his right hand still on the wheel, he reached across her with his left hand for the door handle, caught it, and slammed the door shut, hurling her back on the seat and immobilizing her. She felt pinned like a butterfly. "Let me go," she cried helplessly, her face distorted in pain. "Please, please, let me go."

He halted the car in the deserted street, and grasped her

by the shoulders. "Listen to me," he said gently and moved closer to her. Her eyes were tightly shut, and the tears streamed between her eyelashes and down on her face. "Open your eyes and look at me," he said in the same gentle voice. Through a film of tears she saw that his eyes were fixed on her and full of concern. "I don't know who you are," he said, "but I want to help you. Those people back there were trying to kidnap you or kill you. Would you like me to take you to the police?"

She shook her head.

"Are you afraid of the police?"

She simply stared at him, unable to speak.

"You haven't been involved in any crime, or any dirty business?" He smiled, but his gray eyes were hard and penetrating.

"No," she finally managed to say. "I haven't done anything."

He took his other hand off her shoulder. "Don't be afraid," he said soothingly, and very gently caressed her cheek with the tips of his fingers. "I'll help you. Your name is not Françoise, but if you want me to call you that, it's okay with me. And I won't ask you any more questions, or maybe just one more. . . . Do you have any place to go?"

"No," she whispered.

"We can take care of that." He stroked her face again, as one would do to reassure a frightened child. "Will you trust me?"

She nodded.

They drove on. Bradley started to tell Sylvie something about himself, while she struggled to regain her composure. He worked for USIS. "That's the strong right propaganda arm of the U.S. State Department," he explained. After a few years in Brussels and London, and a stint in the home office in Washington, now he was on leave—"a long vacation," he said pleasurably—before the start of his second tour, in Rome this time. He told Sylvie that he was an architecture buff—had even spent a year in architecture school, and whenever he was in London, he took the opportunity to see some of its most famous buildings and monuments. He'd spent the afternoon admiring again some of the masterpieces of Sir Christopher Wren. In the evening he had gone to an Alec Guinness play, and afterward had decided to take a stroll—the weather was surprisingly pleasant, for London in January. He had gone to Westminster Abbey and crossed the river for a better view, but the fog had spoiled it all, so he had drifted over to Lambeth Palace. "I heard shots and a woman screaming. Then I saw those goons dragging you into their car. Well, I couldn't just stand there. . . ."

He paused, narrowed his eyes, and continued in an even voice: "How did you come to be mixed up with the Russians?"

"The Russians!" She started in amazement and caught his arm. "You say they were Russians? How do you know?"

He seemed surprised by her reaction. "You didn't *know* they were Russians? I don't speak Russian myself, but I've heard enough foreign languages in my life to know that they were shouting in Russian. Does that surprise you?"

She tried to think. Could it be in any way related to the document Richard had found? It seemed too farfetched, and yet that was the only explanation that came to her mind. But could she trust Bradley and tell him about it?

She realized that he was still looking at her, waiting for her to say something. "Yes," she said finally. "Yes, it does surprise me."

They left the car at the corner of Curzon Street. "We shall have to walk a few blocks," he apologized. "I can't leave a stolen car under my balcony. The management is very strict."

"Where are we going?" she asked.

"Park Lane," he said. "I'm staying at the Hyde Park Club. USIS people use it quite a lot. We even get a special discount." He paused for a second. "Now," he continued, his tone suddenly very practical, "the suite has three rooms —two bedrooms and a living room; I mean, a drawing room—in between. You'll get one of the bedrooms, of course. The connecting door to the drawing room can be locked from the inside. You'll have your own bathroom and your own private door to the elevator. So you'll be perfectly safe, even from me." He grinned. "Anyway, I'll be right there in case you need anything."

She was too exhausted to argue. Not that she trusted him. That business about USIS and Sir Christopher Wren was all very well, but where had he learned to steal a car like that, or to fight against men with guns . . . "professional killers," he'd called them. Still, she had nobody else now that Jennifer was gone, and she couldn't go on fighting forever. She felt like she was on the verge of a full-fledged breakdown.

She walked with him into the club, a big white building with a freshly painted façade. At the last moment, before they stepped into the brightly illuminated lobby, she asked him, on a purely feminine impulse: "Aren't you married?"

His face clouded, and his voice sounded dull and toneless. "I used to be. I lost my wife and my little girl in an accident."

"I'm sorry," she murmured.

He simply nodded and showed her into the lobby. The night porter smiled at him; he seemed to be pretending not to notice Sylvie. "Good evening, Mr. Bradley."

"Good evening. May I have both keys for room forty-two, the one adjoining my suite?"

"Yes, sir, of course."

"Miss Delorme will be staying here as my personal guest." He handed her the keys.

"Very good, sir. Good night, miss. Good night, sir."

Sylvie had already stepped into the elevator when the night porter coughed discreetly. "Sir?"

Bradley turned around, mildly irritated.

"Well, sir, for breakfast, I mean," he looked around unhappily. "Should we send breakfast for two, or two separate trays?"

"I'll let you know in the morning," Bradley muttered, and followed Sylvie into the elevator.

The room was spacious and lavishly furnished in Scandinavian style: redwood-paneled walls with two exquisite replicas of sixteenth-century matchlocks hanging over the fireplace, Danish brown and beige leather sofas and chairs, including the inevitable huge reclining armchair with matching footstool, a large low bed incorporating a nightstand and a dressing table, a deep pearl-gray carpet with an abstract design in black and deep brown. The glowing electric heater in the fireplace was the only concession to artless British practicality. Over the bed hung a painting of two hands caressing a dog's head. The dog, vaguely resembling a Borzoi, had its tongue lolling out, and its eyes half closed with pleasure; but Sylvie was more interested in the way the artist had represented the man's hands: calloused peasant's hands, with lean bony fingers and broken nails. Their shape suggested raw physical force, and yet their tender caress of the dog's furry neck inspired a feeling of affectionate protection.

She stood in front of the painting for a long moment. That's what she yearned for so desperately now: two loving, protecting hands that would reassure her and shield her from the horrible nightmare that had started yesterday morning. In her heart she still hoped a miracle would happen, that she would awaken and find that it was indeed nothing but a nightmare.

She couldn't sleep, so she turned one light back on, dragged the big armchair over to the window, and sat there in the semidarkness, wrapped in her coat in spite of the warmth radiating from the fireplace. She was too exhausted to think, so she just stared out the window, watching the black branches in Hyde Park swaying in the winter wind. Sometime in the early morning the fog dispersed and a light rain began to fall. The outlines of the trees and buildings were clearer now. She could see Marble Arch off to the right, but everything still looked gray and wet. She fell asleep just after the first light of dawn.

The sound of persistent knocking on the door abruptly recalled her from a dreamless sleep. "Who is it?"

"It's me," was the cheerful answer. It took her a few moments to remember where she was. "It's almost noon and your breakfast is getting cold. Do you want to open the door?"

"Just a moment, James." She removed her coat and ran into the tiny black-tiled bathroom. She looked in the mirror and gasped.

Her face was swollen and battered. There were two large cuts, crusted with blood, on her forehead. The details of the night before came back to her memory and she shuddered. Yet, she couldn't go on indulging in self-pity forever. She had been lucky that James had been there when it happened and had saved her life. Sylvie washed her face carefully and hastily applied some makeup to her bruised cheeks. She took a deep breath and walked into the bedroom.

"Coming," she announced, and unlocked the connecting door. The drawing room was spacious and cozy, with large windows, and a log fire burning in a fireplace, which reminded her vaguely of home. James Bradley, looking crisp and fresh in an open-necked white shirt and gray woolen trousers, took her hand and led her to the table. There was coffee and tea, a basket of freshly baked rolls and croissants, and covered plates which gave off the tantalizing aroma of fried eggs and bacon. "I ordered breakfast for two," he confessed, and smiled. "I hope you don't mind, Françoise."

"No, I don't," she smiled in return. "And it's not Françoise. It's Sylvie. Sylvie de Sérigny. This time it's the truth," she added shyly.

"I like that better," he said solemnly.

She wondered what had caused that spontaneous impulse to tell him her true name. Maybe it was the reassuring combination of a nicely laid breakfast table and the warmth radiating from the young American, who was so casual and friendly.

She didn't speak again until she had wolfed down half of her breakfast. "And have you been telling me the truth?"

He raised his eyebrows in mild surprise. "Of course," he said. "Why should I lie to you?"

"I don't know. You just don't look much like a bureaucrat, what with those muscles and scars and . . ." She wanted to say the way you can kill people with your hands. Instead she said, "The way you have of dealing with people you don't like."

"Oh, that." He nodded. "I see what you mean. Before I came to USIS I was in the Marines for five years. First an instructor for basic training, then an officer in a combat unit in Vietnam."

"That scar you have on your cheek . . . is that from Vietnam?"

"Yes, the battle of Hué. A VC with a knife. Missed my eye by half an inch. Lucky he just had a knife."

"And what happened to him?"

He looked at her speculatively, without answering.

"And why did you quit the Army?" Sylvie pressed.

"The Marines." He sipped his coffee. "I didn't feel very proud of fighting that war, so I didn't renew my contract. Also, I was married by then, and the separation was hard for both of us."

She could see that he was reluctant to talk about his wife. "And do you like your work now?"

He shrugged. "More or less. Nothing exciting really, but you get to know something about other countries, languages, culture, and so on. That's the good part."

They chatted for a few minutes, until he suddenly grew serious. "I have some news for you that might—I say *might* —be good."

She was on her feet. "What? Jennifer?"

"Yes. There was quite an item in the morning paper. Your friend is alive. . . ."

"Thank God!"

". . . But she's still in a coma in the hospital. I went back for the late edition, but they still didn't say how good her chances were."

"All that matters is that she's alive," Sylvie said eagerly. She turned to the window. "Did they say anything about me?"

"They said the police were looking for a girl. They didn't mention any names, but when they pry a little bit in Jennifer's personal life, they will certainly find out about you."

She didn't tell him that she was already wanted by the police. "And those . . . those Russians?"

"They must have cleared out before the police arrived." He paused. "My guess is that if the police found out Russians were involved, they wouldn't release that to the press. They won't risk a diplomatic incident without real proof."

He came to her and put his hands on her shoulders. "Now listen, Sylvie. I have to go out now, but I'll be back in an hour. And remember that I'm on leave, so I'll be able to spend as much time with you as you want. Anyway, you can't go out by yourself. I suggest that you stay here during the day. I'll go out and get anything you need—clothes, cosmetics, books, cigarettes. Later on I think we'll be able to go out for dinner someplace without causing too much of a stir. So you won't be a full-time prisoner. Is that okay with you?"

"That's fine." She tried to smile, but laughed nervously instead. "I wanted to tell you . . . James, you've been so good to me. I don't know how to thank you."

For a moment there appeared the same look of pain that she had seen in his eyes the night before, then he smiled, and it was gone. "No need to thank me," he said. "You are the best thing that could happen to an American in London. Just a few stitches and some cold compresses on your face, and you might even look pretty. Who knows?"

He kissed her casually on the cheek, grabbed his jacket, and was gone.

Two nights later she woke up screaming.

During those two days life had settled into a routine that seemed almost normal. For most of the day James would stay with her and talk to her about his life in the States— his years in college, the Marines, all the places he had been. On both evenings they had gone to a small Italian restaurant where the proprietor had whisked them over to a table in a quiet corner. Sylvie's chair faced the wall. She was wearing a rather nondescript black outfit and a plain woolen coat that James had bought for her, and she had pulled her hair back in a bun; her face was still puffy and swollen, which made her look much older. Although he never acknowledged it, James was very much on the alert when they went out, and closely examined everyone who came into the restaurant. Going through the morning paper became an important ritual, but there did not appear to have been any important developments. James called the hospital twice a day—Jennifer's condition was stable, but she still hadn't regained consciousness. He made each of the four calls from a different phone booth to minimize the risk, and, as he explained to Sylvie, he had given the name of an American freelance journalist of his acquaintance—"The guy's a notorious pest, so if the police check up on him, and he denies making the calls—no one's going to believe him."

Those first two nights she had taken a pill and slept soundly. On the third night she tried to get to sleep by herself, without any "outside help," as Jennifer used to say. She fell asleep almost immediately, and at first her dreams were dark and confused. Then there was a flash of brilliant, painful light. . . . Richard's body was lying on the floor; she turned away—there was a black shadow on the wall, strong fingers caught at her throat. She heard Jennifer's voice—"Sylvie! Help!" She tried to run toward the sound, but her feet were still rooted to the floor, the Russians were getting closer, and she couldn't move. . . .

She was awakened by her own terrified screams. Her body was bathed in cold sweat, and she was trembling all over. The room was dark and silent; formless shadows were creeping on the wall. She jumped out of bed, ran to the door, groped wildly for the lock, and stumbled into the drawing room. She blundered past the dark shapes of chairs and table till she found the bedroom door. Her bare feet made almost no sound, but she had hardly stepped into the bedroom when James sat up in bed with a start, eyes wide open, body alert and tense, as if ready to spring. She came closer. "James, it's me." Her voice quavered. And suddenly her whole body was wracked with sobs. She forced herself to speak. "Please let me stay with you, I'm so frightened!"

He got up and drew her to him. "Don't be afraid," he

said gently; he took her up in his arms and carried her to the bed.

She lay there for a long time, wrapped in his arms, until all at once she realized that she had stopped crying; she was not even trembling. At first she lay still, unable to speak—she just wanted him to hold her close, to protect her from her horrible dreams. . . . Later, when she tried to assemble her memories of that strange night, she was unable to tell how or when they became sexually aware of each other, how and when they started touching and kissing with growing passion, and how their bodies merged in torrid frenzy. In her mind everything became blurred and confused. She didn't actually remember making love to him. When she came back to her senses, he was lying on top of her, tenderly kissing her face, while she clung to his warm body with all her force.

He rolled over to the other side of the bed, pulled her close to him, and held her. She felt warm and secure nestled against his warm body. "*Je suis bien avec toi,*" she murmured sleepily.

He smiled at her. "*Moi aussi.*"

She didn't want to keep anything from him. She started to speak and told him everything from the moment she met Richard Hall at that Christmas party until he rescued her in front of Lambeth Palace. She related to him the full story, not omitting a single detail. He listened without saying a word, occasionally caressing her face, sometimes nodding in understanding. When she had finished, he said softly: "You did the right thing. Go to sleep now. In the morning we'll talk about what to do next."

But much later, when he heard her breathing evenly in her sleep, he got up quietly from the bed, wrapped a towel around his waist, and went out of the room, closing the door soundlessly behind him. The living room was bathed in silvery moonlight. He walked slowly over to the phone, and dialed the direct line to call the overseas operator. "Can you put me through to Washington, D.C.?"

Five minutes later, after speaking with a succession of operators and reeling off a long string of letters and numbers, he finally got through.

"I'm with the girl," he whispered. "I have the full story."

"The document?" the voice on the other line asked.

"She's got it."

There was a short silence. "Did she read it?" asked the voice finally.

"Yes."

There was another pause. "Get the document," the voice said levelly. "The girl has read it, so she must be killed. We'll let you know when."

The line went dead.

James Bradley carefully replaced the receiver on its cradle. A slight sound behind him made him whirl sharply around, right arm instinctively raised, ready to strike. Sylvie was standing in front of him, arms hanging loosely at her sides, not even trying to conceal her nudity. Tears were streaming down her cheeks.

"You, too, are one of them," she said.

Part Two

THE
BOOK
OF JAMES

6

LETTER

No, he was not one of them.

Not really.

James T. Bradley, thirty-five, from Santa Isabel, California, was one of the most cunning and lethal field agents of the CIA. And certainly, as his superiors unanimously acknowledged, the most violent one. Yet, his ferocity didn't stem from his impetuous character, but from his fiery motivation. It was spelled revenge—a sheer, persistent, all-consuming, and never-satisfied lust for revenge. It had started five years ago, after a car accident near the Atomium monument in Brussels. Or what had looked like a car accident.

He had not lied to Sylvie. He had been a captain in the Marines and he had fought in Vietnam. After his marriage he had asked to be transferred to a position where he could be close to his wife. If his request was not granted, he was ready to resign his commission.

The Marine Corps didn't want to lose him. They had appointed him to the NATO planning board in Washington, and later he was dispatched to serve in the NATO headquarters in Brussels. Since the ousting of NATO from France by an angry De Gaulle, and its transfer to Brussels, the city had become a dangerous battlefield, where secret agents from East and West schemed and played their deadly games. Captain Bradley, now responsible for the security of an important section of the NATO communications network, soon became a top-priority object of the

KGB. In one of the most cruel episodes of the spook war, Russian agents cold-bloodedly murdered Bradley's wife and his five-year-old daughter in what was supposed to look like a tragic car accident.

James Bradley never fully recovered from the death of his wife and daughter. The cruel assassination lit in his heart an overwhelming urge for revenge. He left the Marines and joined the CIA. After his initial training was over, he asked to be assigned to F-3, the operational anti-espionage unit, dealing mainly with Soviet espionage abroad. He made no secret that he had a private account to settle with the KGB. His superiors correctly assessed the potential value of such an operation. Subtly exploiting his hatred for the Russians, they assigned him to some of the most daring and perilous missions. Bradley was largely responsible for the destruction of a Soviet espionage network in the West German Army, later directed less spectacular operations in most of the countries of Western Europe with even a brief foray into Czechoslovakia.

In five years he had been betrayed, ambushed, and twice wounded; still, he had survived. Five years in his line of operation were much more than the average life span of a field CIA agent. For two years the agency had asked him to move to another job. His cover had been blown a few times, he was known to the opposition, and his life was in danger. But he didn't seem to value his life at all. He just wouldn't quit.

Four days before, he was urgently summoned to a meeting in Bill Hardy's office. It was early morning when the phone rang in the isolated Virginia cottage, where he had been living since the death of his wife and daughter. He had grabbed his winter suitcase, which was already packed, affectionately patted Nimrod, his big German shepherd, and stomped through melting snow to the road. The agency car arrived almost immediately and after picking him up, hurtled over the slick country roads at suicidal speed. The only conversation during the ride had been the driver's message: "We have a confirmation on your orders, sir. Someone will be taking care of your house and your dog, as usual." He had grunted in response, in no mood to start chatting about the weather and last night's movie on TV. At Langley they were waiting for him, and he was ushered immediately past security and into the director's office. An impressive group were there: Robert Owen, Deputy Director for Intelligence, Herbert Kranz, Deputy Director for Intelligence, Jeff Crawford, head of the USSR Department, and Hardy himself. His own direct superior, Roger Taft, head of F-3, joined them a minute later, with a thin blue folder tucked under his arm.

Bradley took in those in the room with a swift glance and noticed a common trait in all of them: They all looked dead worried. Even the urbane, elegant Robert Owen looked untidy and preoccupied. He was unshaven and wore a crumpled shirt under his expensive suede jacket. Jeff Crawford, wiry and hawk-faced, was pacing up and down the room, muttering to himself and occasionally glowering in the direction of Bill Hardy. Their bitter rivalry was common knowledge at Langley. Herbert Kranz, his fist beating a nervous tattoo on the armrest, was slumped down on the black leather sofa. He was peering through his thick glasses with the helpless look that made Bradley think of a distraught professor. Bill Hardy was the only one who even pretended to look calm and poised, but the overflowing ashtray on his huge mahogany desk, and the impatient way he was lighting a fresh cigarette, made even the pretense entirely superfluous.

The room became suddenly quiet when Bradley walked in. Hardy broke the silence. "Good morning, James. We haven't got time to go into a lot of background on this, I'm afraid. You're going to London, old man. The KGB there are on red alert. They are trying desperately to get a hold of a document, a letter that was stolen from the British National Archives."

"The archives are called the PRO—the Public Record Office," interjected Herbert Kranz, with characteristic pedantry. Hardy threw him a murderous look and went on: "What is important is that the KGB didn't succeed in getting the document. Some graduate student walked off with it. A couple of KGB agents got him right away and killed him, but did not retrieve the document. Now they are chasing his girl friend all over London. They know more about this than we do at this point, so we have to act on the assumption that she's still got it. And we'd like to get it back."

"Just a moment, sir," said James. "Let me get something clear. Why did those two—the student and the girl—steal the document?"

Hardy shrugged. "Frankly, we have no idea."

"Are they working for anyone?"

Hardy waved the suggestion away. "Not as far as we know." He turned to Roger Taft. "Have you got something for us, Roger?"

Taft took a glossy slip of paper from his folder and handed it to Bill Hardy. "Telex just in, sir. The girl is French, her name is Sylvie de Sérigny. She was picked up by the police two years ago after an IRA bombing attempt. She was involved with an Irish terrorist who was killed in the attempt. She was questioned and released. Left the country. Returned about a week ago."

Hardy frowned, but then quickly dismissed this new development with a second wave of the hand. "Rubbish," he said grudgingly. "The IRA doesn't want that document and has no use for it." He turned to Bradley again. "Let me make it clear that although this letter is almost seventy years old, and seems utterly obsolete, it contains vital information, which can endanger the very security of this country. Do you understand me, James? The very security of this country. You must find this girl before the Russians and get this document!"

"Any suggestions on how I'll find the girl, sir?" He couldn't refrain from a jab of irony. "And if it's so urgent, why not use somebody from the London station? They have two F-3s for emergencies."

Hardy lit another cigarette. "They're going to be working for *you*, plus a few reinforcements from Brussels and Bonn. And SIS and the Special Branch—they are all cooperating with us on this. As for finding the girl, the IRA connection that Roger mentioned should make things easier. There should be a file on her—names of friends, usual hangouts, the like. That should help. The British are not going to make any active move against the Russians. They don't want to and we don't want them to. They will just look the other way if we decide to use some muscle. And the situation might get pretty rough. I want someone there who can handle it."

"But . . ." James started to say.

Hardy shrugged his shoulders. "Sorry, James, no more questions. There is a Concorde flight in two hours from Dulles. Roger will ride with you and give you the rest of the information on the way to the airport." He got up, walked Bradley to the door, and held out his hand. "This is an important mission, James. Believe me, probably the most important in your career. Good luck."

Bob Sulke, a huge baby-faced Texan, head of the London station, accompanied by a sour-faced straight-backed British liaison officer from the Secret Intelligence Service, was waiting for Bradley when the plane arrived at Heathrow late that evening. During the ride into the city in an unmarked embassy car, they brought him up to date. Sylvie de Sérigny was still a fugitive, and the Russians had apparently lost track of her themselves. On the other hand, her IRA affiliation had proved very useful. Her file listed her former address as a small residential hotel in Kensington, a onetime IRA safehouse. A photograph of the girl was attached.

"Got the photograph?" James asked curiously.

Sulke grinned as he switched on the overhead light and reached into his attaché case. "You bet."

The face that looked out of the grainy enlarged print was obviously angry, terrified—and extremely beautiful. "Very nice," James murmured appreciatively. Bob Sulke nodded. "Luck of the Irish," he quipped. The SIS officer was not amused.

"The hotel in Kensington has been under surveillance," Sulke remarked. Bradley nodded and asked: "What about tonight?"

"Nothing useful," Sulke said. "We've got you a suite at the Hyde Park Club. You're supposed to be from USIS, by the way, so don't do anything to dishonor the service." He grinned again. "Think you can handle that?"

They dropped him off at the Hyde Park Club. He had dinner brought to his room, watched the late news on television, and went to bed early. At eight in the morning he was awakened by the telephone. It was Bob Sulke in an exuberant mood. "Get off your butt, boy! We're gonna pile into that nice new car at nine and head over to Kensington Gardens." He paused. "She made a phone call—public phone—just went back inside. We can move in and get her."

"No, not yet," Bradley replied. In spite of what Hardy had said, he still hadn't ruled out the possibility that she was working for someone else, and the phone call just confirmed his suspicions. "Let's wait and see if she makes a contact."

That's what they did, most of the day. Four detectives of the Special Branch shadowed the girl in relays, while James followed closely in a radio car. She wandered around town, went into several shops, bought a purse, some cosmetics, and a few other small articles, and had a quick lunch in a sandwich shop. In the late afternoon she killed four hours in a cinema offering a double feature. A little after eleven she hailed a cab.

"Here's where I come in," Bradley said to his companions. "If she's going to make contact, she'll be damn careful. We'll follow the cab. When she gets out, I'll take it from there. If I need any help, I'll let you know."

He followed on foot as far as Lambeth Palace and watched as the black car pulled up and the redhaired girl got out. When the Russians grabbed Sylvie, Bradley moved into position for the attack.

Everything had come off perfectly.

Until two minutes ago.

Until the moment that he turned to face this defenseless girl, so vulnerable in her nakedness, soundlessly crying in quiet despair. An innocent girl he was supposed to kill cold-bloodedly, because she had happened to read an old letter. His wife and daughter had been innocent too. He was a tough man, not easily moved. Most of his tenderness, most of his deep emotions, had died with them. His human impulses had been blunted and dulled; life, including his own, had lost its sanctity in his eyes. Yet, standing in front of this wretched girl, he knew he would never kill her, never allow her to be killed. *Not again*, he said to himself.

He took his jacket from a nearby chair and put it around her shoulders. Then he led her by the hand to the rug in front of the fireplace. "I want to tell you a story," he said. He thought he noticed a flicker of surprise in the lifeless eyes, but maybe he was mistaken.

He cleared his throat. "Do you want a cigarette?" She slowly shook her head.

"It happened about six years ago," he began. His voice was hoarse and unsteady and he groped for the right words. "An American officer, serving in NATO headquarters in Brussels, was sent off to Washington to pick up some very important documents. Those documents were classified top-secret and dealt with a defense system for Western Europe that had just been worked out in the Pentagon.

"It was pretty late when his plane got in. His wife didn't come to meet him, so he drove home alone. The house was empty. His wife and little girl were gone. As soon as he walked in the door the phone rang." A film of cold sweat covered his forehead. "A man's voice said that his wife and daughter had been kidnapped. They would be released if by 4:00 P.M. the next day, he delivered the full set of documents, or their photocopies, to . . . to a certain address. If not, they would be killed."

Sylvie moved in the darkness. She had her eyes on him now. "The officer was warned that if he alerted his superiors, or the police, his wife and child would be executed right away. That's what they said: 'executed.' "

He ran his fingers through his hair. His hand was trembling slightly. "The officer didn't deliver the documents. He alerted his superior officer, and within an hour a combined operation was launched by the Belgian police and the secret services to find the kidnapped persons. The officer participated in the search for a couple of hours—then the police told him to go back home and wait for the phone call.

"The kidnappers called several times the next day, each time threatening again that his wife and daughter would be killed if he refused to comply. Then they put both of them on the phone, just for a few seconds. That was the last time he talked to them, ever. At 4:15 there was another call. A man said that there had been an accident near the Atomium monument. Then he said: 'It was all your fault. You alone were responsible for their deaths.' And he hung up."

Old scars were opening deep inside him and the pain was sharp and vivid, as if it had happened tonight. "The bodies were found in his wife's car, and it looked exactly like an accident. The child was still hugging her favorite doll. It was actually made of rags, but she loved it dearly and used to call it Princess Agatha."

He felt a warm hesitant touch on his hand. He didn't react. "After that happened," he continued, "the officer joined his country's intelligence service with only one thought—to take revenge against the . . . bastards who had murdered his family. But he also swore that never again would he allow an innocent person to die for a piece of paper—any piece of paper."

He fell silent. His eyes focused on the glowing embers in the fireplace. Small blue flames were flickering on the surface of the charred logs and were quickly fading out in thin wisps of smoke.

Sylvie got up and noiselessly walked to her room. A minute later she was back, wrapped up in a bedsheet. She knelt beside him and put something in his hand. It was a piece of paper, all crumpled in a ball, smaller than a human fist. Bradley put it down on the rug and carefully unfolded it. The paper was thick and yellowish, and its texture was unusual. The reddish glow of the embers cast a wavering light on its surface that was covered with bold, old-fashioned handwriting.

It was the PRO document.

15 November, 1910
His Royal Majesty
King George V

Your Majesty,

I dare bring to your attention a most unusual event that took place lately, and could be, if properly exploited, of considerable benefit to the Kingdom.

Among the foreign envoys who came to attend the funeral ceremonies for your late father, His Royal Majesty King Edward VII, in May this year, was Count Golitzin, chief adviser to the Grand Duke Michael, the brother of the Czar of Russia.

The Grand Duke left our country a week after the funeral, but Count Golitzin remained behind. His strange behaviour aroused the suspicion of His Majesty's Secret Service, and I instructed our agents to conduct a thorough investigation of the Count's activities. Finally, during the night of July 17, our agents obtained a search warrant and forced their way into the flat of a young man, Thomas Alexander, in St. James's Lane. They found the Count in the middle of an homosexual act with young Alexander. Both men were placed under arrest.

Count Golitzin urgently beseeched us to hush up the affair, which in his words could result in a most disastrous scandal. I confronted him with all the material evidence about his unlawful activity. He agreed, in return for our discretion in the matter, to become our agent in Moscow and to spy for our Service in the Royal Court. Consequently, he was released and left England. After travelling on the Continent, he returned to St. Petersburg three weeks ago. Our agent in the British Embassy contacted him on my orders, and the Count confirmed his readiness to fulfill his obligation. As he has resumed his functions of chief adviser to the Grand Duke, we believe that he can supply us with most vital information.

By the present letter, I request, Your Majesty, the authorization to carry out this intelligence scheme, and I remain, humbly, your obedient servant.

Sir Archibald Montague
Head of His Majesty's Secret Service

James read and reread the letter, written so long ago by a master spy to a young king. It was clear why that letter was considered a state secret in 1910. Its publication might have stirred up an unprecedented international crisis and easily could have toppled the already wavering regime of Czar Nicholas II. But all that was almost seventy years ago! How, he thought, could this document dealing with people long deceased and a defunct regime affect in any way the national security of the United States today? Why was the letter reclassified in 1950 and again in 1975? And why was it worth the life of an innocent girl? What other secret lay behind the obsolete request sent to the King of England by Sir Archibald Montague?

At the same moment that James Bradley mused over the strange contents of the London letter, an impromptu meeting was going on in Bill Hardy's office. It was late evening in Virginia. The same senior officials who had seen James Bradley off on his mission were there. Bill Hardy was in a better mood now and turned the meeting over to Roger Taft, who jubilantly informed his colleagues that the letter was in the hands of James Bradley. "I have already talked to London. The letter will be over on the first flight out of London tomorrow." Hardy nodded contentedly.

Half an hour after the meeting was over, a black car pulled smoothly into the garage of a house in Chevy Chase. A man got out from the car, unlocked the connecting door into the house, and let himself in. He didn't put on the lights, but moved in the darkness with the easy confidence of someone who knew the place well. He walked into the study, sat down behind a large walnut desk, and reached for the telephone. He dialed a number in New York City. A cautious voice answered.

"Yes?"

The man spoke quickly: "James Bradley. Room 42. Hyde Park Club, Park Lane, London. He's got the girl and the letter."

"Yes."

He placed the receiver on its cradle, then produced a sleek golden Colibri lighter from his vest pocket and lit a black Swiss cheroot. The flickering flame illuminated for a split second the sardonic smile that touched his thin lips.

7

MOLE

The blackest hours of night had stealthily taken over the sleeping city. Dark shadows crept in, chasing away the last silvery patches of moonlight and plunging the room into a thick mass of total obscurity. The fire in the hearth was gone, and the few surviving embers lurked under a thick layer of powdery ashes. Sylvie and James were huddled in a heap of covers and pillows by the fireplace. The only light in the room was the occasional flare of a match and the wavering glow of Sylvie's cigarettes. She lay quietly, her head on James's chest, her eyes closed drowsily. It had been ages since she had felt so relaxed. She trusted this man who lay motionless on his back, focusing his eyes on the ceiling, while his long fingers gently played with the loose strands of her hair. His story had moved her deeply, and her intuition told her that he was sincere, that he wouldn't let her down. James too was pervaded by a strange, long-forgotten feeling of being at peace with himself. The only thing that he had left out of his story was the sequel—the almost intolerable burden of guilt that had been gnawing him ever since the death of his wife and daughter; the terrible thought that he might have saved their lives had he been less devoted to official duties. Now that he had decided to save this girl's life, even by disobeying his orders, he felt the deep conviction that he was doing the right thing.

Her regular breathing told him that she had fallen asleep. He carefully removed the cigarette from her hand and threw it into the fireplace. He had asked her to go to bed, but she had refused. "I like it here," she had murmured in a little girl's voice.

And so, quite inadvertently, she saved both their lives.

He didn't hear the furtive steps in the corridor, nor the whispers exchanged between the two men before they took up positions by both doors of the suite's bedrooms. But at the very moment the door was kicked open and somebody leaped into the bedroom, James was on his feet, moving instinctively in the direction of the sound, his hand groping for anything that could serve as a weapon.

It took the blond killer barely a second to realize that James's bedroom was empty and to dive toward the living-room door. In daylight James wouldn't have had a chance in a million to escape. The killer had a gun in his right hand and clutched a stiletto in his left. But at night, Bradley had an invaluable advantage: his eyes were accustomed to the darkness. The killer hesitated a split second on the threshold; only too late did he notice the shadow closing on him. The sharp poker James had grabbed from the fireplace pierced his throat with tremendous force and plunged deep into the wooden frame of the door, pinning him there like a horrid marionette, jerking to its grisly death. The gun and dagger slipped from his inert fingers and dropped with a dull thud on the carpet floor.

"James!" Sylvie screamed. She had awakened the very moment James had sprung from his place, and now cried in terror as the figure of another man appeared in the doorway of the second bedroom. Startled by her voice, the man fired twice at random, the silencer making a plopping sound. A third bullet hit the already dead body of his comrade, frozen in its last spasm. James rolled over, grabbing the gun that lay by his feet, and began firing even before he got to his knees. He swiftly pumped four bullets at the bulky figure, and the man staggered and fell forward, clutching his belly. James stepped over the body and ran to the outer door of Sylvie's bedroom, crouched down for a second in the doorway, then jumped into the lighted corridor. A third man was by the exit to the service stairs. James fired twice and missed. The man immediately disappeared.

He stepped back into Sylvie's bedroom, slammed the door behind him, and propped the heavy armchair against it. He hurried into the living room. "Sylvie?" he called, trying to control his voice. "Where are you? Everything's all right. They're gone." She didn't answer. He discovered her cowering by the window, her head down, eyes closed, her arms tightly clutching her knees. Her whole body trembled. He stroked her head. "Don't be afraid," he said gently. "It's all over." He picked her up, and started to carry her into her bedroom, stepping gingerly over the body of the second gunman. He put her down on the bed. "You're safe here. I have to go back in the other room for a minute." Her eyes were open now but she didn't answer.

Bradley shut the connecting door behind him and switched on the lights. Even he blanched slightly at the sight of the blood-soaked corpse limply hanging like a side of beef. He bent over the man on the floor. His eyes were closed, but he was still breathing, and his feet were twitching in weakening spasms. He had two bloody wounds in the belly. James picked up the gun that lay by his side. He tried to calculate how much time he and Sylvie had. No one could have heard anything. His suite was the only one on that floor, the killers had broken in through the back entrance; and the shots had been fired by guns with silencers. As for the killers' friends, he knew they wouldn't have another try after losing two men. At least, not right away.

He searched both gunmen's pockets thoroughly, but, as he expected, he found nothing but a few loose banknotes and a clip of bullets.

He grabbed the wounded man by the hair and shook him roughly. He opened his eyes. James pried the man's jaws open and thrust the tip of the gun barrel into his mouth. "Who sent you here?" he asked, slowly. The man was Russian—he could tell by his wide face and his heavy jaws—but they wouldn't put a man out on the street who didn't speak English. "How did you know I was here? Speak!"

The man opened his eyes, but kept silent. "Talk," Bradley spat out savagely. "You may still live through this if you don't do anything to annoy me." He jerked the man's head up, forcing him to look at the gory cadaver of the other killer. The man gasped in horror. "Talk! Who told you?"

The man opened his mouth, but didn't speak for several seconds. "Don't know. . . . Phone call from New York . . . an hour ago. . . ."

"From whom? Give me the name!" James grabbed him by the shoulders and shook him roughly. "The name!" he repeated. But the wounded man just muttered something unintelligible.

James let him drop back to the floor and got up. The man didn't know the name, he thought, he couldn't know it. The information must have been supplied by the Russian agent in New York who had got it from someone high up, probably in Washington.

He went over to the small bar in the far corner and poured himself a tall glass of vodka. His mind was working feverishly now, leading him step by step to the inevitable conclusion: he had been betrayed. Nobody in London knew that he had the document. The only person he had told was Roger Taft, in Langley, who would have immediately reported it to Bill Hardy and the inside circle. The Russian said that the source was in America. That could only mean that there was a traitor, somewhere at the very top level of the CIA! It had to be one of those who had been told about his phone call right after he had put it through. But who? He reached for the telephone, then quickly withdrew his hand, as if bitten by a snake. His impulse had been to call Roger Taft. But what if Roger himself was the source? Or somebody even higher?

Bradley realized now that his life and the life of the girl were in constant danger, unless he could find out who the traitor was. And that was something he couldn't do. He couldn't call Washington. Any contact he made with the agency would be intercepted by the Russian mole and the assassins would be sent after him, one more time. And the mole could be anybody. He couldn't call London station either. He couldn't tell Bob Sulke: "Don't report about me to Langley; there is a Russian mole there." Sulke would alert the director's office on the double.

He couldn't stay in the open. He saw clearly that only one course of action was open to him: go underground. Clear out of this place, cut all his contacts with the agency, and try to figure out the riddle of the London letter. If he could discover why it was so vital for the security of the United States, and what interests were at stake, he might get a lead on the identity of the double agent in Langley. The man who fingered him for the Russians, barely an hour after his phone call, disregarding the most elementary precautions, must be scared to death. He must be fighting for his life.

He went back into Sylvie's bedroom. She was sitting on the bed, blue eyes staring fixedly in front of her. He sat down beside her and started to talk in a soft, persuasive tone. They dressed hurriedly and in a few minutes they left the suite and walked quietly down the service stairs to the street. There were already signs of morning activity in the elegant old houses on Dunraven Street, and a milkman was whistling cheerfully as he set down big white bottles on the tidy doorsteps.

* * *

They were eating breakfast in the noisy self-service cafeteria at King's Cross Station. "This food is lousy," James explained, "but the place is packed with arriving and departing passengers, as you can see, and the crowd is our best protection." She nodded and made a brave, but unsuccessful, effort to smile. "What are we going to do?" she asked.

He saw that there was no use mincing words. They were both hunted now, both cut off from their closest friends.

"Well, I've found out quite a bit tonight, but first I'd better bring you up to date." He quickly sketched in the details of his mission, though he didn't feel there was any point in mentioning that he was expected to arrange that Sylvie's body would be discovered by the police, or the KGB, sometime over the next few days. "Those two gunmen," he concluded, "were kicking in the door about an hour or so after I talked to Roger Taft. . . . Roger Taft only reports to four, maybe five, men—the CIA inner circle, if you will. That suggests very strongly that one of those men is a Russian mole."

"What is a mole?" she asked.

"A mole is a high government official—usually in the intelligence service—who happens to be working for the other side. He works his way up patiently, until he reaches a top position that gives him access to the most crucial secrets and even to decision making. That's what makes him so dangerous."

"Do you suspect anyone in particular?"

He shook his head slowly. "He must be one of the five or six top men in the agency. All I can say for sure is that he'd have to be pretty damned desperate to take a risk like that."

"Then what are we going to do?" she repeated.

"Maybe you should just split, Sylvie. I'm the one they're going to be after now. Why don't you stay with your Irish friends for a while? They can get you a passport and you can just go home to France, and forget the whole thing."

"But how can I?" she asked miserably. "How can I forget about Richard . . . and Jennifer? I've seen more blood and horror in three days than I'd hope to see in a thousand lifetimes. . . . And how long can I stay with the Irish? A week, two weeks? I can't go home and you know it. You said yourself that the Russians may be waiting for me. I've read the letter, remember?"

He pondered. "You might be right," he agreed. "But staying with me isn't going to be any easier. . . . I'm very hot just now," he smiled dryly. "My presence might be hazardous to your health."

Sylvie merely looked hurt. "I hate begging and I hate asking for favors, James. You did help me and you saved my life. I might be a nuisance to you, I know. But, please, let me stay with you. I don't have anyone else." She added in a hesitant voice: "Maybe I could be of some help.".

He wanted to protest, but he realized that there was a great deal in what she said. In fact, she was absolutely right. She had no place to go, and he couldn't let her down now.

He looked closely at Sylvie. "I only was thinking about your safety, believe me. I don't want you exposed to any more danger. But . . . if you're ready to risk it, I'll be delighted to have you along."

She sighed with relief and pressed his hand. There were tears in her eyes.

"And don't start crying again," he said gruffly. "That won't help. We are in a terribly tight situation, Sylvie. Very powerful forces are involved, and you've seen how very ruthless they are. Try to keep your head and not panic. That's the best help you can give me."

She nodded, but her voice was still shaky. "What do you intend to do now?"

"First," he said, "I know a place where we can lie low

for a while. This afternoon I'll try to get through to Bill Hardy, the director of the agency. It's a chance I must take. I trust him. He can't be the mole. That sort of thing happens only in lousy spy novels." He took a sip of lukewarm coffee. "I'll tell him what's happened and ask him to investigate, discreetly, the top men acquainted with my mission. I won't tell him where I am, and I'll call back in about a week. By then we may have made some headway with Count Golitzin. . . ."

She interrupted him. "What if Hardy doesn't believe you?"

"Why shouldn't he?"

"I don't know how things are done at the CIA," she said uncertainly, "but your boss surely trusts his inner circle more than one of his field agents."

He nodded.

"He might be more inclined to think that you just fell for me, ran away, and are trying to gain time. Last night you told me about your past, and you said you were a very lonely man. Your director certainly knows that." She looked embarrassed, as if she wasn't sure she should be saying this.

"You have a point," James conceded.

"So, if you call him, he might decide to mobilize both the American and the British services to find us and get the document." She looked at him quickly and added: "Am I talking nonsense?"

"No," he admitted, and furrowed his forehead in thought. "You are not talking nonsense. That is a possibility." The other danger that she didn't mention, he had of course already considered. If he called Bill Hardy now, even though he trusted him he could not be sure that the mole would not learn about their conversation and alert the KGB. In no time they'd start hunting him and Sylvie all over England, and he'd be too busy saving their skins to spend time investigating the London letter.

"Maybe it will be better not to contact anybody in Washington for the moment," he said tentatively. "We'll just hide for a few days. They'll find the bodies of the two gunmen and they'll figure that we were kidnapped by the KGB. The KGB, on their side, will assume that we have flown back to the States."

"That's perfect," Sylvie said eagerly. "While they are kept busy checking the false trails, we can get going on our investigation."

He grinned at her fondly and touched her cheek with his fingers. "Hey, you know what? You are absolutely right and I'm glad we're in this together."

Some color came back to her face. "That's the nicest thing I have heard from you since we met," she acknowledged. Bradley stood up. "Let's go out to the platform. Train's due any minute now." They left the cafeteria and quickly walked to the departure hall. Ten minutes later, their train set out on its run to Cambridge.

Number 19 Princess Elizabeth Road was a two-story cottage that might once have been white or yellow or even pale-gray, before time, neglect, and the remorseless English climate had covered its peeling walls with a thick patina of rain-streaked soot. Several of the roof tiles were missing; Sylvie noticed that one or two had slipped down and lodged in the gutter, from which they protruded like jagged, broken teeth; the ornamental gable on the right was cracked and sagging badly. Weeds had long since appropriated the tiny garden, and the few surviving myrtle shrubs in the hedge had clearly been languishing for a gardener's touch for many years.

They crossed the garden. Three stone steps led to the enclosed porch; the upper one was broken and rasped in protest under James's weight as he yanked the old-fashioned bell pull. A window curtain fluttered and an owlish face peered at them suspiciously through the left window. Hesistant footsteps approached the door, which slowly opened, disclosing a tiny dark hallway. The face that peered out of the shadows was owlish indeed—a wide forehead, two feathery tufts sticking out past both ears, hollow cheeks and nutcracker jaws covered with a bristly gray stubble out of which peered two big, round eyes whose pale irises were strongly magnified by the thick wide-rimmed lenses perched on the very tip of a small beak nose. A few wisps of untidy gray hair floated above the pale forehead. This extraordinary apparition was wrapped in a thick black woolen shirt; a tweed jacket with leather elbow patches hung loosely on his narrow shoulders, and his legs were encased in baggy corduroy trousers. He blinked once or twice in the morning light.

"Professor Collins, I presume?" said James amiably.

The old man's face brightened with recognition. "Goodness gracious!" He broke into a broad smile, revealing two rows of large uneven teeth. "James Bradley! My dear fellow! What in heaven's name are you doing here?" He clasped James's hand warmly and reached up to pat his shoulder. "What a pleasure, what a splendid surprise!" Professor Collins hopped delightedly from one foot to the other. He skipped about Bradley and almost bumped into Sylvie, who was trying to suppress a smile. Deeply confused, he stopped his impromptu jig and bowed ceremoniously. "I beg your pardon, young lady. I do hope you'll excuse this . . . this rather extraordinary outburst of an eccentric old man. But you must understand . . ." He quickly looked at James, and asked: "May I tell her?" James nodded soberly.

"You must understand that James saved my life once, not so long ago."

James made the introductions: "Professor Anthony Collins. Miss Sylvie de Sérigny."

Anthony Collins looked at Sylvie with interest. "French, eh?" He shivered and looked abashedly at James and Sylvie. "But we mustn't stand out in the cold like this. . . . James, what can you be thinking of?" He smiled. "Simply push me ruthlessly aside and step into the library." However, he stepped through the door ahead of them and they exchanged glances and followed him down a short hall into a huge library that appeared to take up the ground floor, and, to Sylvie's surprise, was kept in impeccable order. From floor to ceiling there was not a single patch of bare wall, even the spaces above and below the windows, that was not taken up by bookshelves or filing cabinets. There were two more banks of shelves and cabinets on either side of the room, leaving only a narrow aisle in the center which led toward two large desks, covered with papers, books, lamps, and an ancient typewriter. One of the books was open, and Sylvie glanced curiously at the intricate characters.

The professor smiled at Sylvie. "Chinese, you know—Li Po, my favorite poet." He made a proud, sweeping gesture toward the bookshelves as solemn as a general reviewing his troops. "Most of them are, actually . . . this is the most comprehensive private collection of Chinese books in England, perhaps in Europe." He turned to James. "You have never been here before, have you, James?"

"No, I never have."

"Well," the professor clapped his hands, "why don't we sit down? I would have asked you into my Chinese room"—he smiled again at Sylvie—"Yes, indeed, I have a Chinese room—lacquered cabinets, some very nice, old carpets, a number of scrolls I'm quite proud of, Ming vases—real ones with dragons. . . ." He stopped in midsentence and motioned to two straight-backed chairs near one of the desks. "However," he continued ruefully, "I'm afraid it's a bit untidy at the moment." He looked expectantly at James. "So perhaps—if you can stay, that is—we'll look in there later on."

"We'll stay," James said quietly. "Just for a little while."

The grin disappeared from the professor's face and he looked at James with concern. "Some sort of difficulty?"

James nodded.

"Serious?"

"Quite." The professor fixed him with a mild, quizzical stare, until James added: "But we're on the side of the right guys, if that's what bothers you."

"Doesn't bother *me*," Collins said, "but it is gratifying to know. Perhaps we might have a cup of tea and talk about it?"

Sylvie got up. "I'd be glad to help."

Collins shook his head. "You stay right here, mademoiselle, and leave that pleasure to me." Sylvie followed with her eyes as he disappeared through a small door at the other end of the room.

"What a wonderful old man!"

"Well, there's a great deal more to him than that," James remarked. "Or," he added thoughtfully, "I should say there *was*. This wonderful old man was one of the best brains in the British Intelligence Service. He is one of the few survivors of the old guard. In the thirties they used to recruit brilliant young dons at Cambridge and Oxford, and that's how they got him. After the war they had no more use for him, and he drifted back to his Sinology. But in the sixties they called on him again—as the greatest living authority on China in this country, they needed his expertise when the Chinese broke with the Russians and started flirting with the West. Now, of course, he's over seventy, been retired for a couple of years. . . . But did you see his eyes light up when he saw us standing there on the doormat?"

"Did you really save his life?" Sylvie asked.

James nodded. "In a way, yes. Four years ago the service sent him to Peking to exchange some information about Russia with the Chinese spooks, since Russia had become the common enemy. The project misfired, but the KGB didn't know that. They were terrified by the prospect of an alliance between the secret services of China and the West. On his way back from China, his plane stopped at Geneva and there a KGB team kidnapped him. They held him in a villa at Cornavin near the airport."

"Why?"

Bradley raised his eyebrows. "Why? They wanted to squeeze him dry, that's why. They would have killed him after."

"And what was your part in all this?"

"Unofficially, it was a joint project. We cooperated with the British behind the scenes. When Collins disappeared I flew from London—I was based here for a while—to rescue him."

"At the cost of a few lives, of course," she said quietly.

James shrugged and looked the other way.

Professor Collins returned, pushing a tea trolley, his face beaming with pleasure.

An hour later, the old scholar took off his glasses and wiped them absently on the hem of his shawl. "Amazing," he said reverently, his eyes still riveted on the creased document that lay in front of him on his desk on top of the still-open volume of Chinese verse. "Absolutely amazing."

"What do you make of that, professor?" James asked.

Professor Collins nodded slowly. "Well, you might say that I have a vague inkling." He frowned pensively. "Yes, it might be that, but . . ." He sighed and ran his thumb over his bristly jaw. "I never had anything to do with the

Russian section, and the names don't ring any bells. On the other hand, I know the methods we used; I even devised quite a few myself." He chuckled at some distant memory. "Anyway," he said briskly, "I think we can easily solve it in no more than a few hours."

"It's as easy as that?" asked Sylvie doubtfully.

"My dear girl, my experience has taught me that ninety percent of the solution to a problem like this is looking for it at the right place."

"Which is?"

The professor got up from his chair and started to pace around the room. "We have to find out about this Count Golitzin—what happened to him and to his descendants, if any. That will be relatively simple because Golitzin was a nobleman, after all, and a rather important officer at the court of Czar Nicholas. There must be detailed records about him and his family. Now, if we start . . ." He paused for a moment. "We *should* start with the records of the Okhrana—the secret police, you know. All the originals are at the Hoover Institute in America, but they have all the microfilms—including the translation—in the library of the British Museum. They should also have all the volumes of that book—" he frowned—"*Histoire* . . . no . . . *Généalogie de la Noblesse Russe*. That's it. A very useful set of books, which will tell you anything you'd care to know about the Russian nobility, including what's happened to them and their families after the Revolution of 1917."

"Who would compile a book like this?" asked Sylvie curiously.

"Well, the Russian émigrés, who else? They wanted to keep a record of their own people who escaped from Russia after the Communists took over and scattered all over the world. They also use it to trace down the descendants of Russian aristocrats still living in Russia. They enjoy publishing details about their achievements—such as they are—to show the world that they are still the superior class, even under Soviet rule."

Bradley raised his eyebrows skeptically.

"I know, I know," Collins said hurriedly. "I agree that this is rather silly, but the essential thing is that the material is there, and that it is accessible. Now, I can't go and look for it myself. That would cause too much speculation in certain circles. You can't go either—" He looked to James. "You don't look much of a scholar. But you, mademoiselle ..."

James was instantly on his feet. "She can't do it. The police are looking for her all over London!"

A complacent smile appeared on the owlish face. "They are looking for a blue-eyed brunette, but they wouldn't look twice at a short-haired bespectacled blond. We can change the color of her eyes, if it comes to that—colored contact lenses, like those film actresses wear. We can start with a trip to a shop where they sell costumes and theatrical properties. We have one even in Cambridge, for the drama school."

Sylvie lit a cigarette nervously.

"I shall give you a letter of recommendation to the chief librarian at the BM. I'll say that you're a student of mine. Your name will be ..."

"Françoise Delorme," Sylvie said quickly, and exchanged a look with James.

"Françoise Delorme, fine. Let's say you are trying to locate certain documents about the relations between Czarist Russia and China before the Revolution. These documents were at that time in the files of Count Golitzin. Today they might be in possession of a member of his family. That's why you are so interested in him. Does that sound plausible to you?"

Sylvie nodded. "I'll be glad to be of help."

* * *

It was easier than she had expected. When she arrived in London the next morning, she felt very confident about her improvised disguise. The chief librarian at the British Museum, a white-haired, stern-faced elderly lady, was very impressed with Professor Collins's letter and asked the curator of the Slavic Reading Room to lend his personal assistance to Miss Françoise Delorme. The index of the Okhrana documents didn't yield anything. But the short paragraph they found in Volume III of the *Genealogy* was all that Sylvie needed. She was back in Cambridge by dusk.

She gratefully removed her short blond wig while Anthony Collins read aloud the passage she had copied in her notebook.

> Golitzin, Count Alexei Andreievitch, born in Novlikovo, 1861. Chief adviser to the Grand-Duke Michael, 1901–1916, killed in Orel in 1917, during the revolution. Wife—Princess Maria Hippolytova Mishkina, born in Nijni Novgorod, 1876, died in Moscow, 1925. One daughter, Irina, born 1896, left Russia in 1916 to join the exiled communist leaders in Switzerland, returned to Russia with Lenin and his group in 1917. Was known as one of the closest companions of Lenin and Trotsky. Committed suicide in 1937, at the age of forty-one. Briefly married to communist agitator Vladimir Suvorov. One son, Arkadi Suvorov. . . .

"What?" James grabbed the notebook from the professor's hands. His voice trembled with excitement. "Arkadi Suvorov! I can't believe it. Suvorov is the count's grandson?"

"Do you know him, James?" inquired Collins, in a calm, detached tone that sounded almost genuine. Sylvie had been tossing her long hair back and forth, and only half listening. She stopped, her head tilted to one side, and looked at James in amazement.

"Do I know him!" He got to his feet and began pacing around the room. "Why, I've been fighting this man for the last five years of my life." He closed his eyes, and quoted verbatim the succinct digest in the top secret KGB directory in Langley Woods. "Arkadi Suvorov. Reputed to be one of the master brains at the KGB. Promoted to the rank of general at the age of forty. Violently anti-American. Credited with the most brilliant coups of Soviet intelligence in the United States during the last ten years. Present position, assistant-director of the KGB First Chief Directorate, dealing mainly with the United States."

"Good heavens!" gasped Anthony Collins under his breath.

Sylvie's gaze shifted quickly from Bradley to Collins. "I'm sorry," she said. "You've made it rather clear that Suvorov is a very important KGB man, but I still don't understand the connection with the document—why it's so important, I mean."

Collins smiled gently. "Do you see the connection, James? Do you see the link between Suvorov and Golitzin— apart from ties of blood, obviously."

Bradley bent over the table and examined Sylvie's notebook again. "Frankly, no," he admitted finally, puzzled. "I'm surprised to learn that Golitzin was Suvorov's grandfather, but . . ."

Collins began to murmur in a low voice, as if arguing with himself: "That's what I thought from the start. We used to call those people the hundred-year spies."

Bradley was still puzzled. "The hundred-year spies? I still don't understand."

"You will, my boy, you will." Collins got to his feet and

looked carefully at his watch. "I shall have to leave you now. I have a lecture to deliver. I still teach, you know. But if you wish"—his eyes lit with a sly yellow fire—"I'll give you a clue. Just a little clue, and I can promise you by the time I'm back, you'll solve your mystery."

He left the room with an air of expressible contentment.

"Who needs a clue?" James groaned as soon as the professor was out of earshot. "What kind of game is he playing with me? I'm in no mood . . ."

. Sylvie touched his shoulder. "Calm down, James. Let him play his little game. He is an old man, who longs for the days when he was a master spy. You told me yourself he misses the thrills. He is so happy to be of any help. Let him break the news to you in his own way."

Bradley looked at her sharply, and was about to speak when Collins returned to the library. He had already put on a shapeless old duffle coat. He handed James a threadbare clothbound volume. "The Book of Books," he announced, tapping significantly on its cover. "The Bible. And in here, my dear boy, is your solution."

James stared at him balefully, but refrained from speaking.

"Open it to the Book of Exodus, Chapter Thirty-Four, Verses Six and Seven. Then you'll understand."

The old man smiled a last time, and was gone.

"What the hell!" James shrugged, picking up the Bible, and flipped hastily through the pages until he found Exodus 34. "Here it is," he said. "Verses six and seven."

He read aloud: "And the Lord passed by before him, and proclaimed, 'The Lord, the Lord God, merciful and gracious, long-suffering, and abundant in goodness and truth . . .'" He glanced down the column, then repeated aloud the last few phrases: . . . "'visiting the iniquity of the fathers upon the children, and upon the children's children, unto the third and to the fourth generation.'"

He stopped and closed the Bible, the words still echoing in his thoughts. *Visiting the iniquity of the fathers upon the children, and upon the children's children.*

And then he knew.

"Blackmail," James said disgustedly, "just another case of plain, filthy, old-fashioned blackmail."

Sylvie looked at him curiously. "I don't follow it," she said, and slowly lit a cigarette.

James leaned over the table. "Once you have the key, you can solve it easily." He patted the cover of the Bible. "The professor was right. The key is in the verse. It spells blackmail. You see, the daughter of Golitzin, Irina, kept paying for over twenty years for the one night that her father spent with a young queer in London. The British spooks started the operation by forcing Golitzin to spy for them. Then the revolution came, and he died, and Irina became a big shot in the Communist Party. The British realized that Irina could be very useful, so they used Golitzin's record to turn the pressure on her."

"On Irina?" Sylvie frowned in disbelief. "I don't understand. Why should she care anything about that? They had nothing on her, did they? She rebelled against her father, ran away. I suppose she must have loathed him."

James shook his head. "She loathed a nobleman who served the Czar," he explained. "But what could she do when they confronted her with evidence that that very same nobleman was a homosexual and a British spy? It could mean shameful disgrace for her. Or worse, the firing squad!"

"Oh, come on, James!" she broke in. "They'd shoot her for something she hadn't done? You're going too far."

James looked at her ironically. "Believe me, I know what I am saying. Haven't you ever heard of the reign of terror in Stalin's days? The purges of hundreds of thousands of Russians, many of them heroes of the Revolution, just because of a suspicion, a rumor, a remote family connection with what he called 'an enemy of the Revolution'? Did you know that the best military man Russia had, Marshal Tukhachevsky, and hundreds of the most brilliant Soviet generals were slaughtered like mad dogs just because Stalin suspected they were too friendly with the Germans?"

"And Irina . . ."

"Irina was the daughter of a British spy. If Stalin had gotten word of it, he would have ordered her executed on the spot. He shot Communist leaders by the dozen for much less than that. The man had delusions about imperialist spies and saw them crawling all over the place."

"That's the most despicable trick I've ever heard of! To force this poor woman to betray her country like that? How could they do such a thing? And how could she—"

"She couldn't," James broke in. "They must have squeezed her too hard, and she killed herself."

"Disgusting," Sylvie repeated in utter indignation. "It makes me sick." She ground out her cigarette in the heavy pewter ashtray and looked over at her notebook, still lying open on the table. "Now, just a moment," she went on, her eyes lighting up with a fresh realization. "Collins called them *the hundred-year spies*. That means that Suvorov . . ."

James nodded slowly. "The blackmailers start in on the third generation. After Irina dies, they started the blackmail all over again, on a new subject. Her son."

"But you said that Suvorov was one of the chief men in the KGB!"

"And most certainly the greatest spy we ever had in Moscow," James said. For several minutes his face had been glowing with suppressed excitement; now he placed his hands on Sylvie's shoulders and said, "Do you realize what this means? You have stumbled upon one of the greatest secrets of the CIA!"

Her face was still puzzled. "The CIA? I thought that the British were using him."

He released her and moved away.

"Well, we must have inherited him from the British some time ago, probably during the Cold War. England was pulling back and turning into a second-rate power, and we were taking over her bases, networks and who knows. . . . We probably got Suvorov, too, as a special bonus—the plum in the pudding." His smile faded. "That's why Hardy kept telling me how important the letter was and why both sides were after you, and anybody else who might just have glanced at it."

She looked at him intently. "Both sides, James?"

They heard the front door open, and Professor Collins, humming a merry tune, stepped into the hall.

Shortly after midnight, the winter winds gathered over the North Sea, churning up the choppy waters of the Wash into a froth of whitecaps, then rushing southward, sweeping over the flat, watery plains of the Fen country and along on the banks of the Cam. They howled in the swaying treetops and shrieked in the narrow lanes of Cambridge, fiercely rattling the tiles on the gable roofs and drumming on the dark windowpanes.

James still lay wide awake in the tiny guestroom on the second floor. Sylvie was in the next room, and through the open communicating door he could hear her even breathing and see the tangle of dark hair on the pillow. Bradley smiled. But no rest for the wicked, he thought to himself. . . . The disturbing, random images that circled in his brain had resolved into one—the face of Arkadi Suvorov, the first and only time he had seen him in Belgrade, three years before. Suvorov was using then the cover of a junior member in the Soviet delegation to the annual congress of World Youth Federation, which was a none-too-well-disguised Soviet front organization. The agency had rushed James and two other operatives to the Yugoslav capital to watch Suvorov and to take note of any unusual contact he might make. The mission failed; they had barely caught a glimpse of Suvorov before he effortlessly eluded their surveillance. Yet the details of Suvorov's face remained engraved in James's memory: his smooth ivory skin, clear forehead, the thick, wiry gray hair, and shrewd brown eyes became the personification of the enemy, of the ruthless organization he was fighting. And tonight he had discovered that Suvorov was his ally—an unwilling ally to be sure —but an ally all the same. And such an invaluable asset that his superiors were trying to protect him at all costs.

All his superiors but one. The mole. The one who sent him on his mission, that morning in Langley, barely six days ago. Their faces sailed before him, one after the other: the cold stare and the ironic mouth of Bill Hardy, the handsome features of Bob Owen, the permanently worried expression of Herbert Kranz, the bitter eyes of Jeff Crawford, and finally, over and over again, the lean youthful face of his direct boss, Roger Taft. It had to be one of them, but which one? For the first time in years he was completely thrown off course. Since the deaths of Sandra and Lynn, his wife and daughter, he had no other home than the agency. It was his only haven, his base, his return address, the place where his only friends were. But in that very base, among those closest friends, someone wanted him dead. The faces of those people he had learned to trust completely gradually dissolved into blank oval shapes and formed an opaque wall in front of him. And as long as he didn't identify the secret foe among them, they all symbolized treason and danger.

A pale beam of moonlight filtered through the lace curtains, and a tree in the garden, swaying and shaking in the wind, cast a grotesque shadow on the white wall. A cruel memory drew him back six or seven years, to his daughter, who had awakened on a winter night, screaming with fear. "Daddy!" she cried. "Daddy, the animals!" He had run to her bedside, and had hugged her for a long while, explaining to her that there were no animals on the wall of her room. It was just the shadow of a friendly tree that was dancing in the night. But it had taken her quite a long time before she peeped stealthily underneath his arm and hesitantly joined in his laughter at the clumsy tree that couldn't dance so well.

And then in Brussels, he had heard that same little voice crying over the phone, filling his heart with unbearable pain. "Daddy! Daddy, please come and get us. Please take us home. Daddy, I'm scared. . . ."

He had seen and heard those sights and sounds, in each smallest detail, over and over again on the inner screen of his conscience. The only screen he couldn't turn off. The only details he couldn't erase from his memory. Most painful of all was the realization of why he had done it, why he hadn't just given the damned papers to the Russians and saved his family. The reason was his own father, a man he was so ashamed of he ran away from home at the age of eighteen.

Thomas Warren Bradley was a meek, self-effacing country lawyer for whom life was a perpetual losing battle. His unhappy life was reflected in the grayness that characterized his whole appearance: cheap gray suits, unhealthy gray skin and sad eyes, and the routine grayness of his work. His few appearances in court were not successful; he had lost most of his cases. Thereafter, he preferred to stick to his back-alley office and make his living out of giving mundane legal advice to Santa Isabel's less affluent citizens. He was a taciturn, shy man, with few friends. Even at home, in the presence of his wife and children, he seemed to feel awkward, and after supper would retreat to his small den, where nobody bothered him. Yet, he had deep respect for his wife and obviously cared for James and his two younger brothers. James loved him in his own way, and tried to listen with respect to the rare advice his father gave him; but from childhood he knew that for whatever he wanted in life, he would have to count only on himself.

James didn't know much about his father's past—just that he had been born in Albany, and after law school at a state university, had settled in Newark. He courted his secretary for two years and probably never would have dared to ask her to marry him if he hadn't been drafted into the Army. World War II was at its peak. Bradley was commissioned as a staff officer and sent to Europe. During a surprise attack on the headquarters of his brigade, he was captured and spent the last months of the war in a German prisoner-of-war camp. On his return from Europe he saw his two-year-old son for the first time, and made the only major decision in his life—to move to California.

From the moment he saw his firstborn, he never called him Jim or Jimmy. It was "James" from the start, and Lorraine Bradley complied good-naturedly. The opposite of her husband, she was outgoing and jolly and didn't take life too seriously. That made it easier to run a household on a meager income and raise three children whose father didn't even dare to reprimand them.

A precocious child, strong and independent, James learned quite early to solve his problems alone. Their house was quite isolated, about twenty miles from town, and he spent most of his time outdoors. He grew up a loner, silent and introverted, a boy apart, living in his own world, seldom seeking the company of other youngsters. Yet, he was surprisingly popular at school, because of his straightforwardness. And he was the best quarterback the school football team had had for years. He used to train daily, with fierce determination. He knew that his achievements as a football player were his ticket to college. And he had dreamed of studying space technology and working for NASA, the fascinating organization where science fiction was becoming reality.

And all of a sudden all his hopes, all his future, were irreparably shattered.

Nothing in his father's behavior or in their placid small-town life could prepare James for the shock that was in store for him. It happened in the spring of his last year in high school. It was a Monday morning, and he arrived at school a little later than usual. He immediately sensed that something was wrong. In the school yard, his friends avoided him. They were clustered like bee swarms around some copies of the morning newspaper. Finally, one of the boys, Chuck Griffith, approached him. Chuck was one of his few good friends. He was very pale and upset. "Did you read the paper, James?" he asked, his eyes avoiding him.

"No, I didn't," James answered, puzzled.

"You'd better," Chuck advised, handing him the crumpled local sheet and guiltily walking away.

It was on the front page. "LOCAL LAWYER REVEALED SECRETS TO NAZIS IN WAR," screamed the headline. His father's picture accompanied the article. With trembling lips, James read the story. A collection of German documents, captured at the end of the war, had been published in New York the previous week. Among them was a report from the chief interrogator in the Ramstein POW camp. The report, which was extensively quoted in the article, pointed out that most American prisoners refused to disclose any information except their name, rank, and serial number. But a certain second lieutenant, Thomas Bradley, when interrogated, was in such a state of panic he had broken down immediately and given names and code appellations of field units and details of operational plans he had handled. "His full cooperation would certainly be of great importance to the Reich," the report concluded.

Had he been older, more experienced, James would have understood that the breakdown of his father had nothing to do with treason or spying. He was only a weak man unable to face stress and pressure and not the only one to do so. It was just his bad luck that some local editor had spotted his name in the index of the book.

But James judged the world and his own family with the cruel idealism of youth. He was unable to forgive, to feel compassion for, a weak human being. On the spur of the moment, overwhelmed with shame and despair, he decided to run away. He couldn't face his friends. He couldn't face his father.

The same day he hitchhiked to San Diego and enrolled in the Marine Corps. He wanted to prove to himself that he was different from his father—that he could fight for his country and never betray it. Not until two weeks after he started basic training did he write to his mother to tell her why he had left home.

In his barracks, in San Diego, he got the telegram about his father's suicide.

Sylvie stirred in her sleep, but she did not awaken as Bradley, clearing his thoughts of his bleak memories, walked softly over to her bed and stood for a long moment, watching her sleep. The coverlet had slipped down, leaving her shoulder bare and he pulled it up again carefully, then looked out the window. It was almost dawn.

He dressed quickly and went out. He walked for a mile before he came to a phone booth. He had the change ready in his pocket, and he reached for the receiver.

The number of the direct office line was unlisted—there was no need to go through the routine ritual of passwords and identification procedures. The telephone was picked up immediately on the first ring. Doesn't he ever go home? Bradley said to himself.

"Hello." The voice was cold and reserved.

"It's me, Bill. James Bradley."

"James!" Hardy sounded genuinely excited. "Where are you? What's happened? We've been worried sick about you!"

"I'm alive and I'm in England." He looked at his Rolex chronometer, which he had placed on top of the phone. Knowing Hardy well, and the sophisticated equipment the agency had available, he figured he had exactly two minutes and seven seconds before Hardy would have the call traced. The second hand had swept out ten seconds exactly before Hardy spoke again.

"What about the girl and the letter?" Hardy nervously asked.

"I have them both."

"We found the bodies in your apartment and we feared the worst. How, I mean . . ."

James cut him off. "No time for that, Bill. There's just one thing I want you to know. There's a Russian mole at Langley—maybe in your office. He sent those KGB men after me, literally an hour after I talked to Roger."

"A mole? What are you talking about? Oh, come now, James, the Russians could have traced you by a thousand ways. Be reasonable."

"I am being reasonable," James said slowly, repressing a rising wave of anger. "One of the killers talked before he died. The tip came from Washington right after I talked to Roger."

The chronometer told him fifty-three seconds had passed.

"James," Hardy said soothingly. "There's no mole here and you know it. Let's sort this thing out. Tell me where you are and I'll send someone out—someone we both trust."

Sylvie was right, James thought bitterly. *Hardy doesn't believe me.* "No deal." He drew a deep breath and added quietly: "I worked on the meaning of the letter, and figured it out."

There was a short silence, then Hardy's voice returned coldly: "Have you, indeed?"

"Yes. I know who Golitzin was. And his daughter. And his grandson. I know that Arkadi Suvorov is your top man in Moscow, and that you obviously want to protect him."

There was a long silence at the other end of the line.

"Very clever. Congratulations, James."

One minute and twenty-eight seconds.

"His name is in a sealed envelope in the hands of a friend I trust. If anything ever happens to me or to the girl, it will be released to the paper the next day." Hardy would probably suspect that was a bluff, but he could never be absolutely certain.

"Are you crazy?" the director roared. "Are you out of your mind?" James visualized him, at the other end, his ascetic face distorted with fury, and yet his calculating mind swiftly overcoming his seething wrath.

And it did. "What do you want?" Hardy asked in a low voice.

"Lay off me and the girl."

"But . . ." For the first time, the director sounded desperate. "For Chrissake, I need that letter, James."

One minute and fifty-nine seconds.

"The letter can wait, Bill. First, find the traitor who tried to get me killed." Bradley slammed the phone down.

*   *   *

The unmarked helicopter almost skimmed the treetops as it approached the southern slope of Catoctin Mountain in Maryland. Although it was almost midnight, Bill Hardy found his bearings easily: a snow-covered clearing in the birches, a narrow hiking trail, the familiar shapes of three hickory-grown hillocks, and finally the thin line of the wire-topped fence that marked the perimeter of Camp David. The pilot spoke a few words into the mouthpiece projecting from the rim of his helmet. Hardy sighed.

The night flight had unexpectedly reminded him of the past when Camp David was still called Shangri-La and he was a fledgling Secret Service agent on his first real assignment. He was assigned to serve as bodyguard to a mysterious foreign personage who was coming to confer with President Roosevelt in the magnificent isolation of the presidential retreat. The visitor turned out to be Winston Churchill, and Hardy was to learn, much later, that the result of the meeting had been the decision to launch Operation Overlord in France. More than thirty-five years had passed, and here he was, at the peak and perhaps also near the end of his career, rushing to bring bad news to the President.

He had gone over his conversation with Bradley again and again during the forty-minute flight from Langley Woods. And he still had no solution to suggest to the President. His operation had washed out completely because of a young sonofabitch who used to be his best field agent. The helicopter descended smoothly, flew over the L-shaped roof of the fieldhouse, and landed inside the diamond of bright-blue ground lights. Hardy jumped lightly to the asphalt and walked briskly toward the service car that was waiting in the parking lot. The driver nodded amiably, and the car darted forward.

On both sides of the road the powdery snow gleamed softly in the moonlight. There were still lights showing in the windows of a few of the cabins, and plumes of wood-smoke rising from the fieldstone chimneys. The car seemed to plunge abruptly into a thick grove of trees and then pulled up in front of another cabin, larger but certainly no more pretentious than the others. This was Aspen Lodge.

The President, dressed in an old pair of slacks and a blue cashmere pullover, was waiting for him. "Take a chair, Bill," he said, indicating a second armchair drawn up in front of the huge fireplace. His eyes were half closed, his arms folded across his chest, and his long legs stretched out lazily in front of the fire. "Want a drink?" He waved a bony finger in the direction of the Sheraton cabinet in the far corner.

"I'd rather not, Mr. President," Hardy replied stiffly.

"Suit yourself, Bill." The President slowly opened his eyes and examined him speculatively. "You wouldn't have come all this way from Washington if it wasn't urgent. So go ahead."

Hardy perched uneasily on the edge of his chair and began to give a careful précis of the events of the last two days, ending with Bradley's phone call. "And he even hung up on me," he concluded angrily.

While Hardy was talking the President remained completely still. Now he rubbed his eyes with the palms of his hands and stretched, then fixed a cold, mournful eye on Bill Hardy. "Do I understand that the man you selected blew the whole project?"

Hardy helplessly shrugged. "He appears to have cracked the document and has found the link to Suvorov. I'm afraid I can't control him. I don't know where he is, and he has threatened to blow the whistle and make the story public."

The President's eyebrows lifted slowly. "Is he likely to do that, Bill?"

"If he doesn't, the girl could."

The President shook his head. "What a mess," he said softly. "What a damned mess." He looked gravely over at Hardy. "Are you sure you can't locate them? There must be a way."

"I can see no way, sir," admitted Hardy.

"And you have no solution to offer?" the President asked, his eyes still fixed on Hardy's face as he rose slowly from the armchair.

Hardy frowned, but didn't answer.

The President suddenly stood up. "Then get Suvorov out of Russia!"

Hardy jumped on his feet. "Get him out, sir? But . . . but that is not possible! That would defeat the whole purpose. . . . I can't see how we can do it. . . ."

"How you do it is your problem!" exploded the President. "There is no other choice, dammit! Get him out!"

Part Three

THE
BOOK
OF SUVOROV

9

KIOSK

In the thick curtain of fog that hung over the murky waters of the Black Sea, the blurred shape of the huge tanker looked like a ghost ship, hovering over the waves in her endless voyage of doom. She slid smoothly forward, briefly emerging from a thick patch of grayish mist and plunging into another, her horn mournfully heralding her approach. A growing flock of sea gulls followed close in her wake, over the trail of bubbling froth that she left behind.

From the bridge on the elevated aft portion of the ship, two men peered into the fog through powerful binoculars. They stood behind the watch officer, exchanging quiet remarks in stilted English. The younger of the two, tall and loose-jointed, wore a captain's cap. The long, pale-yellow hair that hung on the nape of his neck, his large cheekbones, upturned nose, and pale blue eyes attested to his Nordic origins. His companion was shorter but broad-shouldered and vigorous. His large face was smooth-skinned, yet its stark features and the piercing brown eyes were those of a strong, tough man. A lock of rebel gray hair fell over his forehead. He was wearing a heavy, dark-blue sailor's jacket and placidly smoking a bent sandblast pipe.

"It starts to clear," the captain observed casually. "We'll have a beautiful day in Istanbul."

"How can you tell?" asked his companion.

"The *poyraz* doesn't blow anymore," the captain said, and went on to explain: "That is the northeast wind, coming from the Black Sea into the Straits. The Turks fear even more the Black Veil, an icy gale from the Balkans, that can freeze the Bosphorus solid. But we have this morning a mild *lodos*, blowing from the southwest. You can notice that it already tears the fog in patches." He rolled up the sleeve of his loose black pullover and looked at his watch. "The sun will rise in a few minutes and burn away the mist. As soon as we enter the Bosphorus, the fog will disappear, like magic." He grinned boyishly.

"What is that?" the other man asked suddenly, pointing off to the right, where a yellow light flickered in the thinning fog.

"Rumelifeneri, the lighthouse on the European shore. In a moment you'll see the second one, on the Asian side."

The other man brought down his binoculars and looked off to port. He puffed at his pipe with visible satisfaction and did not speak until he made out the glow of the other lighthouse. "Here it is."

The captain nodded. "Anadolufeneri."

"That's where the military zone starts, right?"

"From here for about five miles."

"Are they still photographing every ship that goes through?"

The captain nodded again. "Routine. If you don't want to be seen, this is the time to go below. You can come back on the bridge in fifteen minutes."

The other man left the bridge without a word. He had no desire to appear in a photograph taken by Turkish Military Intelligence. In Istanbul second-mate Ivo Kinnen— with his Finnish passport and his seaman's papers for the Liberian tanker *Eleonora III*—was already running enough of a risk. There was no sense in taking even the slightest chance that a faceless speck on the tanker's bridge could be identified as Arkadi Suvorov.

* * *

He hadn't even had time to prepare for the trip. Two days before he had scarcely settled in at the new headquarters of the First Chief Directorate in the northern outskirts of Moscow, when he was urgently summoned to Andropov's office; the director had chosen to remain at Dzerzhinsky Square. Suvorov drove quickly through the heavy Moscow traffic, left his car in the cobblestone courtyard of Lubyanka, and hurried through a succession of corridors to the new wing of offices. Kalinin was also waiting for him in Andropov's plush suite on the third floor, and their conversation was cut short the moment he walked in. Andropov remained seated behind his large mahogany desk, and greeted him with a perfunctory nod. Kalinin acknowledged him with a broad, hypocritical smile, which Suvorov returned in the same spirit.

"Take a seat, Arkadi Vladimirovitch," Andropov said absently, not turning his eyes away from the contents of the manila folder he had spread out on his desk. Finally he took off his glasses, and leaned back in his chair. "We have an emergency mission for you," he announced, and Kalinin nodded soberly.

"You're going to Istanbul," Andropov went on.

Suvorov permitted himself to register a mild surprise.

"This has to do with the 'Nemo' operation." Kalinin was speaking now. "You remember of course the plans on the nuclear detection system you brought from Istanbul in seventy-two."

"What's wrong with them?" he asked aggressively.

"Nothing's wrong," Kalinin replied. "The Americans have merely decided to shift their underwater equipment to a different location. A new building project will be starting up south of the fortress in April. And they're worried about security."

"The source?" Suvorov asked, filling his crooked pipe.

"The same one who sold you the plans in seventy-two. The American."

He frowned. "He's still there?"

Kalinin nodded. "And he won't talk to anyone but you." He reached across Andropov's desk and picked up a single sheet of paper. "He approached our resident last Monday and offered him the new plans, for double what he asked last time. Our resident agreed, but the American refused to meet with him or anyone else he doesn't know. He would make the exchange only with you."

"He's afraid he'll be recognized," Andropov reflected. "You're the only one who's ever met him face to face, and since you would be running a greater risk if you attempted to trace him in Istanbul . . ."

Suvorov looked skeptical. "It's quite annoying," he said slowly. "I am very busy now, with the SALT talks coming."

"I know." Andropov seemed irritated. "Kalinin doesn't want to let you go, but it's important. You'll be away for only three or four days." He glanced at a yellow memo on his desk. "Tanker *Eleonora III*, Liberian registry, sails from Odessa this afternoon. Captain's a Finn; he'll look after you. In two days you'll be in Istanbul—with Finnish papers. You'll make contact and that same evening continue on to Salonika. You'll fly back from Athens."

Suvorov nodded. "How do I make contact?"

Andropov handed him an oblong slip of paper containing a few typewritten words: Ciçek Pasaj: 1:30 P.M.

"Do you know it?" Kalinin inquired.

"Flower Passage? Yes, of course."

Kalinin looked at his watch. "It's time for you to get ready, Arkadi Vladimirovitch."

He was halfway out the door when Kalinin added cheerfully: "I've asked our technical man, Komarov, to join you. And two of Polevoy's lads. I have to protect my best man, right?" He laughed unconvincingly.

Suvorov smiled back at Kalinin, hoping that his face didn't divulge the sudden fury that made his blood simmer.

"What did I tell you?" the captain of the *Eleonora* chuckled contentedly.

Twenty minutes had passed since Suvorov went below to his cabin. When he stepped back on the bridge, he was startled by the extraordinary metamorphosis of the sea and sky that surrounded them.

It was a glorious, perfect morning. The sky was clear and blue, the sun had only just cleared the blue hills of Anatolia, and the wooded slopes on the shores of the Bosphorus were turning from gray to green. The officer of the watch pulled open the sliding glass panes of the bridge's panoramic windows, and a crisp, invigorating air rushed in, sharpened with a slight tang of salt. Suvorov looked astern. The sea was calm and the mass of fog lay far behind, checked by the southern breeze at the very entrance of the straits. The tanker had just crossed the southern perimeter of the military zone and was clearing its way through a colorful crowd of fishing boats, yachts, and ferries. Closer to the shores, the water had an odd, milky color, like thin porridge. Suvorov raised the binoculars, and the color resolved into a thousand trembling, whitish globes bobbing up and down in the still water. Puzzled, he looked at the captain.

"Jellyfish," the captain explained cheerfully. "Millions of them, carried down by the currents from the Black Sea. Quite common at this time of the year." Suvorov wrinkled his nose in disgust.

The strait was gradually narrowing and the exotic sights around them were quickly changing. The rolling hills on the Asian side had a pleasant pastoral look: thick woods, tilled fields, vivid villages plunged in a luxuriant vegetation, tiny mosques pointing their needle-shaped minarets toward the sky. The European shore had a more modern appearance, dominated by magnificent villas, extravagant residences, and tourist resorts. Yet the crumbling wooden *yalis* perched at the edge of the strait, with their tiled roofs, porched windows, jutting balconies, were a constant reminder that this place was the very gate of the Orient.

The ship sailed past the coquettish village of Tarabya. Waiters in long white aprons were already busy setting the tables in the long succession of fish restaurants on the waterfront. In the distance, to the south, Suvorov's trained eyes made out the round, jagged shape of the Rumeli Castle main tower. He reached confidently for the nearby phone, dialed a number, and spoke softly a few words in Russian. Two minutes later his assistant, Komarov, joined him on the bridge. He was much younger then Suvorov, a thin man with drooping shoulders and a large baby face, crowned with sparse blond hair carefully combed to conceal a bald spot. He had wide-spaced light-brown eyes and a soft, full-lipped mouth. His innocent good looks were somewhat marred by a permanent sullen expression. He was a quiet, dull man in everyday life; yet his razor-sharp mind and scientific savvy had made him one of the most coveted new recruits by the various directors when he first joined the KGB eight years before. He had been finally assigned to the First Chief Directorate on the assumption that he was one of the few electronics scientists able to cope with the supersophisticated American spying devices.

Suvorov greeted him with a quick smile and pointed at the gun emplacements of the distant castle. "You have seen this place in photographs," he stated briskly. "That's the Rumeli Hisari, and on the other side"—he took his pipe out of his mouth and pointed with the stem toward the second castle, almost hidden in a clutter of tumbledown wooden houses on the opposite shore—"its twin brother, the Anadolu Hisari."

Komarov did not turn to look, but fixed his eyes on the bottom of the Rumeli wall, close to the waterline.

"That's the narrowest part of the Bosphorus," Suvorov added.

Komarov nodded. "Seven hundred and fifty meters. . . . Quite shallow, too, only fifty-five meters. That's why the Americans chose it for their detection system. Oh, here it is." Weathered by the southernmost bastion was a small one-story building, surrounded on three sides by a wall topped by a wire fence. The Turkish flag hung loosely from a peeling mast, and a small sign announced in Turkish and English: REPUBLIC OF TURKEY—OCEANOGRAPHIC RESEARCH INSTITUTE.

"Oceanographic Research, indeed," Komarov observed mockingly. "Three underground galleries, communicating through airlocks with the bottom of the strait. They go down almost every night to service the detection system."

Although annoyed at being lectured by his subordinate, Suvorov couldn't help putting in a question. "Could those devices detect anything else except atomic material?"

Komarov shook his head. "No. The only purpose of the system is to detect the passage of nuclear material through the straits. The Americans know that this is our main access to the Mediterranean and they are ready to pay a heavy price for immediate information on the transport of nuclear warheads by our navy. Right beneath us is equipment worth millions."

Suvorov raised one eyebrow. "I didn't think it was so expensive. A few radars, a couple of Geiger counters, and . . ."

Komarov smiled, trying not to look condescending. "It's much more complicated than that, Arkadi Vladimirovitch. Geiger counters are good only at a limited range, and only if the nuclear warhead is not shielded by any insulating material. But sometimes the warheads are transported in lead containers, or in a specially constructed compartment of the vessel. In order to establish with certainty that an atomic bomb has passed through the straits, the Americans use quite a wide range of devices: radars and Geiger counters, as you said, electronic sensors, scanning apparatus, infrared magnifying cameras to photograph unusually shaped hulls that might store nuclear material. They also use a rather clever gadget that bounces a stream of particles off the hull, then they do a spectroanalysis, and if certain particles have been absorbed, it indicates the presence of fissionable material."

"But you told me once that if we know the exact location of this system we can neutralize it."

Komarov paused before answering. "I'd say that there are ways of jamming or neutralizing most of the equipment," he said cautiously. "That's if we want to conceal the warheads' transport, of course. In 1973, after the October war in the Middle East we slipped a few warheads through the straits, only to scare the Americans. You certainly recall that. We didn't use any precautions on purpose, their sensors sniffed the stuff immediately, and in five hours Nixon had the Sixth Fleet and the Strategic Air Command on Red Alert."

"Yes, I remember that," said Suvorov wryly, and decided it was time to remind Komarov who was in charge. "The seventy-three display was my idea."

The shot scored and Komarov fell silent, his face more sullen than ever.

Eleonora sailed under the tall Bosphorus Bridge, then past the miniature Ortakoy mosque that seemed to float on the water aboard its spotless quay of white stone. At the approach of the classic Dolmabahçe Palace the strait gracefully curved to the southwest; the movement of the ship created the illusion that the hills, woods, and houses blocking the sight were pulled to the right like an enormous picturesque curtain. And there, right in front of them, appeared the magnificent city of Istanbul.

The seven hills of the fabled old city stretched one behind the other, their hundreds of dome-roofed mosques and sleek minarets bestowing an air of living legend on the skyline. The ramparts of the ageless sea walls, with their half-ruined towers and gates, still rose ominously around the tip of the Stamboul peninsula. The rays of the rising sun turned into liquid gold the smooth surface of the crooked inlet separating the new city from the old, thus justifying the poetic name given it by its ancient rulers: the Golden Horn. The colorful mixture of sights—red-tiled roofs, dome-covered bazaars, crooked little streets, antique towers, baths, Islamic schools, wisps of smoke rising from the street-corner charcoal grills, throngs of people—all blended together into a breathtaking, living fresco that projected into the senses of the visitor the magical pulsating beat of the unique city.

Suvorov pulled the strap of the binoculars over his head and handed it to the officer of the watch. For a moment he observed the maneuvers of the tanker, starting its approach to one of the Galata wharves. Then he turned to Komarov. "Be ready to disembark at 12:30," he instructed him dryly. "Civilian clothes, tie, tourist camera. And take care that our two gorillas"—he drew back his lips in contempt—"do the same."

He stepped into the small elevator on his way back to his cabin.

At precisely 1:30 P.M., Arkadi Suvorov left the crowd of dark, mustached Turks on the busy Istiklal Street and stepped into the Çiçek Pasaj. It was a tiny cobbled alley, partly sheltered by decrepit marquees of glass or tin. Small *lokantas*—Turkish taverns—and fast food kiosks lined both sides of the passage, but most of their business was done outside. The patrons were seated on low wooden stools clustered around marble slabs set on top of barrels. Harried waiters were running to and fro with salvers laden with beer mugs, bottles of wine, or goblets of *raki*. Young boys served the traditional Turkish appetizers, *mezes*: fried mussels, broiled shrimps, spicy shish-kebab, fried cubes of kidney, spleen, and liver as well as brain salad and grilled slices of *kokoreç*, a Turkish sausage made of intestines. Circulating between the tables, children sold skinned almonds and garlic-smelling pickles. Radios blared monotonous Oriental melodies and groups of students took up the refrains of plaintive popular songs or got up and danced to the music of the strolling accordion and *saz* players, encouraged by the rhythmic hand-clapping of their neighbors. Suvorov was satisfied. This everchanging kaleidoscope of sights and sounds, with people flowing in and out by both exits of the passage, was the ideal place for a covert contact.

He moved with the crowd until he spotted an empty stool. He sat down and ordered a *raki*, the typical Turkish aperitif. Out of the corner of his eye he noticed Komarov and the other two KGB agents sitting at a nearby table. He had told them an hour ago: "You stick close to me, but not too close. Never talk to me. I'll talk to you, if I have to. In no case should you interfere, unless I ask you to."

"Will the exchange take place at Çiçek Pasaj?" asked Shevchenko, a middle-aged Ukrainian with protruding chin and lifeless eyes.

"No," Suvorov had answered flatly. "The man just wants to make sure he is not walking into a trap of any kind. Elementary precaution. He will no doubt make contact, fix a second, maybe even a third, meeting place elsewhere, and finally bring the papers. And I am ready." He patted the inner pocket of his jacket where there was an envelope with twenty thousand American dollars, supplied by the accounts section of his department.

He finished his drink and looked around. The crowd was slowly moving past his table, but nobody tried to approach him. He left twenty lira on the table, got up, and moved toward the other end of the alley. Jostled by the crowd on all sides of him, he didn't notice anything unusual until he suddenly felt a slip of paper being pressed into the palm of his left hand. He closed his fist, but didn't turn around. Only when he had walked out of the passage and into the open air market in the next street did he look at the paper: Mekan Street, near Galata Tower. *Right at Number 73.*

He glanced casually over his shoulder. Komarov and the two bodyguards were twenty yards behind him. He walked back to the Istiklal Street, and hailed a cruising cab. "Galata Kulesti," he mumbled, and the driver nodded. The cab was an old Ford from the early sixties with rattling doors and a coughing engine, but the driver seemed to be very proud of it. Glued to his dashboard and even windshield were trinkets, miniature dolls, key holders, and cheap compasses. All during the ride he held the wheel with his left hand, while his right hand gently patted and cleaned his collection of worthless baubles.

Suvorov didn't even glance at the impressive Galata Tower, miraculously preserved from the thirteenth century, but hurried down the narrow, crooked Mekan Street. He felt uneasy; there were no tourists around and he hated to attract attention. The further he advanced downhill, the more crowded the street became. He wondered why there was not a single woman in the crowd, only men and young boys, some of them looking pretty agitated.

He understood why when he turned right at number 73. The iron gate controlling the access into the muddy lane was wide open. On his left was a small hut bearing the sign, POLIS, and a policeman was casually chatting with a stout, thickly veiled woman. On his right stretched a long succession of seedy houses, and a crowd of men and boys clustered by the large windows on the street level. A short glance at the merchandise displayed behind the hand-painted signs, VISIT 50 LIRA, informed him that he was in the red-light district of Istanbul.

Whores of all ages, sizes, and colors sat, ate, chatted, or moved in the bare, shabby rooms. Some of them were wearing cheap gowns, others walked around naked, except for tiny underpants. Most of the women were obese, and an air of vulgarity exuded from their worn-out faces, heavy breasts, and thick waists. Only a few were slim, petite, flat-chested, their almond-shaped eyes attesting to their Far Eastern origins. Some of the prostitutes were quite old, in their sixties, and moved gracelessly in their cubicles, mim-icking and grimacing toward the windows like monkeys in a cage. In one of the windows Suvorov saw two young girls who couldn't have been older than fourteen.

Very few men ventured into the whorehouses. Most of them stood in silent groups, gaping at the women, moving aside to let one of them cross the lane and purchase some food and drink from the street vendors. A skinny black whore, her curly hair dyed with henna, brushed past Suvorov and caught the hand of a blushing boy, who had been staring at her. She flashed at him a demure smile, revealing a gold tooth, provocatively shook her breasts, and dragged him in.

At that moment another tiny note was pressed in Suvorov's hand.

He bought his ticket in the box office under the turret-topped Middle Gate and walked unhurriedly into the sec-ond court of the Topkapi Palace. His Russian guardian angels let a group of elderly German tourists enter first, and followed slowly.

Suvorov advanced along the cypress-lined main path without bothering to contemplate the splendors of the ancient dwelling of the Ottoman sultans. He barely spared a glance for the massive structure of the harem, crossed the Gate of Felicity into the third court, and looked at his watch. It was 4:15 P.M.; he had fifteen minutes to kill. The note was quite explicit: "4:30 sharp. The Baghdad Kiosk." After a short hesitation he turned to the right and entered the Imperial treasury along with a group of chattering German tourists. He walked through the display rooms, looking with cold eyes at one of the most fabulous treasures in the world. Before him stepped an elderly English guide, a gaunt man in an untidy black suit, who was pointing out the highlights of the treasury to a horde of British nuns. They uttered the appropriate exclamations at the sight of the Gold Bayram throne, the statuette of the gold elephant with its load of gems, and the huge Spoon diamond, its eighty-nine karats of pear-shaped facets sparkling on the velvet cushion. He followed them indifferently, his thoughts drifting far away. The only item that drew his attention for a second was the famous Topkapi dagger. The three huge emeralds encrusted in its handle diffused a deep-green glow on the slightly bent gold sheath that was ornate with pearls and diamonds.

He looked at his watch. It was 4:26.

He left the treasury room and marched briskly toward the Pavilion of the Blessed Mantle. He crossed the tiny chamber, sacred to hundreds of millions of Moslems all over the world because of the Mantle and sword of Muhammad displayed among precious rugs and curtains embroidered with holy verses. Through a second door he emerged on the sun-drenched marble terrace that offered a breathtaking view of the Golden Horn and the new city. In front of him, surrounded by a vault-roofed balcony and topped by a round dome and a slender minaret, stood the tile-and-marble-walled Baghdad Kiosk.

An old guard came out of the kiosk and barred its access with a chain on which hung the sign CLOSED FOR REPAIRS. Suvorov waited for him to go away, then looked quickly over his shoulder. Komarov stood ten yards behind him, staring woodenly at the Galata Serail from the tiny Iftariye balcony, whose bell-shaped gilt dome blazed in the sun. The two others assumed the attitude of weary visitors strolling idly on the terrace.

It was 4:30. Suvorov effortlessly stepped over the chain, opened the wooden door, and went into the Baghdad Kiosk.

Komarov lit a cigarette and sat down on the bench in the Iftariye. Shevchenko, the Ukrainian, did the same. They smoked in silence. Five minutes passed, then another five. The marble terrace was completely deserted, and the sounds of voices and steps from the nearby kiosks slowly subsided. Somewhere near, the noise of a car engine rose to a crescendo, then faded away. A uniformed guard came to the terrace. "Will you please excuse us?" he apologized with a smile. "It's 4:45 and in winter we close the palace at five o'clock. You have another ten minutes' walk to the main gate."

Komarov returned his smile, but as soon as the guide left, he nervously beckoned to his companions. "I don't like that," he whispered. "He has been gone for fifteen minutes. How long can this damn transaction take?"

Shevchenko looked worried. The other agent, a burly, sunburned Latvian, said quickly: "Let's go in."

Komarov hesitated for a moment, then said: "Let's go."

He leaped over the chain and opened the door of the Baghdad Kiosk. In one quick look he took in everything: the octagonal structure, the intricately ornate walls, the cabinets in the arched niches, the low divans, the wrought-iron brazier in the middle, and the massive bronze chimney-piece. And the second door, which was wide open, on the other side of the room.

He ran across the room, his two companions sticking to his heels. They bolted through the open back door onto a balcony overlooking the neglected garden of the fourth court. A wooden scaffolding, used probably for repairs, rose from the garden, twelve feet below. The Latvian clambered down with feral suppleness and darted into the deserted garden. Ahead of him stood the outer wall of the palace. From a small parking lot in the middle, a narrow asphalt road led to the service gate, which was wide open. The Latvian kneeled and put his hands on the ground. Then he turned and looked in dismay at Komarov and Shev-chenko, who ran toward him.

"It's warm," he shouted. "A car has waited here, with its engine running."

"Oh, no," groaned Komarov. He suddenly remembered the engine whine he had heard, ten minutes before. He sprinted to the service gate and stared out at the deserted road.

Shevchenko viciously cursed. "He did it," he snapped furiously. "The sonofabitch defected."

10

PHONE

The band struck the last, triumphant chords of the "Internationale," the Revolutionary Workers' Anthem, and their echo slowly dissolved in the immensity of Red Square. A moment of total silence followed, and the crowd massed on the sidewalk facing the Lenin Mausoleum stirred with expectation, many craning their necks in the direction of Gorky Street. Suddenly the dry thunder of drums reverberated through the loudspeakers, beating the tight measures of a military march. The band chimed in with the opening notes of the Red Army song, and at that very moment a wave of red banners surged into the square. The soldiers and militiamen posted all along the Kremlin wall snapped to attention and saluted. The parade, celebrating the twenty-fifth anniversary of the Warsaw Pact, had just begun.

A second detachment of soldiers in various uniforms followed, bearing the flags of the Soviet Union, Bulgaria, Czechoslovakia, East Germany, Hungary, Poland, and Romania—the seven members of the treaty. Behind them, in perfect ranks of fifty, marched the contingents of the signatory countries: Bulgarians with white-green-red badges, Poles in their traditional peaked caps, Hungarians in their new dark-blue uniforms, and helmeted goose-stepping East Germans. A smart column of Russian paratroopers, outnumbering the other nations' detachments by ten to one, closed the infantry portion of the parade. They wore green combat uniforms, jump boots shined to perfection, and round fur caps. Their gloved hands clutched the famed Kalatchnikov assault rifles, which were strapped to their chests. As the column approached the Lenin Mausoleum, the Red Army Chorus, massed by the Kremlin wall, intoned "Moskva Maya," the most popular march of the Second World War. The front line of the column was now level with the rectangular structure of the mausoleum; in a sharp movement 5,000 men turned their heads right, slapped their palms on the wooden butts of their rifles, and presented arms to their leaders, who reviewed them from the front terrace of the building.

The foreign military attachés and the newspapers' correspondents, standing on a low podium by the mausoleum wall, also looked up. On top of the severe facade of gray and red granite blocks stood the most powerful men in Russia. The observers were familiar with the strange fifty-year-old tradition of the Russian power game: each man's position on the terrace relative to the present ruler was the most accurate indication of his current standing in the Soviet hierarchy. Consecutive photographs of previous years' parades permitted one to follow the careers of many an ambitious leader, at times gradually approaching the ruler and moving to the top—and at other times sliding away from the focus of power and down to oblivion, disgrace, or even the firing squad.

This year's power display disclosed two major changes: an alarming drive to the center of hard-liner Gusnov, a bulky, craggy-faced party boss, who most certainly coveted Brezhnev's position; and the relative disgrace of Politburo member and KGB chief Yuri Andropov, who had been relegated to the far edge of the terrace and stood there with a wooden face, clutching the stone parapet as if it were a lifebuoy.

Most of the foreign guests quickly assimilated the new Kremlin order, then shifted their attention to the impassive face of Leonid Brezhnev. That was why only a few of them noticed something strange happening at the very height of the spectacle. A lean man with a scrawny face, partially concealed by dark glasses and a large-brimmed hat, appeared behind Andropov and whispered something in his ear. The KGB director tilted his head closer. His face grew livid, then he nodded, turned, and disappeared along with his mysterious companion.

The stranger was Alexei Kalinin.

"Suvorov," Andropov muttered hoarsely, the profound shock painted all over his bloodless features. "Suvurov. The most brilliant man in the service." His shock abruptly turned to uncontrollable fury. "The bastard," he spat out, "the filthy, treacherous, double-crossing bastard."

Kalinin looked at him blankly but didn't say a word. They were standing by the Kremlin wall, near the section where outstanding Soviet citizens were buried. A stand of snow-laden firs and a cordon of militiamen concealed them from curious onlookers.

In the ominous silence that settled between them, they heard the Red Army Chorus reach the finale of the martial song.

> ... *Strana Maya, Moskva Maya*
> *Tuy samaya, lubeemaya!*

The last notes of the march died abruptly, but the spell didn't last. The roar of engines and the rattle of chains quickly filled the square. The T-76 tanks were opening the motorized part of the parade.

Andropov's wrath focused now on Kalinin. "If you had just got that damn letter in time, I would have crushed him like a snake!" He drove his right fist into his open palm. "But all I got from you were promises." He spitefully mimicked Kalinin's confident voice. "You'll send your best agents to London! You'll get the document in twenty-four hours! You'll find the girl!"

He drew a deep breath. "Rubbish," he cracked. "First, a young bitch, who is not even an agent, fools all of you. Then, an unarmed American kills your best men in the Hyde Park Club! And now, to top it all, Suvorov defects under the very noses of your agents. You'll pay for that, Kalinin. I'll have you court-martialed for incompetence!"

Kalinin kept quiet, head slightly bowed.

"Why don't you say anything?" raged the KGB director. "I know, you don't have anything to say. But what am I going to say to the Secretary General? That the man we recommended for the Lenin order is a traitor?"

"I think that Tovarishch Brezhnev will be rather pleased that Suvorov was the mole," Kalinin unexpectedly remarked in a very soft voice.

"Pleased?" Andropov glared at him in dismay.

Kalinin nodded. "Suvorov was Gusnov's protégé," he pointed out matter-of-factly. "And Gusnov is getting quite embarrassing lately." He paused, letting that sink in, and continued: "The Secretary General will certainly seize this opportunity to settle his account with Gusnov. On thinking about it, Suvorov's defection is the best thing that could have happened to Tovarishch Brezhnev."

Andropov threw him a calculating glance through half-closed eyelids. He didn't react, but Kalinin sensed that the message had seeped through, and his boss's fury was starting to abate. "I admit that we blundered," Kalinin conceded. "Yet, it was more a matter of bad luck than incompetence."

"I can't believe it," Andropov growled, but his tone had notably mellowed. "You worked with him daily. How come you didn't suspect him?"

"Oh, but I certainly did," Kalinin quickly put in. "Why

do you think I objected to his trip to Istanbul? Why did I send three people with him? You may interrogate Shevchenko, if you wish. I had briefed him explicitly about the danger that Suvorov might defect."

"You had?" Andropov flared up again. "And you didn't report a thing to me?"

"How could I?" Kalinin asked morosely. "I had no proof, no lead, nothing. Just a suspicion. If I had made such an accusation, you would have thrown me out of your office."

Andropov lapsed into a long silence. "The defection was masterly planned," he bitterly admitted.

Kalinin nodded. "Yes, that hoax about the detection system was very clever."

"The plans were phony?"

Kalinin pondered. "No. The plans that they gave him in seventy-two were genuine. The CIA wanted to bolster Suvorov's credibility, so they let him have the plans. They must have conceded that sooner or later we would find out about the underwater detectors, so they handed them to us on a platter. But the new tip about their intention to remove the sensors to a different location—that was phony, of course. They must have panicked, they wanted him out, they looked in his file and got the idea about Istanbul."

"And it worked perfectly." Andropov sank into the masochistic mood that Kalinin knew only too well. "He must be in Langley Woods by now."

Kalinin shook his head. "No. They don't operate that way. They'll debrief him in Europe before they fly him to America. But they will not do it in Turkey. The Turkish government is very careful. The CIA will whisk him out of Turkey as soon as possible. . . ."

"Maybe they already have."

"Yes, maybe they already have," Kalinin agreed. "They'll take him to one of their bases in Europe for a first debriefing. It's a matter of a week or so."

Andropov looked back toward Red Square. It had started to snow again. The last tanks of the armored column were rolling past St. Basil's Cathedral. Five huge trucks emerged from Gorky Street, pulling heavy trailers behind them. On each trailer lay the giant cylindrical body of an SS-14 missile, its massive warhead sharply pointing forward.

The KGB director scowled at Kalinin. "Do you know what will happen when Suvorov talks?"

"I know," Kalinin admitted. "But he won't talk, comrade director."

Andropov stared at him skeptically.

"I'll find him," Kalinin said firmly. "I'll find him and I'll kill him, if it's the last thing I do."

"Hello? Anybody in?"

James and Sylvie, eating a light dinner in the kitchen, hadn't heard the key turning in the lock and the soft footsteps of Professor Collins. He stood in front of them now, still wearing his duffle coat, and carrying a small valise in his left hand. His face was devoid of expression.

James leaped to his feet. "Did you get them?" he asked.

The professor dropped the valise. He removed his right hand from his pocket and produced a package, which he flung down with a flourish on the table.

"You've got them!" Sylvie jumped up to embrace the professor, while James merely remarked, "You should have gone on the stage instead of becoming a professor." But there was no malice in his voice and he clapped the professor's shoulders warmly while Sylvie busied herself with the package. It contained two used American passports in the names of Mr. and Mrs. David Adams, of Phoenix, Arizona. James flipped through the pages, examined the entry and exit stamps of various European airports, and frowned at Sylvie's photograph in her blond wig, and his own, sporting a bushy mustache. "It's rather amateurish—good for one time only, though."

After James's conversation with Hardy they had begun to make plans to leave the country. Sylvie had no papers at all, of course, and his would be quite a bit worse than useless. The British would certainly be watching the airports and ports. He didn't know anyone who could provide them with fake passports, and although Collins had still a few contacts from the past, James was reluctant to involve him further.

Sylvie had come to the rescue, mentioning that Mrs. O'Shaughnessy had offered to obtain papers for her from the Irish underground. She didn't dare, though, to visit the apartment hotel in Kensington Gardens, and James wouldn't let her telephone. They concocted a simple plan: Professor Collins traveled with Sylvie to London and left her in a cinema. He then took a cab to 27 Kensington Gardens and rented an apartment. He handed Mrs. O'Shaughnessy a written message from Sylvie, containing a few personal allusions that completely guaranteed its authenticity. Two hours later the Professor and Mrs. O'Shaughnessy met in a crowded self-service restaurant in Oxford Street, where Sylvie joined them. Mrs. O'Shaughnessy seemed pleased rather than surprised when Sylvie asked for two passports and handed over their photographs. She returned directly to Cambridge and the professor stayed in his new apartment for the weekend. That Monday morning he had arranged to pick up the passports, and now he was sampling the first smile of his success.

"I have some more news for you," he said, smiling at Sylvie. "Your friend Jennifer is out of danger."

He was awarded with another passionate embrace, as perhaps had been his intention.

"Did you see her?" Sylvie asked excitedly.

"No," the professor said. "That would have been too

risky. But I did call the hospital and spoke to one of her nurses. I instructed her to convey Anne Bee's warmest regards."

"Did you call from the hotel?" James asked quickly.

"Really, James." The professor's voice carried an edge of rebuke. "You know me better than that. I called from a pay phone. I also know something about tracing calls." He shrugged. "Anyway, I don't think you are going to be bothered any further. The heat is off you both, and I doubt that either the CIA, or the KGB, are looking for you anymore."

"What the hell do you mean by that?"

"I mean that document of yours has become something of a dead letter. . . ." The professor casually produced a copy of the *Evening News* from his valise. The banner headline told all: KGB MASTER SPY DEFECTS, and below that GENERAL ARKADI SUVOROV SEEKS POLITICAL ASYLUM IN THE UNITED STATES.

James grabbed the paper and skimmed through the first few paragraphs. "So that's what they did," he said under his breath. "After I called Hardy they must have decided to cut and run, and then smuggled Suvorov out of the country."

"I take that to mean that nobody cares about this letter of yours anymore. That closes the file on Suvorov, right?"

"Wrong," Bradley replied tartly. "The Russians won't give in without a fight. They must be hunting Suvorov all over Europe now. We're not out of the woods yet."

"By now he must be already in Washington," Sylvie suggested.

"No," James looked again at the *Evening News*. "You see, they don't mention where Suvorov is. My guess is that they'll have a debriefing session in Europe somewhere before they get him over to Langley. . . . And my second guess is that the KGB is on red alert all over the continent to locate him and blow his brains out before he speaks."

"Why?" Sylvie asked, her face puzzled.

"Because they want to save their mole, that's why," snapped James impatiently. Then, quickly regaining control over himself, he said, "I'm sorry. I'm too tense. I'll try to explain. There is a Russian mole in Washington, we know that. The KGB would do anything to protect him. Now Suvorov might have some ideas about the mole's identity. Even if he hasn't, he might remember unusual incidents or bits of information that could lead us to the mole. If I were the KGB director, I would do anything in my power to find Suvorov and silence him before the debriefing."

"So?" Sylvie suddenly realized that James was already preparing his own plan.

"So I've got to find him first," he said.

The bedside telephone in the small Georgetown apartment had a soft, almost musical ring. Yet, at the first sound Gene Ackerman was wide awake and calmly picked up the receiver. Twelve years with the agency had taught him to sleep lightly and to awake immediately, even if it was 3:30 A.M., as the luminous dial of the alarm clock indicated. "Yes," he said softly.

"Is this Mr. Ackerman of United Steel?" He immediately recognized the voice of his best friend.

"No," Ackerman said. "Right name, wrong number."

He hung up and quietly slipped out of bed. The heaviness of his enormous bulk was compensated by an animal suppleness; his smooth, unhurried way of moving was deceptive. He glanced over his shoulder at Joan, who was fast asleep, curled like a little girl under the heavy blanket, with only the top of her nose and a wisp of strawberry-blond hair emerging from her cocoon. He dressed in silence, threw over his shoulders a heavy lambskin coat, and went out in the night. The question and the answer over the phone had been for years a secret code between him and his friend from F-3.

Gene walked to a phone booth about three hundred yards down the street. He stepped in and waited, enjoying the delicate taste of a Manikin cigarillo. Five minutes later the phone rang. He lifted the receiver.

"I am calling from Europe," James Bradley said slowly. "My time is very short and I can't tell you the whole story. You have to trust me. It's important."

"What the hell's happened to you?" Gene asked. "Where have you been?"

"Listen." Bradley's voice sounded tense and preoccupied. "I'm in hiding because high up in our company there's a mole working for the opposition. He almost had me killed."

Ackerman didn't react.

"Are you with me?" Bradley nervously asked. "I repeat: High up in our company . . ."

Ackerman cut him short. "How high?"

"Very, very high," Bradley said carefully. "Now the rest. This man will do all he can to prevent an important official of the opposition from coming to this country. Actually, he may already have signaled to the other side where that official is hiding now. Do you read me?"

"I do." It was easy to understand. The double agent in the CIA upper echelons would try to prevent Suvorov from reaching safe haven in the United States.

The faraway voice of Bradley went on: "You must let me know where this official is hiding. I must go there at once. He is in danger."

A skeptical expression slowly settled on Ackerman's face. "You sound rather melodramatic," he remarked.

"I don't give a damn if I do," Bradley tartly answered.

"The boss doesn't believe me. Nobody else but you can help me."

"What proof do you have that something might happen to him?" Ackerman was still unconvinced.

"No proof," Bradley admitted. "Just a hunch."

Ackerman paused, dropped the butt of his cigarillo and stepped on its glowing tip. He ran his hand over his balding skull. Bradley's story seemed too farfetched, but it wasn't like him to make up stories of any kind. His face calm, poised, almost perpetually stamped with the shadow of a cynical smile, emerged in front of Ackerman. He wasn't a man to panic easily. But what if something had happened and he was in the hands of the opposition?

"Are you alone?" Ackerman referred again to their private code.

"No, I am not." It meant he was. If he had been under pressure, or held prisoner, he would have answered: "Yes, I'm alone." Simple reversal code, but very effective. "Listen," Bradley pressed. "I haven't cracked up. I am dead serious and the stakes are very high. I must get there."

Ackerman drew a deep breath. "Okay, I'll stick my neck out for you, just this time. Remember the affair we were on together three years and . . . and five months ago?"

A short silence followed. Finally, Bradley spoke: "I remember."

"Same place."

"Good man," Bradley sighed with relief. "Take care."

The line went dead. For a long moment, Gene Ackerman dully contemplated the receiver he held in his huge fist.

In the tiny booth at Heathrow Airport, where he had been feeding half-crowns to a pay phone, Bradley turned to Sylvie de Sérigny. "We are boarding the first flight to Nice."

"He is there?"

"Close enough," Bradley said. "In Beaulieu. There is a nice secluded villa on the beach that I know pretty well."

In Chevy Chase a hand picked up the telephone and dialed a New York number. The man didn't wait for his party to identify himself.

"Tonight," he said. "Between midnight and a quarter past. Villa Dolorès. Route du Golfe. Beaulieu."

"How many guards?"

The man paused just long enough to light a black cheroot with his golden Colibri. "Two inside," he said. "Nobody outside."

"That's good," the voice said.

The young immigration officer at Nice–Côte d'Azur airport cast a bored eye over the handsome couple who stood in front of his booth, and mechanically stamped the passports of Mr. and Mrs. Adams. They collected their suitcases and walked casually through customs. "Thank God, there's no security check on luggage," whispered James, and Sylvie nodded. His heavy Colt Python .357, especially chambered for .38 cartridges, and a box of handmade special loadings lay wrapped in a woolen sweater on the bottom of his suitcase. This modified version of the Magnum was big and heavy and could become quite cumbersome at times; but he had stuck with it ever since the faraway days when he was a Marine captain taking target practice at the shooting range in San Diego.

The spacious arrival hall of the airport was crowded with incoming tourists, mostly well-off and middle-aged, flocking to enjoy the sunny crispness of the off-season Riviera. James's eyes quickly monitored both levels of the lobby, but except for the routine shift of two *inspecteurs* of the DST—the French FBI—lounging by the Hachette newsstand, the place appeared to be clean. He removed his fake mustache in the men's room. He was startled to feel quite confident now that he had left England. The chances that anyone would look for him here were pretty remote, and he decided to risk using his credit card and his real name when he stopped by the car-rental counter. At the Hertz stand they had a large selection, including a number of vintage convertibles, which were quite popular among the more ostentatious vacationers. He chose a powerful Mercedes 450, with the thought that something might go wrong that would cause him to leave Beaulieu in quite a hurry.

He threw his suitcase into the back seat of the silver-gray Mercedes. Sylvie was already in the front seat, eagerly turning the radio dial. Her eyes were shining and her cheeks were flushed with excitement. Sylvie had been in an expansive mood ever since the moment the plane had taken off from Heathrow. He understood why she was happy. She was going home, convinced that at last she had finally awakened from her nightmare. He didn't share her optimism. *She's in this pretty damn deep,* he thought to himself, *and the rest of the trip may not be so carefree.* As he looked at her radiant face he felt something toward her he was reluctant to admit even to himself.

He tried to drive his personal feelings from his mind and concentrate on the mission ahead. They headed out of the parking lot and drove off toward Nice. It was a pleasant winter day, and the palm-lined Promenade des Anglais was thronged with tourists. At the Place Masséna he double-parked the car and walked into an optical equipment shop, where he bought a pair of powerful field glasses. Then he gunned the car up the winding Basse Corniche. Fifteen minutes later, Mr. and Mrs. Adams checked into the deluxe Hotel Métropole, overlooking the rock-strewn beach of Beaulieu-sur-Mer.

"I'll be back in a couple of hours," he told Sylvie. "We can have a late lunch on the terrace."

"I'm coming with you."

He shook his head and smiled. "You'd better hit the boutiques in the lobby and find yourself some clothes." He smiled. "They don't appreciate girls in jeans in the Métropole restaurant. And I feel like having lunch with an elegant lady."

"You will," she said lightly, "but I warn you that jeans are my favorite clothes. Remember that."

"I will," he said seriously. The peculiar note in his voice made her raise her eyes and watch him cross the plush lobby to the glass doors, and go out beyond into the midday sunshine.

The Villa Dolorès was a low Spanish-style building with whitewashed walls and a red-tiled roof. It was built on top of a cliff overlooking the sea and was surrounded on three sides by a screen of pine, oak, juniper, and exotic shrubbery. The large bay windows of its facade looked out on an arcaded veranda and kidney-shaped swimming pool. A lush green lawn sloped gently down to the edge of the cliff. The entire villa was surrounded by high, thick walls topped with broken glass. The only access to the gravel driveway that looped around to the rear of the house was a dirt road that led through a heavy iron gate.

James lowered the field glasses. He knew the place well, every inch of it. He tried to visualize the oblong living room with its soft lights, rustic furniture, and worn rugs, where so many defectors and agents returning from operational missions had been debriefed. He was also well acquainted with the few vulnerable spots in the security system. And in addition to that, he knew the only vantage point from which the villa could be observed: the place where he was now, the old stone belfry of the four-hundred-year-old church of Sainte Marie de la Mer, in the tiny village of Dupré, three miles east of Beaulieu.

He concealed the binoculars under his jacket and hurried down the stone steps of the belfry. He had everything he wanted. Gene Ackerman was right: the villa was operational. From his observation post he had counted seven guards patrolling along the wall inside the estate. From experience he knew that there were three more outside concealed from his sight, and two bodyguards inside the house who would be with the defector twenty-four hours a day. Also, according to regulations, two senior agents, in charge of debriefing, were in the house.

At 1:30 the security shifts had changed. Four Peugeot 604 sedans arrived and stopped outside the gate. One by one, ten men had come out of the cars to be checked by the two guards at the gate, and then each had moved off toward a different position, where he would remain the next six hours. The off-duty agents immediately got into the cars and drove away. The security was tight as ever, he noted with satisfaction; but then, he didn't expect any foul play in broad daylight. If his assumption was correct, and the mole knew of Suvorov's whereabouts, a KGB attempt to kidnap or kill him would be made only during the night. The obvious advantage given to the defender was seriously handicapped by darkness.

The push is going to come, he thought, as he was driving back to Beaulieu, either tonight or tomorrow night. The Russians knew that the CIA current routine was to keep the defectors in a safehouse for a week before flying them to America; but they wouldn't be sure that in Suvorov's case the agency wouldn't fly him to Langley earlier. The Russians had to seal Suvorov's mouth as quickly as possible. They were engaged in a race against time.

And so was he.

He left the car with the doorman, walked through the lobby, and went out to the terrace. Far below, the surf was breaking over the rocks in a small cove sheltered between two outcroppings of land. The air was heavy with the fragrance of Provence. A beautiful woman, her black hair cascading over her bare shoulders, the contours of her lithe body accented by a long white dress of clinging fabric, was sitting at the far end of the terrace, staring out at the sea. She turned to him and smiled.

He felt again the bittersweet throb of pain and long-forgotten tenderness, as he smiled back at Sylvie de Sérigny.

The maître d'hôtel, a suave, well-fed Corsican, seriously discussed the menu with James and Sylvie, and they finally settled on a *mousse de saumon*, a grilled turbot, and a bottle of Sancerre. As soon as he left with the order, Sylvie leaned eagerly over the table. "Well?"

"He's there, all right."

"Did you see him?"

He shook his head. "They didn't even let him out for a swim in the pool. The whole place is swarming with security."

"But you're still worried?"

"Yes. I'm going in tonight. It's the night I fear. During the day he is safe."

She started to speak, but he raised his hand. "You are not coming with me, Sylvie."

A hurt look crept into her eyes. "Why not?"

He fiddled awkwardly with his fork. "Look, I just want to get you out of this. You had your share of horror in London. All that is over now. Your friend is safe, you are back in France, nobody is stalking you anymore. Go home, stay with your mother, get out of this lousy business. It's a cruel game, Sylvie; it's not for you." He was about to add: "And I don't want to lose you, as I lost Sandra," but he caught himself. Someone had once said to him: "You can't lose something you don't have." And he didn't have her. They hadn't made love since that night in the Hyde Park Club. He felt it would be taking advantage of her dependence upon him. And since then their relationship had evolved into something unclear, undefined. They were close, intimate—and yet, they were still strangers. If he only could take her hand and say to her: "Don't go away," but he didn't know how. Sometimes it was more difficult to take a girl's hand than to take her body.

Sylvie was looking at him sharply, her head tilted to one side, as it always was when she was trying to fathom some deep mystery. Finally she spoke. "I'm not going back home, James, if that's what you're thinking about." She smiled. "Don't forget that I've been in this longer than anyone—and you are not going to make me miss the ending."

He was about to ask if this was the only reason she wanted to stay but decided it wiser not to. Instead, he said sharply: "Now listen, no matter what you say, it's for me—and not for you—to decide if you are staying or not. I'm saying that you are going home: I'm going into the villa tonight, and it may be pretty rough." An angry note appeared in his voice. "There won't be anything for you to do there."

Her eyes flashed with frustration. "You're being unreasonable and you know it," she shot back. "We've already had this conversation in King's Cross Station. I asked you then to let me stay with you. I said I might be of some help. You didn't take me terribly seriously, of course. You said that the best help I could give was to stop crying all the time." She lit a cigarette and inhaled deeply. "Well, I haven't cried much since then. But I turned out to be rather more use to you than you expected. I was the one who went to London to look up those books at the British Museum. To tell you the truth, I was scared even with my disguise. And I was the one who got the passports. Don't forget."

"I don't deny—" he started to say, but she went on heatedly.

"Well, then don't . . . I don't mind telling you this affair scares me, and these plots and counterplots and double-crossing disgust me. I didn't ask to get involved. All I wanted to do was escape and forget. But things turned out differently. We are in this together, James. I can't go home now, knowing that you might be in danger. I'd never forgive myself if something happened to you."

"But do you know what going into the villa means?" he persisted.

"I'm not talking about going into the villa. . . ." She looked at him impatiently. "Really, James, you are so stupid sometimes . . . I want to be there, to hang about outside just in case you need me for something. And if you say no, it's entirely possible that I'll be there anyway . . . with or without your permission." She suddenly bit her lower lip, her voice broke, and she averted her eyes.

He sighed deeply, but didn't insist further. There was something firm and stubborn beneath her feminine softness, and he felt that any further arguing would be useless. He knew that she couldn't be of much help tonight, and yet she was right in a way. She was still his only ally. Besides, he admitted to himself, somewhere deep inside he wanted her to stay close, lest her departure break the still fragile bond between them.

He did not reply, and Sylvie knew that she had won. She looked up brightly and asked, "What's happened to our lunch? I'm ravenous."

As if on cue, a waiter in white jacket appeared with the salmon mousse and poured smoky white wine into their glasses. She sipped from her glass, closed her eyes, and turned her face toward the sun. A blissful smile spread across her face.

"I can't believe it," she said. "I just can't believe it."

He looked at her uncertainly, and she explained: "Here we are sitting out in the sunshine, having a wonderful lunch in one of the most beautiful places in the world. Everything's just perfect: the weather, the food, the ambience . . . I can't believe that only last night I was running for my life, after the most horrible experience I've ever had. It's like being on a different planet, James."

Bradley didn't answer. He was trying to remember how many times he must have said the same thing to himself. . . . *When I was pretending to be a normal person,* he said to himself, *and I'd walk into a restaurant, and sit down and realize that I wasn't out to get anybody, and nobody was out to get me. . . . She can't see now . . . that in an hour or so, we're both going right straight back where we came from, to that world that seems so unreal, so distant yet impossibly close.*

And he wondered what was in store for the girl he loved.

They concealed the car in a clearing off the main road and continued on foot, through the fir trees. He was dressed in black: a zippered leather jacket, turtleneck pullover, leather slacks, and soft moccasins. When they reached the foot of the wall, he looked at his watch and whispered: "It's half past eleven now. I'm going over. Then I'll try to find Suvorov and talk to him. You wait outside. If anything funny happens, run to the car and get the police." She suddenly moved toward him in the darkness and her soft lips found his mouth. "Take care, James."

He caressed her face, then moved away and crouched down in front of the wall. He had decided to try the northwest corner, where the trees were taller and the hedge especially thick. The guards patrolling along the northern and the western walls always stopped short, about ten yards from the corner, because of the thick vegetation.

He climbed effortlessly to the top of the wall; the leather gloves protected his hands from the jagged shards of broken glass. He rolled over the top and landed softly in a dense clump of hibiscus bushes. He held his breath, listening for any unusual sound that might indicate he had been seen or heard. But everything seemed normal. The first stage of the penetration had been successful.

He lay down on the ground and considered his next move. . . . He couldn't go nearer the house now without attracting the attention of the guards, but in about half an hour, at midnight, the guards would change and people would be moving around. He would have a few minutes and could make his way to the villa unnoticed. Suvorov would probably either be in the living room or, if everything seemed quiet, he might even be outside on the front lawn by the pool. That would be his opportunity to talk to him.

His thoughts focused on the mission he had undertaken. Not only must he protect Suvorov from the KGB but he must also try to discover the mole's identity. He was almost sure that Suvorov didn't know the mole's name. If he did, he would have warned Washington long ago. Yet, he might be aware or at least suspicious of the mole's existence and know some useful information that might give him a lead as to his identity.

But would he get a chance to talk to Suvorov? And would Suvorov cooperate?

In the villa's brightly illuminated parking lot the engine of a car began to rasp. Then a second car, a third, and there was a steady drone of the engines. He looked at his watch and frowned in surprise—it was five minutes to midnight. The night team hadn't arrived yet, but somebody was already warming up the engines. What the hell was going on? Bradley started to rise cautiously to his feet. Why did they start the cars in the goddamn parking lot? The regulations stated explicitly that those cars should be used only for emergencies. . . . The guys that went off shift were supposed to go back in the same cars that the relief shift came in. Something very strange was happening.

He heard footsteps and soft voices on his left, and he

could make out the silhouettes of two men hurrying toward the parking lot. Nobody had replaced them, and they were just walking away from their posts. Puzzled, he stealthily followed them, keeping close to the trees, his dark clothes blending with the dark shadows. He reached the edge of the small grove, where it bordered the parking lot. The three cars, one big American limousine and two Peugeots, were only yards away. Stupefied, he watched the security men climb into the waiting vehicles. One after another, the three cars rolled down the gravel driveway and disappeared through the open iron gate. No one was left behind; no one even bothered to close the gate.

The guards were deserting the villa!

A terrible suspicion came into James's mind. Oblivious to the danger of being seen, he rushed up to the villa and peered in through a window. The room was brightly lit. In an armchair, with a large electric heater nearby, sat Arkadi Suvorov.

He was wearing heavy woolen trousers and a brown vest over a gray cotton shirt. A book lay open upon his knees, but his eyes were staring fixedly at the large window. Two bodyguards were sitting nearby. One of them, a hatchet-faced, bony man, smoked a cigarette, leaning back on the yellow cushions of the sofa, his long legs propped up on the round coffee table. A gun was resting on his lap. The other bodyguard was leafing idly through a magazine. From where he stood, James could see only his broad back and the graying fringe of hair at the back of his neck.

The younger man said something, and the gray-haired agent turned. Bradley recognized him immediately: a middle-aged agent from the security division, Burt Bushinski. The three men in the room looked peaceful and relaxed, almost like old friends relaxing together on a long winter's night.

And even before he heard the engines of the cars climbing up the hill to the open gate of the estate, he knew. The traitor in Langley had won the second round. Suvorov was set for the kill.

He hurled himself at the door, but it was not even locked. Bushinski was first on his feet, his gun already drawn. His eyes widened in surprise when he saw Bradley's face. "James! What . . ."

"Get out of here!" Bradley turned to face Suvorov, who stared at him, uncomprehendingly. "Get him out of here! We're under attack!" He didn't wait for them to react. Pivoting on his heels, he ran back to the outer gate. He reached it at the same moment as the approaching cars rounded the last turn on the road and the beams of their headlights converged on the gate. Bradley grabbed the crossbar of the gate and slammed it. He reached for the massive padlock hanging on a ring in the wall, passed the shackle through the protruding staple of the gate, and snapped it shut. The first of the two Citroëns was only yards away when he threw himself back, rolled across the gravel, and crashed behind a bush, the Python already trained on the gate.

The first Citroën, ugly and evil like a monstrous bullfrog, came to a halt in front of the locked gate. All four doors opened simultaneously and several figures disappeared into the bushes on either side of the narrow road. He heard shouts, in Russian, and his last doubts evaporated. It was a setup, all right. One of the Russians hurled himself on the gate, but the heavy iron barely shuddered. He groped for the padlock. James fired twice and missed. The Russians replied with a hail of bullets and Bradley threw himself to the ground. When he raised his head again, the man at the gate fired several shots at the padlock; James got off two more shots, but the Russian had already pushed the gate halfway open, and the Citroën drove through the opening, its front bumper swinging the halves of the gate back violently.

The car brushed past James, narrowly missing him, but he didn't fire. It was useless. There was no one in it but the driver, and the four or five remaining Russians were already storming the villa. A second car was already at the gate, and this time James moved out from the shadow of the low bush that had protected him, and raised his gun, aiming for the driver. The Citroën veered sharply to the left, its tires screaming on the gravel, tore through the hedge alongside the driveway, and ploughed across the lawn. The Russians were trying to block the only possible escape route from the other side of the villa, which overlooked the pool and the cliff. James's reflexes were quicker than his thoughts. Before he had grasped the real purpose of this maneuver, he had dropped to one knee, the Python locked in his two outstretched hands, pointing its ribbed barrel directly toward the barely visible ridge of metal two inches below the back bumper, slightly to the left. The fuel tank.

The gun barked twice. The tank exploded and the car was engulfed in a roaring column of red and yellow flames. A lone human figure, shrieking in agony, detached itself from the burning car and rolled out over the lawn; the car shot straight forward, broke through the low wooden barrier at the edge of the cliff, and plunged into the darkness.

James turned back, still crouching. From the villa came the dry rattle of a heated exchange of fire. He reloaded his gun feverishly and was about to move toward the villa when three figures crossed the arched veranda and passed the brightly lit solarium, by the pool, heading for the dark cluster of bushes on the far side of the lawn. Bushinski went first, holding Suvorov by the arm. The younger agent suddenly crouched at the edge of the pool and raised his gun. Three more Russians emerged on the veranda, firing. The kneeling agent returned their shots, and the closest Russian dropped his gun and crumpled. Then his two companions leveled their pistols at the American. James distinctly heard his groan of pain. He rose to his feet, swaying drunkenly back and forth, then fell sideways, splashing into the black water of the pool. James opened fire, trying to provide cover for Suvorov and Bushinski, who were already close to the bushes. Then Bushinski staggered and fell, his body jackknifed in pain. Suvorov too was hit, and he slowly dropped on his knees, clutching at his right thigh.

James darted across the lawn toward Suvorov, firing ineffectually at the two Russians. One of them also began to run in the same direction. James had almost reached Suvorov, when the defector rose unsteadily to his feet. He was watching the approaching Russian, a pale-faced man with a thin, beaked nose. Suvorov took a step forward. "Kalinin!"

Kalinin fired.

Suvorov clutched his belly and slumped to the ground. Instinctively, James hurled himself on top of Suvorov's body and fired back at Kalinin. The Russian drew back, still firing, and James felt the stinging burns in his chest and left arm as two bullets intended for Suvorov tore into his flesh. He squeezed the trigger over and over, but his hand trembled, a red veil blurred his vision, and he gasped in agony. Behind him, quite close to his ear, Suvorov was groaning wearily: "Kalinin—*predatyel . . . predatyel. . . .*" James summoned up all his strength and started to drag Suvorov into the clump of bushes, crawling on all fours. He heard shots behind him, and painfully turned his head. He thought he could make out Kalinin's pale face in the darkness, and he knew that he was only moments away from death.

Then he heard, as if from very far away, the blare of a car horn. An arc of blazing light swept through the dark clump of buhes; then an engine roared in his ears, and he lay still. The car came to a stop a few yards away, and the shouts and gunshots seemed to die away. The last thing he remembered before he lost consciousness was a tremulous voice calling his name, and the wide, anguished eyes of Sylvie.

Part Four

THE MAN
WITH THE
GOLDEN LIGHTER

12

WOLVERINE

In his opulent apartment on Rue Chardon-Lagache, Doctor Fabiani was almost finished with his lunch when the phone rang. "I'll take it," he said. He quickly swallowed a last morsel of Camembert, and wiped his lips with a napkin embroidered with his monogram. Anne-Marie, the boys, and even the maid, who stood quite close to the small commode where the telephone was placed, saw nothing strange in Fabiani's reluctance to have another person answer the phone. Frédéric Fabiani, formerly of the anti-Gaullist underground, still had the habits of a hunted man.

He picked up the receiver. "Docteur Fabiani," he announced in a flat toneless voice.

"Frédéric? It's me, Agnès." It was a voice out of his past, a voice he could never forget. He glanced furtively at Anne-Marie and smoothed his graying hair with his left hand in an obvious gesture of perplexity. He couldn't call her by her Christian name, not in front of his wife, and "Madame la Comtesse" would sound too formal.

"Madame de Sérigny," he said decisively. "What a nice surprise."

Anne-Marie looked up at him curiously. He imagined that she did suspect something about Agnès, but she had never spoken of it. On the other hand, she was aware of his special relationship with the Sérigny family.

"Frédéric, I shouldn't have called you like this, but the fact is I need your help. Urgently."

"Something's wrong with Sylvie?" He had seen her name

in the evening paper, something about an unsolved murder in London, and since then he had heard nothing.

"No, Sylvie is all right, *grâce à Dieu.*" She added quickly: "I too am quite well. It's ... it's a friend."

"Is it really all that urgent? I'm quite busy right now, and ..."

"Frédéric, it's a matter of life and death," she said breathlessly. "There's no other doctor. ... It may be a matter of hours. Hugo assured me so often that we could always be able to rely on you."

The reminder of his indebtedness to the Sérigny family left him no choice whatever.

"I'll come," he said quickly. "I'll leave everything and come." He noticed that Anne-Marie and the boys were looking at him anxiously. "Can you describe the symptoms?" he added hastily.

"Wounds," she said after a slight hesitation. "Wounds of the sort you used to treat over there, Frédéric."

Bullet wounds. So that was why she couldn't turn to anyone else. Any doctor treating a gunshot wound was required to report the case immediately to the police. "Is there much bleeding?" he asked.

"Yes. Bleeding and terrible pain."

He reflected for a moment. "You're still taking the morphine pills I prescribed to you after the car accident?"

"No, of course not. ... Those wounds are healed now." He grasped the double meaning of her words.

"Let me think then," he said slowly. ... "Do you take sleeping pills?"

"Yes."

"What kind?"

"Largactil, 50 milligrams."

"Good. Give him two of those now, and if he doesn't respond, another one in an hour. I'll be there by four o'clock at the latest."

"Thank you, Frédéric. I thank you with all my heart. I knew I could count on you."

"Pray, don't mention it," he said, and rang off.

He turned to his wife. "I'm sorry. There's an emergency at the Château de Sérigny. I must go at once."

Anne-Marie rose from the table. "Of course," she said sweetly. "You couldn't possibly refuse after all she has done for you."

While he steered his Peugeot-604 through the streets of Paris toward the access ramp of the Autoroute du Sud, it occurred to him that Anne-Marie must know much more than he thought.

Agnès de Sérigny hung up the telephone and turned to her daughter. "He'll come," she said, quite unnecessarily. "Everything's going to be all right."

Sylvie nodded miserably. Her face was haggard and her eyes bloodshot from fatigue and worry. Barely half an hour before, she had appeared dramatically at the front gate, exhausted after driving for twelve hours, with James lying unconscious on the back seat of the rented Mercedes. She had ignored her mother's frantic questions, and just assured her quietly: "Please, mother, send the servants away." When they were alone, she had helped Sylvie to carry the wounded man to the master bedroom on the second floor. It was unquestionably not the moment to reproach Sylvie because she had not had any news of her in two weeks— except from that horrible story in the papers about the young man who was stabbed to death. Madame de Sérigny had been hovering on the edge of a total breakdown—even though her doctor in Orléans kept her abundantly supplied with sleeping pills and sedatives. Yet, when she came face to face with Sylvie, she appeared perfectly calm. Perhaps she had just embraced her more warmly than usual. All this was horribly wrong, horribly artificial. But she was completely at a loss. She had forfeited Sylvie's love years ago, she blamed herself for that, and she didn't know how to win her back.

She was only concerned now with saving this young man's life, a young man who seemed so important to Sylvie. She hurried to her bathroom, opened her medicine cabinet, and took out a small vial of sleeping tablets. "Give him two of these." Sylvie immediately fetched a glass of water and ran to James's room. Agnès followed after. Sylvie's hands were trembling so badly that she couldn't get him to swallow the pills. "Let me do that," she said. Sylvie obediently stepped aside.

Agnès made sure that he swallowed the pills, then stood up, and smiled warmly at her daughter. "Let's leave him now. He will sleep for the next few hours."

Sylvie shook her head. "I'll stay with him."

Agnès softly stroked her cheek, then turned and went into the small boudoir that had been a kind of refuge for her during all those years of loneliness. She sank into an armchair by the window, then got up again and began pacing and wringing her hands nervously. She could scarcely cope with all that had happened. Sylvie's return with the wounded man and Frédéric's voice after so many years were about too much for her nerves. Lately she had begun to think that a curse hung over the Sérigny family: the death of her husband, her own misery, the succession of tragedies in Sylvie's life.

She stood in front of the square gilt-edged mirror embedded in the wall over the fireplace and bitterly examined her reflection. The burden of unhappiness had badly ravaged a face that had once been so lovely, banned the smile from her lips, and dried the statuesque figure into a thin, hollow-chested body.

It had all started with the arrival of Frédéric that night in 1961. She remembered when Hugo, her husband, brought him to the château and into her life. Hugo served as a combat officer in Algeria. He was opposed to the government's plan to grant independence to the province and was determined to keep Algeria French. In spite of his long-time devotion to De Gaulle, he was secretly cooperating with the Organisation de l'Armée Secrète, an underground group of hard-core nationalists engaged in a violent struggle against the government of the Republic. A young doctor, Frédéric Fabiani, had been involved in several bombings and attempts on the lives of government officials; they said he had even participated in an abortive plot to kill De Gaulle. "He is to stay here in the château until all this is over," Hugo had told her.

Hugo de Sérigny had returned to his unit in Algeria the next morning. And before long, the inevitable had happened. She was lonely and bored, longing for her faraway husband and feeling that somehow life was passing her by. And Frédéric was at hand, a handsome, swarthy young man, with an easy smile, ardent black eyes, and a lithe body. They had both been caught up in a fiery passion, and for a few months Agnès felt again the pulse of life and of happiness. Until one night her little daughter, who was barely nine years old, had awakened and come to her room, interrupting them in the middle of torrid lovemaking. The child had run away, screaming. Agnès, overwhelmed with remorse and panic, followed her to her bedroom and tried to soothe her, but the child had rejected her, kicking and striking out at her with her little fists, bitterly crying for her daddy. Only at dawn did the exhausted Sylvie fall asleep in the arms of her nurse.

A week later an official telegram signed by the Minister of War had informed Madame de Sérigny that her husband had fallen in one of the last actions of the Algerian war. Agnès had run down the steps into the courtyard to her small Sunbeam Renault and had driven away. The accident happened barely one mile from the château. The little car crashed into an oak tree on the edge of the road. Agnès was dragged out of the wreck, alive but with both legs and several ribs broken. She spent long painful months completely immobile in a hospital bed, but she never admitted that she had tried to commit suicide.

When she came back to the château, Frédéric Fabiani was gone. Pardoned by the government after the end of the Algerian war, he had returned to his wife and settled in France. Sylvie had gradually calmed down, and sullenly cooperated in her mother's effort to put the bits and pieces of their life together. And yet, each time that Agnès looked into the deep, hurt eyes of her child, she knew that she had lost her love forever.

A blue Peugeot rolled smoothly into the courtyard. Doctor Fabiani stepped out of it and she went down to meet him.

It was already dark when Doctor Fabiani came out of James's room, followed by Sylvie, her blouse still stained with dried blood. "Your daughter would make an excellent nurse," he remarked to Agnès, who followed him to the bathroom. Sylvie joined them, and leaned wearily on the door frame while he washed his hands.

"How is he?" Agnès asked.

"He'll be all right. We removed three bullets—one from the arm, two from his chest. He's lost a lot of blood, but he's strong. In two weeks he'll be up and out. He needs rest and constant attention." He smiled at Sylvie. "I'm sure he'll get that."

"Are you staying the night?" Agnès asked.

He shook his head. "No, there's no need. I'll be back tomorrow."

Agnès brought him his coat. "I'll walk down with you to your car," she said, and threw a shawl over her shoulders.

Sylvie watched thoughtfully as they made their way down the great Renaissance staircase, then hurried back to James's room. The sedation was beginning to wear off, his entire body was trembling, and his lips muttering inaudible words. She sat beside him and took his hand in hers. "James. James, do you hear me?"

He opened his eyes, and blinked a few times, slowly adjusting to the bright lights in the room. His dilated pupils were covered with a dull film.

"James, it's me," she repeated. "It's me, Sylvie."

He nodded and she felt the faint pressure of his fingers on her hand.

"The lights . . ." he whispered. "My eyes hurt . . ."

She turned off the lights and walked back to the bed. Moonlight filtered through the voile curtain.

James's head moved restlessly on the pillow. "Where . . . What happened?"

"Don't talk," she said quickly. "I'll tell you everything. We are in my mother's house, near Orléans. You were wounded at the villa last night. I brought you here, the doctor's had a look at you and you're going to be fine."

"The villa . . . what happened at the villa?"

"I waited outside, like you told me to," Sylvie began, not sure that he understood what she was saying. "I heard the cars coming and then the shots. I was afraid for you, and there wasn't time to call the police. I didn't know what to do. I was scared to death, and I lost my head. I drove the car up to the villa and I sounded the horn. The gate was open and I went right through, circled around the house and came out by the front lawn while people were still shooting. They got frightened when they saw the car and drove off. They must have thought the Americans were bringing up reinforcements. I found you in the bushes and dragged you to . . ."

He was impatiently pressing her hand, and mumbling something. She leaned over to hear.

"Suvorov . . ." he whispered. "Suvorov. What happened to him?"

"Suvorov?" She was momentarily confused. "I don't know, James. Where was he?"

"Beside me . . . in the bushes . . ."

The image of the gray-haired man lying in a pool of blood reappeared in her memory.

"He was there, James. In the bushes. I left him there."

He moved his lips, but no sound came. Finally he managed to whisper painfully: "Is he alive?"

She remembered his breath coming in gasps, the blood . . .

"I don't know, James," she confessed. "I really don't know."

Two days later, in the early morning, Sylvie stepped into a phone booth in the Poste Centrale in Orléans. An elderly *téléphoniste*, wearing an untidy blue apron, was seated behind an equally ancient switchboard. Sylvie gave her a number in Washington, and she joined the line of people waiting for their calls to be put through.

"Washington, *cabine trois*," the woman barked after a few minutes had passed.

Sylvie squeezed into the booth and took the receiver. "Yes?" a voice answered calmly.

"Is this Mr. Gene Ackerman of United Steel?" she asked.

An hour later she strode happily into James's room. He was still weak and unshaven, but his eyes were clear and he had even succeeded in propping himself on his right elbow, though not without an agonizing stab of pain at first.

"Well?" His voice was still very weak.

"He's alive, James," she announced triumphantly.

"Thank God," he breathed. "Thank God. What happened?"

"Your friend was rather tight-lipped. He did at least tell me that your people returned to the villa a few minutes after the shooting. They found Suvorov and whisked him out of the country. He's in a hospital, in critical condition. Gene says that his chances are good."

"Where is he?" he pressed restlessly. "Which hospital? The Russians will try again!"

She shrugged helplessly. "He wouldn't say, James. He was afraid to talk."

"And the mole?"

She shook her head gloomily.

He slumped back heavily on the bed, and looked up at her helplessly. "Sylvie, they are just going to pull the same thing all over again!"

She looked at him for a long time, then bent down and pressed her lips to his cheek. "James," she said softly, "why don't you give up? Can't we just forget it? They almost killed you and the next time they may succeed. Let them play their grisly games alone. Please. Why don't we get off this crusade, James? It's no good. . . ."

He had become pale and was nervously shaking his head. "No . . . no . . . I can't let them do it. They'll kill him, don't you see? The mole is in Langley, he'll set him up for the kill . . . and there is nobody but me! I must talk to Gene. I must . . ."

She interrupted him, without raising her voice. "I know what you were thinking, James. We must convince Gene to tell us where Suvorov is. But he won't mention it over the phone."

"Then I'll have to go to Washington." He flung the blanket aside, revealing his heavily bandaged chest. He tried to sit up, but gasped in pain. "Oh, shit!" he said angrily, and sank back down onto the pillows. His face was contorted and his skin had become deathly pale from effort and pain.

Sylvie knelt beside him, took a linen towel, and gently wiped the sweat from his forehead. "You can't go to Washington, James. You're still too weak for that. You must stay here and recover."

"But..."

"Calm down, please. Don't be stupid. You won't make it. Besides, they will be expecting you. They'll pick you up at the airport, and that will be the end of it."

"Sylvie, do you understand what's at stake here?"

"I do. I do indeed." She drew a deep breath and thrust her chin forward determinedly. "Leave that to me. As soon as you're feeling better, I'll fly to Washington."

Robert Owen, the Deputy Director for Operations, carelessly dropped his camel's hair coat in the outer office and hurried into Bill Hardy's private sanctuary. "Sorry I'm late, gentlemen."

He was the last one to arrive at the meeting. All the department heads who had been involved in the London letter operation were already there. The director looked at him questioningly. "I've just come from Bethesda, from the hospital," Owens explained, smoothing back his ruffled hair. He paused for a second and added quietly: "Burt Bushinsky died this morning."

"Oh, God!" Roger Taft groaned. "That makes two killed and Suvorov in a coma. Nice operation, I must say."

Bill Hardy intervened quickly before the DDO and the head of F-3 could start hurling accusations at each other, in the best tradition of interdepartmental rivalry.

"He was a good man," he said in a low tone. "We were on several missions together when I was in Operations. Does he have a family?"

Robert Owen cleared his throat. "A wife, a boy of fifteen, a daughter in college."

Hardy nodded. "Bob, will you write the letter? I'll sign it."

Owen was leafing through one of the files he had removed from his attaché case. "I think he deserves a commendation. He did a good job back there."

Bill Hardy nodded again. "I could put him in for the Intelligence Medal." He pressed both his hands, palms down, on the desk, indicating that this subject was closed. "Did he say anything before he died?"

Robert Owen shrugged. "He mostly repeated what he had told the people on the plane. About Bradley suddenly . . ."

"Yes, yes," Hardy cut him short. "Bradley. I suppose that sonofabitch deserves the Intelligence Medal too?"

"That sonofabitch saved Suvorov's life after all," Roger Taft replied blandly.

Bill Hardy swiveled his chair around to face Taft. "I know," he replied evenly. "I know, and when we locate him, I will pin that damn ribbon on him." His voice suddenly lashed with fury. "But I'll do it in prison, where he'll be for insubordination, desertion, obtaining and using classified information without authorization, interfering with agency operations, and . . . "

"Where is he now?" Jeff Crawford interrupted from his observation post near the window.

Roger Taft shrugged. "We don't know. He didn't contact us again after his call to Bill. I guess he flew to France on the day of the attack. We're checking now."

"No records at the airport?" Crawford frowned.

"None. There can be no doubt that he used false identity papers. He might have taken the girl with him. We're still checking with the French police and the hotels in the Beaulieu area. In a couple of days we'll have something."

"But what should really concern us is *how* he discovered that Suvorov was in Beaulieu," Herbert Kranz said.

"I heard a curious rumor," Jeff Crawford said slowly, looking significantly at Bill Hardy. "A rumor that when he called you, Bill, he made some very definite allegations that a Russian mole might be operating at Langley."

"If he did make any such allegations," Hardy said in a cold, even voice, "they are being investigated." He added quickly: "I said *if*."

"But if he did make any such allegation," Jeff Crawford echoed mockingly, "then he was right. Somebody must have tipped the Russians about the Villa Dolorès, don't you think?"

"I don't think I like this conversation, Jeff," Hardy answered. "And I think you may want to reconsider those remarks." He turned his back to him. "Any idea how the Russians got the information, Herb?"

The Deputy Director for Intelligence made a tiny circle with his thumb and forefinger. "Nothing. We only know that the Russian team arrived that same morning. Five back-up agents, nine front-line operatives. They rented two Citroëns. Four were killed when one of the cars exploded, one by the gate, one on the front lawn. We don't know about the wounded. They must have taken them when they cleared out."

"And why was the villa left unguarded?" Taft couldn't resist a jab at Robert Owen.

"There was some confusion about the timetables. The arrival of the next shift at the villa was delayed, we still don't know why. Somebody in the rear base, who apparently didn't know about the delay, called the evening shift and ordered it to return immediately. That caused a gap of fifteen minutes between departure and arrival. We are still checking that."

"If there is a mole, he could easily have arranged that," suggested Jeff Crawford.

His remark was met by an ominous silence.

"How can we make sure that it won't happen again?" Crawford went on. "Suvorov's alive. How can we be certain that they won't try again?"

Hardy didn't look at him. "We have taken every precaution," he said. "Most of the people in this room don't know where Suvorov is at present. I've detached a special detail from F-3. They report only to me."

"That sounds all right," Crawford observed, then needled Hardy again. "In any case, let's hope that if there is any trouble, our dear James Bradley comes through again."

Hardy looked pained but he didn't say a word. Under normal conditions, Kranz reflected, Hardy would have thrown Crawford out of the room. But the snafu was his fault and he had no interest in jeopardizing his authority even more, by starting an open quarrel with one of his department heads. Kranz decided it would be wise to defuse the ticking bomb and changed the subject. "Let's go back to the problem of how Bradley learned where we were moving Suvorov."

"He must have been tipped off by somebody here, somebody who knew of the operation," Owen said.

"Nobody gives out that kind of information to an agent who is considered a deserter," Taft snapped.

"Nobody?" Hardy's voice was heavy with irony. "Nobody except maybe a good friend, someone who has worked quite a few times with Bradley, and who trusts him completely. Roger, you must know who his friends are."

Taft shrugged. "He didn't have many, Bill. There were maybe five or six, from F-3 and from Operations. He was quite close to Stuart Langella and Carl Morton. He had been on a few operations with Ackerman and Stevens.

Maybe Rodney, too, but Rodney wouldn't know about Villa Dolorès."

"That leaves Rodney out, but the others?"

"The others—yes, I think all of them knew where Suvorov was."

After the meeting was over, one of the participants took the elevator to the sixth floor and walked into the personnel department. He flashed his special pass to the guard and was passed into the section where the files of operational agents were kept. He consulted several files and copied a few addresses and phone numbers onto a slip of paper. He left the building and drove to Washington. From a pay phone in a gas station he called a local number. Half an hour later, he entered a quiet cocktail lounge in Georgetown. A small, gray-faced man in a business suit approached his table. He looked like an accountant or a clerk.

The CIA man motioned for him to take a chair, then handed him the slip of paper. "Langella, Morton, Ackerman, Stevens—I want them watched twenty-four hours a day. I want their home phones tapped, and all their movements recorded. You'll report twice a day. If any of them makes an unusual contact, you'll alert me at once. Is that clear?"

"Yes."

"Will you have enough men to do it? It's a big operation, four people."

"I'll manage."

The CIA executive nodded to indicate that their meeting was at an end. The small man quickly left the place.

A black waitress brought a double Chivas Regal to the table. The man sipped it with pleasure, unwrapped a black cheroot, lit it, and put his golden lighter back in his vest pocket.

* * *

As the spacious ZIL limousine sped westward on the Volokolamsk Road, both Andropov and Kalinin sat silently, two icebergs floating in a cold sea of hostility. Kalinin didn't try to start a conversation. He knew that Andropov must feel deeply humiliated because he had been compelled to bring him along to Gorsky Dorog. Andropov had to give an accounting for the Beaulieu fiasco, and his only hope would be to prove that someone else was to blame. Kalinin was supposed to be his chief defense witness, which meant that one day Andropov would have to return the favor. And Andropov, reluctant to be beholden to anyone, already hated him for it. As for Kalinin, he had nothing to fear. He had distinguished himself in the Beaulieu operation and had almost succeeded in liquidating Suvorov. Furthermore, the head of the First Directorate had taken his own precautions and had already found a scapegoat. The chief of his operational squad, Polevoy, was under arrest in the Lubyanka prison, awaiting trial for "gross negligence in the performance of his duties." That he was innocent was totally irrelevant.

The car turned to the right onto a narrow road that stretched in a straight line between two barriers of snow-capped fir trees. They crossed three consecutive road blocks, manned by soldiers of the Kremlin's special guard, before they came to the electrically operated gate of the huge dacha. The duty officer checked their papers. "Drive to the dacha itself," he instructed the driver. "The Secretary will be returning shortly from the hunt."

"Any good game around?" Volodya, the driver, was curious.

The officer shrugged. "A fox or a rabbit, maybe. The Secretary prefers hunting in Siberia."

The car moved slowly. A sleek Lincoln Continental emerged from a side road and they followed it all the way to the dacha, built along the lines of a Swiss chalet. The

Lincoln screeched to a stop, raising a cloud of snow from the deserted parking lot. Kalinin suppressed a smile. He was familiar with the Secretary's penchant for flashy foreign cars and fast driving. He had been given that one as a present from the American President during his visit to Washington the year before.

Leonid Brezhnev got out of the car, carrying a double-barreled shotgun, and waited for them to catch up. He was wearing a heavy blackish-brown fur coat, which made his thickset figure look even more bearlike. His calpac was made of the same smooth fur, and its earflaps hung loosely on both sides of his broad face.

They exchanged greetings. Brezhnev knew Kalinin from former meetings with the KGB supreme council, and welcomed him with a smile. Kalinin felt encouraged enough to venture a question. "A good hunt, Comrade Secretary?"

Brezhnev grunted and made a vague gesture toward the trunk of the Lincoln, hinting that he hadn't come back empty-handed. "Only small game around here," he complained. "Siberia, that's where the big game is. And the excitement too." He made a sweeping gesture over his coat with his left hand. "See that fur? I killed the animals myself. Wolverine. Do you know the wolverine, Kalinin? It's an evil animal. It hides in the taiga all day, and strikes at night. It is cruel, and fearless, but most of all, cunning." He suddenly turned to Andropov. "Did you hear that, Andropov? Cunning. You should meet that animal." His eyes had assumed a cold, spiteful expression. Andropov looked away. He had got the message.

Brezhnev stepped inside the dacha and walked to the big fireplace. Without even removing his coat and hat, he knelt beside the hearth and poked the embers. His heavy muzhik hands deftly examined and weighed the freshly chopped logs, stacked beside the hearth, and he patiently fed the best chunks into the fireplace. A few minutes later, the fire was blazing again and Brezhnev straightened up and clapped his hands contentedly. "Well, let's hear all about it. Kalinin?"

Kalinin glanced at Andropov, who was white as a sheet. The Secretary General had chosen to humiliate him by conferring with his subordinate as if he did not exist.

He began to describe the raid on the villa at Beaulieu and to analyze the reasons for its failure. "We were told that we would have complete freedom of action for fifteen minutes, Comrade Secretary," he pointed out. "We were told that only two guards would be inside the building. Yet when we arrived there were more than two guards at the villa, the gate was locked, and we were expected; nevertheless, we might have accomplished the mission, but an additional American security team arrived almost immediately, and we had no choice but to retreat."

Brezhnev pondered this information. "We were lured into a trap, then?"

"I don't think so, Comrade Secretary. If it was meant to be a trap, they would have let us come in first, then locked us in and hacked us to pieces. It looks to me as if somebody got wind of our approach at the last moment and tried to improvise a counterattack."

"Did the French police interfere?"

"No. They only came later to hush the whole thing up. Not one word filtered out to the press. They must be cooperating with the Americans."

Brezhnev took off his coat and started pacing back and forth in front of the fireplace. He was wearing a loose Ukrainian *rubashka*, tied with a wide belt. "And yet," he said forcefully, "it was a shameful blunder! Three or four Americans defeated a whole squad and killed six of our best men. You should have been equipped to cope with such an unforeseen contingency."

"I completely agree with you, Comrade Secretary,"

Kalinin said. "The attack was poorly planned. I have arrested the officer who was in charge of the operation, and I intend to have him court-martialed."

Brezhnev nodded slowly, then slumped into a sofa. "Well, that's all over and done with. What now, Kalinin? Where is Suvorov?"

"We don't know," he admitted. "Even our man in Washington says it will be difficult to locate him. He's been removed to an American hospital, but nobody seems to know where."

"And we're sitting here by the fire while he's spilling all of our secrets to the Americans!"

Kalinin shook his head. "Not yet, Comrade Secretary. He was unconscious when they found him. We know he's very badly wounded. They won't start interrogating him before he recovers, which might take two or three weeks."

Brezhnev slammed his hand down on his knee. "What difference does that make? So he'll talk in three weeks, but he'll talk!"

Kalinin smiled. "Not necessarily. Not if we devise a plan to smoke him out of hiding. And when he comes out—we'll be waiting for him, and this time there'll be no mistakes."

Brezhnev and Andropov looked at him in surprise. "You mean," Brezhnev asked slowly, "that we can force the Americans to bring Suvorov out into the open?"

"That's exactly what I have in mind, Comrade Secretary. Bring him out into the open, as soon as he recovers."

Brezhnev narrowed his eyes, speculatively. "Are you just speaking in riddles, Kalinin? Or do you have a definite plan? Don't play games with me, I warn you!"

"I have a plan," Kalinin said firmly.

Brezhnev leaned forward eagerly. "Tell me all about it."

13

BAIT

Their twin turbojet engines thundering furiously, smoke and flames spurting from the black afterburners in their split tails, the six MiG-25 warplanes raced down the smooth asphalt runway of the Khabarovsk airbase and took off in quick succession. With their angry voices, fiery breath, sleek bodies, batlike wings, they seemed very like dragons emerging from their dark lairs and climbing into the sky. The citizens of the People's Republic across the nearby Chinese border had always regarded dragons as benevolent, wise creatures—they had no such illusions about the MiG-25.

The inhabitants of the border town of Khabarovsk were more reverent toward their fighter squadron and rightly so, for these jet fighters, nicknamed "Foxbats" by Western intelligence, were the fastest military aircraft in the world. With a top speed of Mach 3 and a maximum ceiling of up to 118,000 feet, outclimbing the most advanced American jets, the MiG-25 easily tipped the balance of power in favor of the USSR; many elaborate schemes, costing millions of dollars, had been devised by American military intelligence to obtain the performance specifications of the Foxbat.

The six MiGs fanned out in formation at an altitude of 20,000 feet, overflew the misty Sichote-Alin Mountains and the sinuous coastline of Primorsky Kray. They were soon over the Tatar Strait, starting their routine morning patrol over the narrow-waisted island of Sakhalin.

When they reached Aniva Bay, the jets gracefully dipped

their sweptback wings and turned to the west, speeding over the Sea of Japan on their way back to base.

Suddenly, the plane that was on the extreme right of the formation peeled off and dove sharply into the sea. At barely 150 feet over the sea the plane leveled off and veered to the southeast. Soon it vanished from the screens of the Soviet radar stations. After frantic calls from ground control remained unanswered, two other MiGs broke from the formation and set off in pursuit. The pilot had no trouble eluding them. When he sighted the island of Hokkaido, the pilot climbed back to 20,000 feet, crossed into Japanese airspace, and appeared over the snow-capped peaks of Sapporo. The Japanese Phantoms took off, to intercept the intruder. But they soon lost sight of him, when he dived again to a dangerously low altitude and plunged into the deep shadows of canyons and narrow valleys.

Twenty-four minutes after entering Japanese airspace, the MiG-25 appeared over the southern tip of Hokkaido and landed at the civilian airport of Hakodate.

Construction workers on one of the runways began to run up to the strange aircraft, but they froze in their tracks when a man in a white flying helmet and gray zippered overalls climbed from the cockpit, gun in hand, and fired a warning shot in the air. "Get back!" he shouted hoarsely in Russian. "I am Viktor Maslinov, a captain in the Soviet airforce! I want to go to the United States!"

By noon, the teleprinters of the news agencies had chattered out the stunning news all over the world: a Soviet pilot had defected to the West with his top-secret MiG-25. The background features that followed emphasized the utmost importance of this unexpected trophy for Western intelligence. They revealed that the last Soviet warplane examined by the West had been a MiG-21 captured almost intact by Israeli forces during the Yom Kippur War. Now, American experts hoped to examine the Foxbat thoroughly —engines, controls, armaments, and electronic hardware.

In Tokyo embarrassed Japanese officials had to face an angry onslaught of the Soviet ambassador and his senior aides. The Russians demanded that Maslinov be immediately handed back to them and the plane returned to the Soviet Union that very day. "Our pilot made an emergency landing on your territory and is now being held prisoner against his will," Ambassador Semionov furiously shouted at Akiro Sato, the Japanese Foreign Minister. Then he hurled a thinly disguised threat at the Japanese: "Japan is acting at the instigation of a third country, and a refusal to honor our request might lead to severe repercussions."

"Captain Maslinov is in custody for having violated Japanese immigration procedures and for possession of illegal weapons," Sato replied formally. "The aircraft is being held by the authorities as evidence in the proceedings against Maslinov and might have to be dismantled to determine the facts of the case." He remained coldly aloof when the Soviet ambassador charged that this was only a legalistic pretext for keeping Maslinov and the plane in Japanese hands.

The ambassador was right. The same morning, only an hour after the Foxbat had landed on Hokkaido, a U.S. government 707 took off at Andrews Air Force Base near Washington, carrying a team of seventeen U.S. Air Force technicians, all from the Foreign Technology Division. The 707 landed at Hakodate that night and the newcomers were shown directly into the improvised enclosure, surrounded by barbed wire, where the MiG-25 was kept under armed guard. The Americans quickly removed the heavy tarpaulins and set to work. They started to dismantle the aircraft, systematically photographing, measuring, and recording every one of its components.

But the technicians were not the only passengers on that flight; there were five more passengers, though they had kept to themselves most of the time. They were Jeff Crawford, the director of the USSR Department of the CIA, and four of his senior assistants. They didn't even bother to look at the Russian plane. Three agents from the local CIA station were waiting for them on the runway in unmarked cars. At nine that evening, the Japanese officers standing guard on the fourth floor of the Hakodate Grand Hotel admitted Jeff Crawford and his party to Suite 401. Victor Maslinov turned off the big television set in the living room and awkwardly came forward to meet them.

He was a tall, muscular young man in his late twenties. His broad, pinkish face was topped by close-cropped blond hair. He had heavy, solid jaws, a small mouth, and alert brown eyes.

Jeff Crawford smiled broadly when he pumped his hand, but his eyes remained cold and watchful. He introduced his men by their first names only: "Jim, Ken, Alex, Glen." Maslinov grinned at them and nodded amiably. "Alex is going to be our interpreter," Crawford said slowly, and Alex Dragunski quickly translated the introduction in soft, mellifluous Russian.

They settled informally on the sofa and armchairs, around a large coffee table. "Shall we drink to celebrate your safe arrival?" Crawford asked invitingly.

Maslinov nodded.

"Scotch? Vodka? Champagne?"

The Russian hesitated for a second. "Scotch," he said finally. He took the Davidoff cigar that Crawford offered him and leaned over the table toward the match. He exhaled the smoke with visible satisfaction. "We also have quite good cigars," he observed. "Direct from Cuba."

A Japanese waiter brought three bottles of Scotch, a few glasses, and some tiny bowls of salted peanuts, along with an ice bucket and a huge bottle of soda water. Crawford served the drinks. "Cheers!" he said. "What do you say in Russian? *Na zdrovya!*" Maslinov solemnly raised his glass. "*Na zdrovya,*" he echoed. He had a deep, strong voice.

Crawford took a long sip from his drink and looked across the table at Maslinov. "We represent the American government, as you have doubtless already guessed. We understand that you want to go to America."

Maslinov nodded.

Crawford took a thin manila file from Ken Barry, who sat beside him, and opened it. "You are Victor Maslinov, twenty-nine years old, born in Odessa, married, one child. Your family lives in Leningrad, where you have been stationed for three years. Your record is good, and you have been promoted to the rank of captain two years ahead of time. You are flying the best plane in the Soviet Air Force, and you were recommended for test-flying. You get a good salary, you have special privileges, and you may have a brilliant career in the Air Force. Why did you defect?"

For a moment Maslinov seemed taken aback by the detailed information in the file. Then he smiled. "You have good information," he pointed out, "but you will have to update it. I was separated from my wife a year ago, and I live alone." He added: "I hope nothing will happen to her and to the boy because of my departure."

"You didn't answer my question," Crawford reminded him drily.

"Why did I defect?" He spread his hands, palms up. "There is no freedom in my country. The Soviet Union is a suffocating place. Nothing has changed since the times of the czars! Only the czars are called by different names today. You can tell the truth only when you are drinking vodka with your friends. And you can't even trust your friends." He added with candor: "Since I left my wife I have been very lonely. I want to start a new life, in a new country."

Crawford nodded skeptically, as if he had heard this kind of thing before.

"Could you help me?" Maslinov asked. "I was told by some friends that you can give me a new identity, new papers, teach me English with a different accent, and even perform plastic surgery on my face, to protect me from the KGB."

Crawford nodded noncommittally. "First, we shall have to ask you some questions."

Ken Barry and Jim Wiggins were already busy stacking files on the table and pinning an enormous map of the Soviet Union onto the nearest wall. Glen Sawyer set a small tape recorder on a nearby chair and connected two microphones, which he placed on the coffee table in front of Maslinov and Crawford. The Soviet pilot waited patiently.

"Let's begin, then," Crawford said when everything was ready. "Your squadron number, the name of your commanding officer, the names of the other pilots . . ."

Seven hours later, Jeff Crawford walked through the deserted lobby of the hotel and stepped into a car that was waiting at the curb. The car brought him back to the airport, where the 707 was already starting up its engines. It took off immediately, with Crawford as sole passenger. At 6:30 A.M. Crawford was whispering into the mouthpiece of the scrambler phone at the American Embassy in Tokyo. He was connected to Langley Woods immediately, and in a matter of seconds Herbert Kranz was on the line.

"Did he talk?" Kranz asked eagerly.

"Oh, he talked all right," Crawford said, but there was a distinct note of reserve in his voice. "Still, I'm not sure if we've struck gold or if we're being fed red herrings."

"What do you mean?" The DDI sounded puzzled.

"We had a very extensive first debriefing," Crawford told him. "We covered a lot of ground: strategic deployment of the Soviet fighter command, missile sites, aerial defense, contingency planning, and underground air bases. A substantial part of the information has been in our possession for quite a while. We verified it on the spot and we are able to confirm it. This is good, solid stuff. But there are still quite a few things we hadn't known."

"For instance?"

"For instance—Maslinov reported seven new missile bases in the Urals and in the Crimea, four new airfields in Latvia and Estonia, and some improvements in the early warning system. But there is one very disturbing item, Herb. He claims that they have just finished testing a Russian version of the cruise missile."

"Where?"

"In Kazakhstan, after early tests in Baikonur. If what he says is true, then our missiles are already obsolete. This means that we'll be in big trouble at the SALT conference."

There was a silence on the line, then Kranz said slowly: "I don't like that. The conference starts in two weeks."

"Exactly, that's why I'm calling you, Herb. This is an emergency situation. We have to check and verify every single word in this guy's deposition."

Kranz sighed. "You think he might be bluffing."

"I don't know," Crawford admitted. "But I know the opposition and I know how they operate. I wouldn't be surprised if all this defection business was a hoax, designed to feed us false information."

Kranz was skeptical. "And they would sacrifice a MiG-25 for that?"

"I wouldn't rule that out," Crawford said cautiously.

"Any suggestion on how we should verify Maslinov's information?"

"Nope. We'll need a first-class source for that. At the very top. And right away."

Kranz paused again. "There's only one who comes to mind," he said finally.

"Who?"

"Tovarishch Arkadi Suvorov, who else?"

In the KGB Center in Dzerzhinski Square, Andropov and Kalinin had been systematically avoiding each other for two weeks, ever since the visit to Brezhnev's dacha. This morning, though, Kalinin asked to see the director for a few minutes. He burst in with a triumphant smile on his face. "They've swallowed the bait, Yuri Vladimirovitch!"

Andropov raised his eyes from the file he was reading. He deliberately took off his glasses and wiped them thoroughly before he spoke. Finally he asked: "Who is *they?*"

"Our man in Washington just made contact," Kalinin said eagerly. "They debriefed Maslinov and they reacted exactly as we had anticipated. They're flying Suvorov from his hideout to meet with Maslinov and verify his information. The confrontation is scheduled for next Thursday night, in their safehouse at Punta Higüero, in Puerto Rico."

A smile of satisfaction briefly flourished on the waxen face of Andropov. "That's very good," he said. "Very good. We flushed him out into the open. Congratulations, Kalinin."

He might really be furious, Kalinin reflected, because it was my idea and not his. But if this was true, it did not show on the director's placid face. "You should make the necessary arrangements with Havana," Andropov added.

"With your permission I'll lead the hit squad myself."

Andropov nodded thoughtfully.

An hour later a cable, drafted by Kalinin and countersigned by the Chief of Naval Operations in the Red Army General Staff, was dispatched to Havana, Cuba. It was addressed to the chief of the Soviet naval base there and read: "Prepare submarine *Aurora* for immediate operation stop Classification top-secret First priority stop Place captain submarine and crew under command Alexei Kalinin arriving with special team and equipment 1700 hours Special Flight Air Force Tupolev-114 stop Kalinin will exercise full control over operation stop objective Puerto Rico stop end."

The same evening Sylvie de Sérigny arrived in Washington.

Her forged passport proved to be as effective as it had been at Nice, and she quickly went through the formalities of immigration and customs. From the airport she phoned Gene Ackerman. At first he seemed surprised and angry to learn that she had arrived, but he calmed down quickly and instructed her to check into the Riverside Motel, a low stucco complex built in Colonial-style, off the George Washington Memorial Parkway. He drove over to see her late that night. She let him into her room, somewhat embarrassed by his obvious suspicion and reserved welcome. He locked the door and she showed him her credentials—a handwritten letter from James, stuffed with facts, codewords, and private references that guaranteed its authenticity. She spoke for about two hours, describing in detail everything that had happened to them since Richard Hall had stolen the London letter, ages before. As she went along with her story Gene's hostility slowly melted away. He listened attentively, asking a question now and then. It was 2:00 A.M. when he got up and stretched his long legs. "That's an amazing story," he remarked. There was now a genuine expression of concern in his eyes. "I've never heard anything like that before."

"Do you understand why James sent me to see you?"

He nodded. "He was right. There's something very fishy

going on. I'll try to do some checking of my own in Langley."

She stuck to the objective of her mission. "Could you tell us where Suvorov is?"

"No," he said. "I can't tell you that for the simple reason that I don't know. He's recovering from his wounds in a hospital, but nobody seems to know where. There were rumors, though, that he might be transferred next week. They were checking a list of safehouses in the office this morning. I might have some hard facts for you in a day or two."

She smiled at him. Her eyes were puffed with fatigue and her lovely face was drawn and pale. "You must be exhausted," he said sympathetically. "Take a shower, go to bed, and get a good night's sleep. Please don't leave the hotel, and have all your meals in your room. The television will keep you company."

She looked startled. "Do you think there's any danger here?"

He smiled reassuringly and shook his head. "No danger. Just standard precautions."

He shook her hand rather formally, and then was gone.

From a pay phone in the motel lobby, a black man dressed in a gray business suit called a number in Chevy Chase. "Mrs. Adams," he said into the phone. "Room 437."

The early morning mist rising off the Loire still enveloped the Château de Sérigny. One could almost hear the clatter of hooves echoing on the cobblestones, and imagine a swashbuckling musketeer or a gracious lady of the court stepping out of the mist, en route to a clandestine rendezvous.

But the lonely figure that appeared on the porch of the castle keep this morning, as he had for the past few days, had nothing to do with the colorful history of France.

James Bradley, still leaning on a cane, wearing knee-high boots and a long sealskin coat that had belonged to Sylvie's father, took his usual stroll around the château. These early morning walks in the splendid forest of medieval ramparts, Gothic facades, and Renaissance turrets had become a source of real delight and growing fascination for James Bradley.

The first time that he had gone out on the porch, leaning heavily on Sylvie's shoulders, he had stopped in the middle of the courtyard, stunned by the scene that confronted him. The Château de Sérigny was a huge rectangular structure, surrounded on three sides by a moat and a low wall. Its white facades, ornamented with pilasters, parapets, and Gothic strip windows, were topped by steep gabled roofs covered with tiles.

Visibly pleased by his enthusiasm, Sylvie had explained that the castle was a characteristic example of a transition style midway between the medieval fortress castles and the *château de plaisance* of a later period; that was why the famous Gilles Berthelot, one of the greatest builders of his time, had intended the château to represent a harmonious blending of Gothic and Renaissance motifs.

Their first outing had been very short and quite painful for him; he was still weak and the slightest exertion made him dizzy. But they were back the next morning, and every morning thereafter, walking hand in hand in the first light of dawn, exploring every corner of the château or crossing the chestnut park to visit the ruins of an ancient parish church. Once he had turned sharply and caught Sylvie watching him intently. There was a look of genuine tenderness in the deep blue eyes, and suddenly he knew that there were no more questions to be asked, no more doubts to be cleared up. He knew he no longer had to fear freeing himself from the memory of Sandra.

Sylvie's departure for Washington three days earlier had

caused him almost physical pain. Not only had he gotten used to her presence; he needed her with him badly. His longing was accompanied by deep concern. He knew he could count on Gene; still, he wanted to make sure that she was safe. That afternoon he was going to phone Gene in Washington, as he had arranged with Sylvie before she left.

He heard Sylvie's mother call his name and he turned toward the house. Agnès de Sérigny was waving to him from the porch. He waved back and walked toward the castle keep. He had come to like this woman, prematurely aged, imprisoned in her palace with a handful of servants, cast down again and again by her daughter's misfortunes. From the start he had noticed how strained and unnatural the relations between Sylvie and her mother were. Still, in the last few days he had gotten the distinct feeling that a change was slowly occurring. Agnès de Sérigny had taken care of him devotedly, and Sylvie responded to her, out of gratitude. The night before, after dinner, Agnès had unexpectedly embraced him. "You are giving me back my daughter, James. And you are bringing her back to life. Her eyes are happy again, as they were years ago." He could only smile awkwardly.

Now she was calling him again, and there was urgency in her voice. "James! Come quick! A phone call for you!"

"For me?" He forced himself to hurry inside. Who could be calling him? Not Sylvie. Gene? But he should never call him here. Unless there was an emergency. Could something have happened to Sylvie? Or was there news about Suvorov?

It was Gene. "Sorry for breaking the rules." His friend sounded taut and dejected. "But I have urgent news for you. Bad news."

"Go on. I'm listening."

"They are taking the new guy out of hiding and bringing him to meet somebody who came over to us from the same firm a few days ago. You must have read about him in the newspapers. That could mean trouble."

James cursed under his breath. So they were taking Suvorov to a confrontation with the Russian pilot. It could be a trap.

"Where?" he asked.

"We used to swim there five years ago. I was with that gorgeous beauty from the place next door. Remember?"

"Of course I do," Bradley said. How could he forget? It had been soon after Sandra and Lynn had been murdered. During the final stage of his training, he had been sent with five other agents to a diving course at Punta Higüero. Gene had then been courting a remarkably beautiful woman from Mayagüez. "When?" he asked quickly. "When is he coming?"

"Thursday night."

That gave him barely seventy-two hours. "I'll be there," James said decisively.

"Are you crazy? Your wounds haven't healed yet. You're hot. They'll pick you up at the airport. You can't come to this country, not yet. Not before we solve the mystery."

"We won't solve it if I don't come. Don't worry, I'll get there all right."

A note of distress and anxiety sounded in Gene's voice. "That's not all the bad news, James," he said cautiously. "There is something else. The girl—your girl—is missing."

"What?" he cried, and a sudden tremor shot through his whole body. "What did you say?"

"Now take it easy. Maybe it's just some kind of a foulup. I'm going over to her place to check it out. I'll get back to you as soon as I can." The line went dead.

Gene Ackerman walked out of the phone booth. A hundred yards down the street, hidden in the deep shadow of a square porch, a man in a dark coat removed the tiny earphones from his ears and pressed the *stop* button on his portable tape recorder.

It had been the only time that Sylvie had disobeyed Ackerman's instructions.

She had spent the whole day in her room, contemplating the Potomac flowing peacefully by her window. For the first time in weeks she was at peace with herself—no panic or pursuit or intolerable dreams. She was beginning to realize how much she had changed during those few weeks. From the hysterical girl who had fled in terror from Richard Hall's apartment, she had evolved into a person who was able to cope with a tough, cruel reality; she hadn't collapsed or run away or become a millstone around James's neck. She had become for him what she had never been for Sean: a partner. Maybe these new qualities had always been there, but she had never been aware of their existence, because she had never had to call upon them. And so she had drifted through life, as a rich, pretty, romantic girl, who acted on impulse and never had to decide anything for herself. Sean had kept her at home as a fragile love object. James had accepted her, although not without a fight, as a true ally. Somehow, it made her involvement with James more complete, more fulfilling. Since that morning in King's Cross Station, she had been striving to prove that she was not just a pretty face, a woman who could be depended upon to utter horrified screams at the appropriate cues, but somebody who could be as efficient and resourceful as he was. She had done it, and the taste of the accomplishment was sweet, almost intoxicating.

Shortly before midnight, she had run out of cigarettes. The idea of calling a bellboy had briefly crossed her mind, but she quickly dismissed it. There was a vending machine on the landing, barely twenty yards away. She had noticed it on the first night. She opened the door and looked out.

There was nobody in the corridor. She left the door un-locked and walked quickly, fumbling in her purse for the change. She fished out the coins and began to feed them into the slot. But she never pressed the button. Someone grabbed her from behind, a wet cloth was pressed to her face and a sweetish, nauseating smell filled her lungs and throat. A spasm of deadly panic gripped her; she tried to scream but no sound came and then everything faded and she slumped, unconscious, into the arms of her assailants.

When she came to the surface again, everything was still blurred and unreal. She had the feeling that she was floating on a gently rolling wave, and her entire body lay under a soft, suffocating mass of cottony substance. She tried to open her eyes, but her eyelids were heavy and wouldn't obey her. She couldn't feel her arms and legs. Muffled voices, coming from far away, touched her ears but she couldn't understand a word. A thought started to form in her mind, gradually shaping into a question, an important question.

Only when she dimly heard a sound like a shriek and felt her body being brutally jolted, did she understand that she was in a car. Someone threw a hood over her head, strong arms seized her body, and she let them drag her away out into the cold, then back into a warm place. She felt like she had been dropped into a chair, and she tried to raise her hand, to warn them that she couldn't sit, that she might fall down.

The hood came off her head and she opened her eyes. Dim, indistinct shadows moved around her. Her eyes slowly focused and started to distinguish objects and human fig-ures, still hazy and distorted. She could make out a desk, and the oval shape of a human face behind it. A single lamp was burning on the desk; the rest of the room was dark.

And then she heard a voice, speaking in French, but

with a heavy American accent. "*Bonjour*, Mademoiselle de Sérigny."

The figure behind the desk got up and came closer. Someone put a cigarette in her mouth. A light flickered in the dark. She looked down. A hand was thrust out of the darkness, offering her the tiny flame of a sleek golden lighter.

For an hour James paced restlessly in his room, his nerves on edge, his face drawn. He tried to calm down, to collect his thoughts, to reason, but he failed. What had happened to Sylvie? Where was she? How did she disappear? Why wasn't Gene calling? He had tried to hide his concern from Agnès de Sérigny, pretending that the phone call had been a routine contact. But her pale face and anxious eyes showed clearly that she had seen through him. She knew that something was wrong. To avoid a painful confrontation, he had walked away, after asking her not to pick up the phone for the next few hours, since he was expecting an important call. Then he had gone to his room and sat down to wait.

Twice the telephone rang and he had gripped the receiver as if it was his lifeline—and both times it was someone from the village calling to ask Madame about tomorrow's groceries. The third call was for him, but it wasn't the call he had been expecting.

A faraway operator's voice said: "Personal call for Mr. James Bradley."

"Bradley speaking," he said hurriedly.

"One moment, please."

Another voice, distant and metallic, filled the receiver. "James Bradley," the voice said. He didn't recognize it. It was not Gene Ackerman's voice. It was a cold, detached voice, which he was hearing for the first time in his life, and which reminded him of another voice, another phone call.

"Yes," he said. His mouth was dry.

"Now that we know where you are," the voice said matter-of-factly, "we'll take care of you when the time comes. But first there's a more urgent matter. You just talked to a friend of yours in Washington. You told him that you intended to arrive shortly in a certain place in Puerto Rico, because a certain person is going to be there."

Bradley didn't answer.

"We just want to warn you," the voice said. "Don't do it. We've got the girl. If you dare come near Punta Higüero, the girl will die."

"Oh, my God." He clutched at the edges of the table with a badly shaking hand.

"Would you like to hear her?" the inhuman voice continued. And even before he could answer, Sylvie's voice burst into the receiver, sobbing, calling his name, uttering incoherent phrases. "James, *chéri*, James, I'm sorry, darling, I love you, don't . . ."

He slammed the phone down and buried his face in his trembling hands. A hoarse, animal wail rose from deep inside him. He was going through the nightmare again. Once again, the same threat: "Comply, or your beloved will die!" He remembered those other calls, in Brussels, when they had said: "4:00 P.M. If we don't get the file by 4:00 P.M., your wife and daughter will die." And the desperate voice of little Lynn, bitterly crying: "Daddy, daddy, come and get us. Daddy, I'm scared . . ." He hadn't come and they had died.

He fell to his knees and pounded the wall savagely with his clenched fists, until his bruised knuckles began to bleed. "Not again!" he kept repeating. "Not again, not again, not again!"

It was past midnight, and the big lonely house at Punta Higüero seemed peaceful and serene. It was an ugly modern structure, two stories of bare concrete and naked glass, towering like a displaced fortress above the white powdery beach and the clear water of the Caribbean. Fortunately, the austere martial outlines of the house were softened and broken up considerably by a luxuriant stand of mangroves and palm trees, as well as bougainvillaea, poinsettia, and golden canarios.

Except for a single window on the second floor and a small lantern on the porch, the house was completely dark. No guards were to be seen around the building or on the beach. The winding path that led from the house, across the park, and along the trees to a wooden pier, some two hundred yards to the south, was equally deserted.

There seemed not to be a living soul around, except for a few lizards and mongooses, which hurriedly disappeared into the grass when a door opened and a man stepped out. He stood still for a second, looked suspiciously around, then followed the path to the beach. He stopped again, surveyed the stretch of sand on both sides, and turned to the south, moving quietly in the shadow of the trees.

He stood barely ten feet away from the spot where James Bradley was crouched, holding his breath. For a split second, the soft light of the tropical moon fell on his face, and James saw him clearly. The man was Suvorov.

His face was haggard, and he seemed to be in pain; yet he went on, toward the pier.

James Bradley followed him cautiously, moving noiselessly behind the trees. His hand, thrust deep into his pocket, gripped his loaded gun. He was a desperate man, grimly aware that he had sacrificed all that was dear to him in this world. Sylvie was certainly dead or dying. He didn't care for his own life anymore. But he was here now, a dangerous, hopeless man, moved by a strange instinct, by a stubborn determination to carry out the mission he had undertaken, and at whatever cost.

He was unshaven, his skin was sticky with sweat and his eyes red-rimmed with exhaustion. His clothes were crumpled and his trousers still wet with seawater. He had assumed, from the moment he left the château, that he had no chance of entering Puerto Rico by air, so he had flown from Paris to Guadeloupe and from there to Santo Domingo. From the airport he had taken a cab to the harbor; it had been easy to find, among the poor Dominicans idling on the wharves, a fisherman who agreed to take him on a one-way journey to a neighboring island. The engine of the boat had failed twice during the sixty-mile voyage; still, they had made landfall without being spotted by the coast-guard. James pressed the wad of dollar bills into the fisherman's calloused hands, then he jumped into the shallow water. He reached the house under the cover of darkness, and patiently waited outside, among the trees. He realized that he was condemning Sylvie to death and probably himself as well. Yet a strange feeling of peace had settled over him. He knew now that he hadn't sacrificed his wife and child because of toughness, insensitivity, or blind obedience to orders and slogans. He was just that kind of man, caring for his country and for what it represented more than for himself and for his own family. And once he had embarked on a mission like this, he would persevere to the bitter end.

Suvorov reached the pier, climbed the four decrepit steps, and slowly walked out to the middle of the wharf. He stopped awkwardly, raised his left hand, and looked at his watch.

From the corner of his eye, James could make out something moving in the trees, as if shadows were advancing in the darkness. He turned to the right, to see better. The grass behind him rustled, and he started, but too late. Someone landed directly on top of him, immobilizing both his arms, almost crushing his bones. "Not this time, my friend," a hoarse voice said in his ear with an unmistakable Texas drawl. "You're not going to spoil everything again. You just stay put and don't move."

At that moment, the pier was suddenly swept by the powerful beams of several floodlights. Suvorov was caught in the middle of the dazzling rays. Five men, dressed in black wetsuits, clambered onto the pier, and ominously converged on Suvorov. At close range they trained their short-barreled submachine guns on the defector and opened fire. Suvorov collapsed, almost hacked to pieces by the fusillade of bullets that had hit him. In a matter of seconds it was over. Like dancers in a well-rehearsed ballet, most of the killers vanished as suddenly as they had appeared, leaving behind the dead body of Arkadi Suvorov. They didn't take the floodlights, though, and the scene of the kill was still bathed in light, like a theater stage.

One of the killers stayed behind. He knelt by Suvorov to make sure he was dead. Then he slowly straightened up, and looked toward the beach. All of a sudden, Bradley realized that he was not alone on the pier. A man in a gray summer suit appeared at the top of the steps, a very familiar figure. He started to walk toward the assassin and his victim.

"Oh, no!" Bradley groaned at the sight of the newcomer.

The killer had seen him, too. And then, unbelievably, he grinned at him, a cold, evil grin, that stirred James's memory. Kalinin! The man who had almost killed him, and Suvorov, in Beaulieu.

But Kalinin didn't shoot this time. He raised his hand and waved conspiratorially to the other man, who was still calmly walking toward him. Then he carefully adjusted his diver's mask and plunged into the water. A minute later, Bradley heard the unmistakable purr of a motorboat engine.

The man in the gray suit stood calmly by Suvorov's body and lit a black cheroot with a golden lighter.

James felt that the grip on his arms had slackened slightly. He gathered all his strength and in a sudden, jerking motion, sharply drove his elbows backward, and the man who was holding him gasped and pulled back his arms. James pivoted, kicked his opponent in the groin, and when the man doubled over in agony, he dealt him a hard karate blow on the side of the neck. The man went limp and collapsed heavily. James wiped his perspiring brow and darted off through the trees. In a few strides he was on the pier, his hand outstretched, pointing his formidable Python at the solitary figure in front of him.

"So we meet again, Mr. Owen," James Bradley said.

The Deputy Director simply looked at him.

"I saw everything. And I *know* about everything. Those killers were Russians, weren't they? You delivered him over to the KGB, just as you tried to do to me, and the girl. Suvorov was our top agent in Moscow—but you got him killed. Nice job, Mr. Owen. Exactly how long have you been a Russian mole?"

Owen looked at him blankly. "You sound like the hero in a bad spy movie," he observed dryly.

"I don't care how I sound," snapped Bradley angrily,

and tightened his hold on the gun. "But you're coming with me back to the house now and you're going to stay put for quite a long while . . ."

"Why don't you put that gun away and calm down?" Owen asked softly. "You'll never get to the house. I have people posted all along the path."

James shifted around instantly, so that Robert Owen was now between him and the beach, shielding him from any well-aimed shot fired from the darkness. "One of your people is lying unconscious back there," he whispered hoarsely. "And if any others try to touch me, I'm just going to squeeze that trigger."

"That would be plain murder, and you won't get away with it." For the first time a note of concern appeared in Owen's voice.

"Murder?" James sneered. "You must be out of your mind. I'll get a medal for doing away with you. I saw you, remember? I've got you red-handed. Now, you'll do as I say, or I am going to shoot you, and you know I mean it."

Owen met his eyes and held them, then nodded. "Yes," he said slowly. "I guess you might do that." His eyes fastened on the heavy gun that trembled slightly in Bradley's hands.

Then Robert Owen reacted in the most unexpected manner. He smiled.

"You've got it all wrong, you know," he said softly. "There was no mole in the agency."

James stared at him, momentarily confused.

"You leave me with no choice but to enlighten you," Owen continued in the same quiet voice. "Have you got the London letter?" He quickly added: "Never mind if you don't. Just let me show you something."

Very slowly, he fished in the outer pocket of his jacket and took out some papers, which he carefully unfolded.

He knelt on the pier and flattened them on the wooden planks. Bradley gaped at them in amazement. They were exact replicas of the document he had gotten from Sylvie, same paper, same ink, same stamp, completely identical down to the smallest dot. Bradley produced his own copy, his right hand still pointing the gun at Owen. He knelt down and put the letter beside the others.

"You can't tell the difference, can you?" chuckled Owen proudly. "First-rate work on the part of the forgery lab. We made some extra copies, just in case."

Bradley's throat was dry. "But ... What ..."

"Don't you understand?" Owen asked. "The London letter was meant for the Russians. We drafted it, forged it, and planted it in the PRO for them to find. One of our men in London tipped them about it through a double agent."

"Why would you forge a letter betraying our best agent?"

"That," Owen said, elated, "you should hear about from the man who dreamed up this whole thing." He turned back.

James looked over Owen's shoulder. A gaunt, bony man with short salt-and-pepper hair stood in the shadow of a mangrove tree. Bill Hardy.

The director stepped onto the pier and came to join them. James looked at him in dismay. "So you're in this together?" he managed to say.

Owen sighed. "I am afraid we'll have to tell him, Bill." He cocked his head at the Python in James's hand. "He might be crazy enough to use this thing."

Hardy nodded. He folded his arms and drew a deep breath. Finally he cleared his throat. "A few months ago, our man in the KGB Supreme Council, code name Pandora, was almost unmasked by Soviet counterespionage. A high official of the KGB, code name Achilles, was on the verge of nailing down evidence that could hang him. I got the President's explicit authorization to save Pandora at all costs."

"I still don't understand," James said. "You wanted to save Pandora at all costs. Fine. So why have him killed?"

Owen shook his head. "It wasn't Pandora we set up for the kill, James," he said very quietly. "Don't you see?"

James looked at the crumpled corpse of Suvorov, and the truth struck him like a thunderbolt. "You mean . . . you mean Suvorov was not Pandora? Suvorov was Achilles?"

Owen nodded. "Exactly."

"And Pandora? Our man in Moscow?"

Owen smiled. "You just saw him waving good-bye to us. Alexei Kalinin, head of the First Directorate of the KGB."

The pawns in this satanic game started to march to their places. The ranks were formed, the colors were reversed. Black was white, and white was black. "So Suvorov suspected Kalinin," James said, "and you decided to get rid of him at once. You forged the London letter to frame him. None of that ever happened."

"Of course not," Owen agreed. "Count Golitzin was not a homosexual and never spied for the British. Neither did his daughter, Irina; she committed suicide for purely personal reasons. And Suvorov himself was the most dedicated adversary we have ever faced."

Hardy turned back and walked onto the pier. James and Owen followed him onto the desolate stretch of white beach. James had lowered his gun. "You had your plan ready," he said, "and just by chance . . ."

"Just by chance that stupid student happened to steal the letter," Hardy grunted.

"The Russians killed him and tried to get Sylvie." James was reconstructing the whole story step by step, but each element was acquiring a totally different meaning now. "So you sent me to retrieve the letter, and then . . ."

". . . And then Bob Owen, here present, set you up for the Russians," Hardy blurted out brutally, without looking over at James. "We wanted them to get the letter, and Bob assumed the role of the greedy Yankee who let himself be bought by the KGB. He fed them good, hard information for quite a while."

"Jesus Christ!" James said. "You tried to get us killed. Me and Sylvie. You filthy bastards!"

"We had to save Kalinin at all costs," Hardy snapped, and repeated forcefully: "*At all costs.* Even if we had to sacrifice some of our own people." He looked awkwardly at James. "You were expendable. We asked you to retire from active duty two years ago. You were burned, you were exposed, and you were known to the Russians. But you refused. So, for this case, we ruled unilaterally that *you* were expendable, like the other two who were killed in Beaulieu."

"But how the hell did you get Suvorov to defect?"

"He didn't exactly defect." Hardy smiled and kicked at a broken white conch that lay at his feet. "You remember your phone call? When you discovered the meaning of the letter? We panicked. We were afraid you'd make good on your threat to leak the letter to the newspapers. The letter was good only as long as Suvorov didn't know about it and couldn't challenge its authenticity. Andropov would have had him arrested, court-martialed, and shot within twenty-four hours. Suvorov wouldn't even have been allowed to answer the charges against him. But if the letter was published in the West, its credibility would have become suspect. Within hours, Suvorov would counterattack and rehabilitate himself, maybe even implicate Kalinin. So we had no choice. We had to get Suvorov out of Russia before the story came out."

"Suvorov didn't defect," Owen said shortly, and then dropped his cigar butt into the sand, where it glowed dully like a firefly. "We arranged for him to be sent to Istanbul, on a wild goose chase, and there we snatched him. It was a clean job."

Bradley nodded grimly. "I see. Everybody in Moscow assumed that Suvorov had defected; thus, he must have been the mole that they'd been looking for all along. Andropov ordered him killed and you, Bob, obligingly let them know that he was in Beaulieu. And put in the big fix with the security staff."

"And then you came gallumping up," Owen shot back, "and spoiled the whole damn surprise."

Fresh images from the night in Beaulieu were returning to James's mind. He remembered the glazed stare in Suvorov's eyes, the first time he had seen him at the villa, minutes before the attack. He had a book lying open in his lap, but he wasn't reading. Of course. He was held there against his will, and must have been stuffed with drugs.

A second image flashed in his memory. The front lawn of the villa. Suvorov looking over at Kalinin, getting up, and taking a step toward him. He must have thought that Kalinin had come to rescue him. And later, when Kalinin fired the shots, he said something. What did he say? Kalinin ... *Predatyel* ...

"What does *predatyel* mean in English?" he asked quickly.

Hardy shrugged. "Bob speaks Russian, not me. Why?"

"*Predatyel* means 'traitor,'" Owen answered promptly. "I think that's the word you're groping for."

James nodded. Suvorov had gotten his crowning bit of evidence against Kalinin too late. Yet, something was still unclear.

"Why didn't you kill him when you found him in the villa?" he asked. "That would seem like the best solution."

Hardy examined him critically. "You should know better, James. First, the Russians had to kill him and watch him die at their feet. That was Kalinin's best alibi. Second, this is a most secret operation, even within the agency. Actually, most of the department heads didn't even know about the plot. They still haven't found out that Kalinin, and not Suvorov, was Pandora. This operation is a kind of inner conspiracy, known to only a handful of people: Bob, me, and a few men from Operations. Your own chief, Roger, didn't even suspect what was really going on. Neither did Jeff Crawford, nor that pompous egghead Herb Kranz. If I want to go on using Kalinin—and believe me, I want to— I can't afford to have the whole CIA bragging about our success. Tomorrow another Philip Agee is going to write a book, and Andropov will roast Kalinin alive in the Red Square."

"And I guess it was Kalinin's idea to send you the Foxbat."

"A brilliant one, I must say. When Suvorov refused to die, thanks to your brilliant diversionary feint, and we had to rush the bastard to an impregnable hideaway, the Russians had to flush him out into the open. Kalinin convinced his superiors to sacrifice a MiG-25, with pilot—who is, by the way, a highly trained KGB agent."

"It was foolproof," Owen chimed in. "Two weeks before the SALT talks the pilot brings us some dramatic information. We have to confront him with Suvorov. This is the only logical thing to do. Suvorov was in the naval hospital in San Juan, so we moved him here."

James nodded. "The killers must have come from Cuba."

They had reached the house. It suddenly struck James that there was something entirely unreal about their conversation. A conversation that had started at gunpoint, over a dead body, had become a confrontation with the men who had coldbloodedly sent him marching off to his death, and was developing now into an amicable discussion among three specialists in the spook war. He shuddered involuntarily. Owen was lighting another cheroot. "During dinner," Owen said, "a note was passed to Suvorov—which said that his escape was all worked out and Soviet agents would pick him up on the pier."

"And he believed it?" James asked skeptically.

"Did he have any choice?" A bloodless grin appeared on Hardy's face. "He played right into our hands. . . . One born every minute, James. You know the rest."

They fell silent. The butt of the Python was moist in James's hand. "So it was all a hoax."

"Right," Owen said proudly. "A beaut. A stunning success. Pandora is alive and well, Achilles is dead and gone. Our only worry was that at the last moment you might step onto the stage for a curtain call."

"That's why we tried to frighten you," Hardy muttered, avoiding James's eyes again. "Bob had your file. The only way to stop you was to hit you where it would hurt most. . . . The kidnapping, the blackmail—the works."

James clenched his teeth. "You may be very very clever, indeed. But you're still not human. You are the most sickening, disgusting . . ."

"Come on, James," Hardy shot back. "I didn't come to hear you pontificating. This isn't *Face the Nation*. You'd better thank God that you came out of this with a whole skin. And that your girl friend is alive."

"Where is she?" The emotion gripped Bradley's throat and seeped into his voice.

"She's fine." Hardy intervened. "But she is going to be the price of your silence. Maybe you don't care about your life, but you do care about hers. She'll be safe as long as you keep your mouth shut. You're never going to discuss Pandora with anyone. If you do, we'll find her, wherever she may be, and we'll blow her brains out. Did I make myself clear?"

James ignored him. "Where is she?" he repeated savagely, and grasped the lapels of Owen's jacket.

Owen and Hardy exchanged glances. "Take it easy," Owen rasped. "Don't get excited." He pointed south. "There's a small house, about a mile down the beach. She's been there since Tuesday."

Bradley released him. Owen smoothed his jacket and with deliberate calm consulted his watch. "The guards must have cleared out already. They had instructions to leave the grounds at 1:00 A.M. We knew it would be all over by then."

Bradley threw the gun at their feet. "You can keep that, for what it's worth." He turned and started running down the beach.

"You can stay there a few days if you want," Hardy shouted after him. "Plenty of booze in the house."

Bradley didn't seem to hear. The Director shrugged indifferently. He picked up the heavy Python, cleaned it, and slipped it in his pocket. "Shall we ax him?" Owen asked quickly. "Early pension or something?"

Hardy flashed his sardonic smile, and turned toward the house. "We can't. He's a damned hero. Send him on a long, long leave, and give him time to simmer down. Who knows? He might still be useful one day."

The crests of the Montañas de Uroyan glowed with the soft pale-yellow light of dawn when James saw the low white house on the beach. He started to run faster. The place was extraordinarily peaceful—only a few sandpipers pecking in the sand and a couple of thrushes singing in an African tulip tree. It seemed like there was nobody else in this whole enchanted piece of paradise.

But then he saw the tall, slender figure, wrapped in a coat twice her size, pacing on the beach and looking out at the sea. The breakers were dying at her bare feet and the morning wind played gently with her long hair. He couldn't shout. He just stopped, his heart thumping wildly, looking at her while a new day was slowly coming to life. And then she turned, and saw him, and stood still.

ARENA

NORMAN BOGNER

"Another *Godfather!* It has virtually everything!"—*Abilene Reporter-News*

The spectacular new novel by the bestselling author of *Seventh Avenue*

Four families escaped the Nazi nightmare with dreams that could only come true in America.
For Alec Stone, the dream was a boxing arena.
For Sam West, it was a Catskill resort—a refuge for his beautiful, speechless daughter, Lenore.
For Victor Conte, it meant establishing a west-coast talent agency.
And for Paul Salica, it meant a lasting committment to another family—the Mafia.
But to young, gifted Jonathan Stone, no dream was big enough. Obsessed by love for Lenore, he would risk all they won—again and again.

A Dell Book   (10369-X) $3.25

The continuation of
the exciting six-book series that
began with *The Exiles*

The SETTLERS

WILLIAM STUART LONG

Volume II of *The Australians*

Set against the turbulent epic of a nation's birth is
the unforgettable chronicle of fiery Jenny
Taggart—a woman whose life would be torn by
betrayal, flayed by tragedy, enflamed by love and
sustained by inconquerable determination.

A Dell Book   **$2.95   (15923-7)**

Dell BESTSELLERS

- [ ] **TOP OF THE HILL** by Irwin Shaw $2.95 (18976-4)
- [ ] **THE ESTABLISHMENT** by Howard Fast........$3.25 (12296-1)
- [ ] **SHOGUN** by James Clavell $3.50 (17800-2)
- [ ] **LOVING** by Danielle Steel $2.75 (14684-4)
- [ ] **THE POWERS THAT BE**
  by David Halberstam $3.50 (16997-6)
- [ ] **THE SETTLERS** by William Stuart Long $2.95 (15923-7)
- [ ] **TINSEL** by William Goldman $2.75 (18735-4)
- [ ] **THE ENGLISH HEIRESS** by Roberta Gellis....$2.50 (12141-8)
- [ ] **THE LURE** by Felice Picano $2.75 (15081-7)
- [ ] **SEAFLAME** by Valerie Vayle $2.75 (17693-X)
- [ ] **PARLOR GAMES** by Robert Marasco $2.50 (17059-1)
- [ ] **THE BRAVE AND THE FREE**
  by Leslie Waller $2.50 (10915-9)
- [ ] **ARENA** by Norman Bogner $3.25 (10369-X)
- [ ] **COMES THE BLIND FURY** by John Saul $2.75 (11428-4)
- [ ] **RICH MAN, POOR MAN** by Irwin Shaw $2.95 (17424-4)
- [ ] **TAI-PAN** by James Clavell $3.25 (18462-2)
- [ ] **THE IMMIGRANTS** by Howard Fast $2.95 (14175-3)
- [ ] **BEGGARMAN, THIEF** by Irwin Shaw $2.75 (10701-6)

At your local bookstore or use this handy coupon for ordering:

Dell **DELL BOOKS**
P.O. BOX 1000, PINEBROOK, N.J. 07058

Please send me the books I have checked above. I am enclosing $_____
(please add 75¢ per copy to cover postage and handling). Send check or money
order—no cash or C.O.D.'s. Please allow up to 8 weeks for shipment.

Mr/Mrs/Miss_____

Address_____

City_____State/Zip_____